WHAT PEOPLE ARE SAYING ABOUT

NOTHING TO CONFESS

"I recommend this novel to all health care workers in the transplant field. This novel will be technically educational even for those within the field. More importantly, it will help them to understand their vulnerability and help them to cope when something unexpected does go wrong. I also recommend this for all medical students, residents, fellows and nursing students who have not yet completed their training. One is perhaps most idealistic at the end of training. In *Nothing to Confess*, Hricik paints a realistic picture that accurately captures the feelings and emotions caregivers feel the first time they have a claim or suit filed against them. The education is worth the read."
Daniel Brennan, MD, Medical Director Kidney Transplantation, Washington University.

"The field of organ transplantation is a fast-moving and complex endeavor that involves hundreds of professionals. Organ donation significantly benefits the lives of thousands of patients each year. In his new novel, *Nothing to Confess*, Dr. Donald Hricik, an internationally renowned transplant physician, successfully portrays the many facets of this field while telling an accurate and compelling story. This book will be a "page turner" for all who enjoy medical thrillers and is a must read for those who have any interest in organ transplantation."
James A. Schulak, MD, Past President of the American Society of Transplant Surgeons.

T0162304

Nothing
to Confess

Nothing
to Confess

Donald Hricik M.D.

Winchester, UK
Washington, USA

First published by Roundfire Books, 2013
Roundfire Books is an imprint of John Hunt Publishing Ltd., Laurel House, Station Approach,
Alresford, Hants, SO24 9JH, UK
office1@jhpbooks.net
www.johnhuntpublishing.com
www.roundfire-books.com

For distributor details and how to order please visit the 'Ordering' section on our website.

Text copyright: Donald Hricik 2012

ISBN: 978 1 78099 802 2

A CIP catalogue record for this book is available from the British Library.

Design: Stuart Davies

Printed and bound by CPI Group (UK) Ltd, Croydon, CR0 4YY

We operate a distinctive and ethical publishing philosophy in all
areas of our business, from our global network of authors to
production and worldwide distribution.

CONTENTS

Prologue   1

PART I
Chapter 1.   A Kidney Transplant – May 10, 2008   4
Chapter 2.   Elroy Kirk's Overdose – May 7, 2008   19
Chapter 3.   A Graduation Party – May 23, 2008   26
Chapter 4.   Preliminary Consent – May 7, 2008   33
Chapter 5.   Seizures – May 24, 2008   48
Chapter 6.   Declaration of Brain Death – May 8-9, 2008   59

PART II
Chapter 7.   A Deposition – January 2010   70
Chapter 8.   An Investigation – May 25, 2008   81
Chapter 9.   Hepatic Coma – May 15, 2008   90
Chapter 10. A Lung Transplant – May 23, 2008   95
Chapter 11. Conference Call – May 26, 2008   100
Chapter 12. Another Deposition: Part 1 – March 2010   103
Chapter 13. Follow-up Conference Call – May 26, 2008   109
Chapter 14. The Life and Death of Warren Mitchell
             – May 28, 2008   113
Chapter 15. CDC Investigation – June 1, 2008   121
Chapter 16. The Case of Anna Korhonen – June 2008   129
Chapter 17. Linda Skaper's Angry Husband – June 2008   138
Chapter 18. Honeymoon in Montego Bay
             – September 2008   144
Chapter 19. The Postponed Deposition – February 2010
Chapter 20. The Anderson Case – July 2009   151
Chapter 21. Liver Rounds – November 2009   164
Chapter 22. Medical Grand Rounds, Cleveland
             Medical Center – April 2010   173
Chapter 23. Caesars' Palace, Las Vegas – May 2010   180

Chapter 24. Cora Mitchell's Decision – May 2010   187
Chapter 25. The Virgin Islands – June 2010   191
Chapter 26. Another Deposition: Part Two – March 2010   201

PART III
Chapter 27. Lance Turner's Demise – November 2010   208
Chapter 28. The Anderson Trial – December 2010   214
Chapter 29. Henry Bolman's Book – 2012   223

Epilogue   227

To all organ donors and the families of organ donors – past, present, and future

Acknowledgements

Many thanks to the faculty and staff of the Transplantation Service at University Hospitals Case Medical Center in Cleveland, Ohio.

Thanks also to Timothy Staveteig for his literary expertise and guidance.

Prologue

In 1999, a report from the Institute of Medicine, entitled "To Err Is Human", concluded that as many 98,000 people die annually in the United States as a consequence of medical mistakes. That is equivalent to the death toll that would occur if three jumbo jets crashed every two days. Malpractice claims are filed by only 1.5% of patients harmed by medical errors. This observation suggests either that Americans are not as "sue happy" as many presume, or that the public remains ignorant about the frequency and severity of medical mistakes. Doctors recognize that there can be a fine line between medical mistakes and *expected* complications. It is when complications are *unexpected* that doctors argue with lawyers most vigorously about who is to blame.

Who is to blame when a medical catastrophe happens unexpectedly?

PART I

Chapter One

A Kidney Transplant
May 10, 2008

Mark Hubbard stretched his back and craned his neck to check the digital clock on the wall behind the anesthesiologist. *1:35 AM. Over eight hours in the OR. And I told Mary Ellen I'd be home for dinner. This has been the kidney transplant from hell.*

Hubbard turned to the chief resident and the intern who were assisting on the case. "Gentlemen, I trust that you can close the fascia and skin? I'm going out to talk to the parents. Make sure to keep his central venous pressure above ten. The last thing this kidney needs is an episode of hypotension."

"Got it, Dr. Hubbard. Maintain CVP of ten to fifteen and no blood pressure drops," the chief resident reiterated – mostly for the sake of the yawning intern who would be caring for this patient through the remainder of the night. Turning back to Hubbard before closing the fascia, the chief resident asked, "Do you want staples or sutures for the skin?"

"Staples, and be sure that the skin edges are properly aligned. Let's at least make the skin closure a successful part of this operation," Mark said sarcastically. *It's the only part of the operation that the patient sees.* "Listen, I know you guys only rotate on the Transplant Service a couple months a year, but you gotta understand that a kidney transplant is truly an *elective* operation, even when we do it in the middle of the night to minimize the organ's preservation time. People with kidney failure can always be kept alive on dialysis without having a kidney transplant. We do the transplants to improve quality of life and hopefully to prolong the patient's survival. But these operations are still *elective* procedures and patients and families expect good outcomes."

The chief resident peered over the top of his mask into the eyes of the intern across the table, rolling his eyes. *It's way too late and I'm way too tired to assimilate these subtle teaching points! Let's just sew and staple and get the hell out of here!* No words were spoken. It was getting near the end of the internship year. The intern completely understood his chief resident's body and eye language, agreeing with a nod and a long sigh that caused his own surgical mask to bellow.

Mark snapped off his bloody gloves, slipped off his gown, and headed for the waiting area outside of the operating room. Like most surgeons, he dreaded talking to family members about bad outcomes. He was especially upset because he went into the operating room thinking that this kidney transplant would be an easy "chip shot." The recipient, Scott Anderson, was eighteen years old and in perfect health, save for kidney failure. He was thin and had an athletic build. The donor was ideal too – a 23-year-old man, also thin and muscular, dying from a massive cocaine overdose complicated by a stroke. He had no significant past medical history and his kidney function was perfect when brain death was declared. *An ideal recipient and an ideal donor. This operation should have been a chip shot.*

Mark mentally prepared his thoughts as he strolled toward the waiting area. *Nothing beyond the standard of care. Just an unusual but expected complication.* That all sounded like language doctors used when dealing with malpractice lawyers. But Mark realized that surgical complications, expected or unexpected, were difficult for troubled family members to digest. *Use lay terminology with these parents and be honest.* This wasn't the first time he had to do this, and it wouldn't be the last.

Earlier in the day – before the transplant operation – Mark met with Scott's mother, Sarah Anderson, to get a quick update on her son's recent health status and to discuss details about the surgery and the anticipated postoperative care. Sarah seemed almost too calm. Mark got an immediate feeling that she had been through more strenuous medical ordeals in her lifetime. To test his hunch, he asked "Do you have a medical background?"

"Oh not really, except for dealing with our sick kids. You see, when Ken and I got married twenty-three years ago, we agreed that we wanted only two children. Scott was our second son. I had a tubal ligation shortly after his birth. Scott's older brother, Sam, developed a brain tumor at the age of sixteen – it was a medulloblastoma in the base of his brain." She glanced up to Hubbard to be sure he understood. He nodded to indicate that he was at least a little familiar with brain tumors.

"Sam died nine months later after lots of radiation therapy and multiple surgical procedures," Sarah went on. "We live west of Lima in a small town called St. Marys. It's between the Ohio-Indiana border and Wapakoneta – you know, home of Neil Armstrong, first man on the moon? So, during Sam's ordeal, Ken and I spent the larger part of a year traveling back and forth here to the Ohio Medical Center for his medical care. Ninety-six point five miles each way to be exact. I hate to admit it, Doctor, but we know this place pretty well...too well."

Mark immediately felt sorry for the Anderson family and wanted to be upbeat. "Listen, Mrs. Anderson, Scott's donor was in ideal shape, and this new kidney should work even better and longer than most kidney transplants from deceased donors," he offered. Sarah was very thankful and appreciative.

Now, as he approached the OR waiting area almost half a day later, Mark spotted Sarah with a tall heavy-set man, presumably her husband. He was pacing the floor and appeared worried. *Jesus, I should have tempered my pre-transplant enthusiasm.* The husband was wearing a crumpled white shirt with rolled up sleeves, an open collar, and an unassembled blue necktie flying at half-mast. Sarah was wearing the same yellow sun dress she wore earlier in the day. She appeared concerned but less flustered than her husband.

"Hi. I'm Mark Hubbard. You must be Mr. Anderson," said Mark, extending his weary right arm to shake hands with Scott's father.

"Hi, yes, Ken Anderson here." Ken was trying to be strong but couldn't keep his voice from shaking. He had been pacing the floor for hours, imagining that he would be bold and harsh with a long list of demanding questions for Scott's surgeon. However, when the confrontation materialized, he melted as he always did when dealing with someone whose professional stature was greater than his own.

He tried to calm down. "I think you met my wife, Sarah, earlier today," he said, almost whispering. "What's going on, Doctor? A nurse came out of the operating room at around 10 PM and said you were having trouble with the blood vessels. Sarah said the operation would take three hours. Is Scott OK? Its way beyond three hours – it's been more like eight. We're worried sick."

"Scott's going to be fine," Hubbard replied. "But yes, we had problems with the arterial anastamosis – the connection between the donor artery and Scott's iliac artery. As part of the routine in preparing a kidney for transplantation, we work with the organ on a back table in the operating room, literally cleaning off the kidney, dissecting fatty tissue from its surface. The surgeon who removed this kidney reported that there was a single artery feeding the organ – that's the usual anatomy in eighty per cent of cases. When we took the organ to the back table, we discovered that there was a small second renal artery that went unnoticed by the procuring surgeon. It was hidden in the fatty tissue. Again, this is not unusual." *Am I being defensive?*

"The procuring surgeons work very methodically to extract the organs from the donor. In this case, the donor's family agreed to allow *all* organs to be harvested – not just the two kidneys, but also the liver, the pancreas, two lungs, and the heart. When there are several teams of surgeons removing organs in sequence, it's easy for the kidney surgeon to miss an extra renal artery, especially if it's small." *Yes, I AM being defensive!*

Mark looked at the Andersons and realized they were only following his story loosely, waiting for a punch line.

"Anyhow, the first arterial connection with the main artery went smoothly. But the second artery was too short for me to create an anastamosis directly to Scott's iliac artery. So we needed to remove a vein from his left groin to use as a jump graft between Scott's internal iliac artery and the shortened artery from the allograft. You'll notice that he has two incisions – one on his lower right abdomen, and another on his left upper thigh where we obtained the vein graft."

Seeing complete confusion on the faces of the anxious parents, Mark found some paper and a pencil at a nearby receptionist desk and proceeded to draw pictures to explain the complicated anastamosis.

"What does all of this mean?" asked Sarah.

"The extra time spent doing the second arterial anastamosis means that at least part of the kidney was subjected to some *warm* ischemia – a lack of blood flow. That's different than the *cold* ischemia that occurs when the organ is preserved in iced solutions."

"So, is the kidney working or not?" asked Ken Anderson, getting a bit agitated once again, and still not fully comprehending Hubbard's technical explanation about the arterial problem.

"The last step of the kidney transplant surgery consists of sewing the ureter of the new kidney into the recipient's bladder after the blood vessels have been hooked up. When the kidney works right away, urine flows freely through the new ureter, literally pissing like a racehorse over the whole operative field before we get the end of the ureter sewn into the bladder," Mark said with a smile, but finding no return smiles from Ken or Sarah. *I guess neither of them has ever seen a racehorse pissing.*

He stifled his smile and went on. "Scott's new kidney wasn't making any urine at the end of the case, so it's not working right now. But you have to keep in mind that about twenty-five percent of kidney transplants from deceased donors don't function immediately. We call it 'delayed graft function' – basically the kidney goes into a state of shock. The organ will recover in over ninety-five percent of cases, but the recovery process can take anywhere from days to weeks. *This is probably not a good time to tell them that it can actually take up to three months.* During that period of 'shock', patients usually need to continue on dialysis treatments. We'll consult our Nephrology Service and they'll follow Scott closely to decide whether he will need dialysis on a day-to-day basis."

"So, sounds like it's just 'wait and see' for now?" offered Sarah.

"In all honesty, I am very concerned about the small second renal artery. It's possible that the portion of the kidney supplied by that artery may be infarcted or dead. As we were finishing the case, the upper pole of the kidney pinked up some, but the lower pole looked dusky and blue. We'll do a Doppler ultrasound scan first thing in the morning and that should give us the answer. If there's an infarction, my hope is that it involves only a small portion of the kidney. If so, it is likely that the remaining normal part of the kidney will provide enough function to get Scott off of dialysis eventually."

"Sounds like a lot of hoping, but I guess we'll hope along with you," said Ken. "Hey, Doc, Scott is scheduled to graduate from high school in a couple of weeks – do you think he'll make it? We'd love to see him walk up that aisle and get his diploma."

"We'll see. I hope so," Mark responded, intentionally overusing the word 'hope.' He could tell that the Andersons were tired and disappointed. So was he. The warm ischemia time mandated by the arterial reconstruction was almost thirty-five minutes, and he was worried about the viability of the entire transplanted kidney. But he was being totally honest with Sarah and Ken. He always tried to be completely honest with patients and families. And there was room to be optimistic in this case because both the recipient and donor were young. There was room for hope.

"Scott will be transferred to the Recovery Room shortly but he probably won't wake up from the anesthesia for another few hours," said Mark. "I'm heading home to catch a few hours of sleep and will be back at 7:30 for morning rounds. I suggest you do the same."

"Dr. Hubbard, as I mentioned earlier, we live more than an hour and a half away, west of here – so we'd actually prefer to stay until the morning," said Sarah. "Maybe we can catch a few winks on the couches here."

"That's fine. The ICU staff can give you some pillows and blankets. Unless you have any other questions, I'll see you in the morning."

Ken and Sarah could not sleep. They were each terrified by the possibility that Scott's kidney transplant would not work and that he would require dialysis treatments forever. They also were concerned that this simple kidney transplant could turn into a prolonged hospitalization. After tossing and turning for an hour, Sarah broke the silence. "Ken, I'm beginning to see those ninety-six point five miles all over again."

The couple was fitfully dozing off on the waiting room couches when an ICU nurse interrupted their broken sleep at 5 AM. She spoke quietly, trying not to disturb another group of visitors that were soundly sleeping in the opposite corner of the room. "Hi, I'm Jane Pollack. Your son Scott has been moved from Recovery to the ICU next door. I'll be his nurse today. His post-op blood work showed a potassium of 7.2. A dialysis nurse is on her way to perform an urgent dialysis treatment. We called Dr. Hubbard and he agrees with doing the dialysis. Scott is waking up, and you are welcome to join him if you'd like."

"Okay, Jane, thanks. I thought the potassium level was normally around 4. Did you say it was 7.2?" asked Sarah, now very familiar with language of kidney failure, dialysis, and related blood test results.

"Yeah, 7.2 is pretty elevated and it can cause cardiac arrhythmias. The good news is that his EKG is normal, but he'll still need dialysis urgently to get the potassium down. Sorry for waking you folks up, but I thought you'd want to know what's going on. Honestly, this is all pretty routine after a new kidney transplant," said Jane, pausing as she recognized that the Andersons seemed a little anxious. She smiled and tried to reassure them that the high potassium level was nothing to worry about, now sitting down to help Sarah and Ken feel more comfortable. "So tell me about Scott's kidney problems."

Sarah looked at Jane and realized they were each about the same age. *I'm sure this nice woman has family stories of her own.* Somehow, Sarah always felt a sense of relief when she was able to divulge her life story to a sympathetic ear. She proceeded to tell Jane about her first son, Sam, and his fatal brain tumor.

"About a year after Sam died, Scott developed the nephrotic syndrome." The look on Jane's face indicated that she was only vaguely familiar with the terminology.

Sarah went on. "It's a kidney disorder resulting from loss of protein in the urine. It leads to massive swelling of the extremities and the face. After all those trips with Sam, Ken and I once again had to travel frequently here to the OMC for treatment of Scott's kidney problem. The clinics and hospitals in Lima said his condition was too rare for them to handle. Scott had a kidney biopsy and it showed a disease called focal and segmental glomerulosclerosis – FSGS for short. For six months, he was treated with prednisone – pretty high doses – but it didn't help. Funny thing is, when Scott initially discovered that prednisone was a 'steroid' he was expecting to beef up his biceps and quads...you know, Schwarzenegger style. But we all quickly learned that prednisone is a *catabolic* steroid, not one of those *anabolic* steroids that some athletes use to build muscle mass."

"I've seen lots of patients who are taking high doses of prednisone," Jane interjected. "The side effects can be really nasty."

"Exactly," Sarah responded. "Scott developed a fat swollen face. He had mood swings – sometimes he seemed irritable and depressed, at other times almost overly energetic. He got terrible acne on his face, and on his back and chest. He had bouts of raging indigestion and needed to take all sorts of antacids and other stomach remedies. You know, Scott was looking like a first-rate running back on the varsity football team, but he had to quit sports during his sophomore year because the kidney disease caused such bad swelling of his legs. He could hardly walk, let alone run."

Sarah was getting teary-eyed and Jane quickly disappeared and reappeared with a box of tissues before encouraging Sarah to continue her story.

"Anyhow, after six months of prednisone, Scott's pediatric nephrologist met with me and Ken to inform us that Scott was developing irreversible kidney failure. He would need either dialysis or a kidney transplant. He wasn't responding to prednisone, despite all of the side effects. And there was no other treatment. She told us that a kidney transplant was the best option, but quickly tempered her optimism by pointing out that there was a chance – somewhere between thirty and fifty percent – that the FSGS would recur in a newly transplanted kidney, possibly destroying it." *It seemed in medicine that good news was always accompanied by some bad news.*

Jane remained attentive, and Sarah continued. "Ken was ruled out as a kidney donor to Scott because he had diabetes. He's been taking diabetic pills and following a diabetic diet for more than eight years now. I couldn't donate to Scott because I have an incompatible blood type. I'm type A and he is type B. And of course there are no other siblings to serve as living family donors."

Sarah went on, after pausing to grab another tissue. "Scott was placed on the waiting list for a kidney transplant from a deceased donor. We were told that it would take between three and five years before he would be called in for a transplant – owing to the large number of patients on the waiting list ahead of him. We've been living through a nightmare of teenage illnesses for over five years."

"So this kidney transplant is really good news for you two!" Jane offered, now becoming conscious of the time and her need to back to the ICU.

Sarah peered into Jane's eyes and said, "You know, Scott is our only remaining child. When we received the call about the kidney that had become available for Scott several hours ago, it seemed like a nightmare had finally come to an end. But then...this bit of bad news from Dr. Hubbard about a problem with the kidney's arterial connection."

Ken had been following Sarah's review of the Anderson family story and finally chimed in. "To think I was worried that the original disease might recur in the transplanted kidney," Ken said to Sarah and Jane. "That was my *big* concern – waiting to see if his FSSG, or whatever it's called, would recur in his new kidney. Now it sounds like the kidney might not work at all."

"Ken, that's not what Dr. Hubbard said,' Sarah retorted. "I thought he said there was a ninety-five percent chance it would work. And it's called 'FSGS'."

"He was talking about statistics, not this individual case with the faulty artery. That artery problem changes everything. Just our luck. Just Scott's luck. Oh, what the hell, let's just keep our fingers crossed and hope that the scan is okay this morning."

"Good idea," said Jane, offering to escort the couple into the ICU. "Man oh man, you guys have really been through a lot. I'm sure everything will go fine with this new kidney transplant."

Scott had been receiving hemodialysis treatments for over two years at a dialysis unit in Lima – hooked up to a dialysis machine for four hours at a time, three times a week. So he and his parents were accustomed to the routine, including insertion of the two large dialysis needles into the arteriovenous fistula that had been surgically created in his left forearm several years ago. Scott was a little lethargic from the general anesthesia, but he was able to converse with his parents who recounted Dr. Hubbard's concerns, including their own rendition of the arterial problems. They had saved Hubbard's drawings and shared them with Scott.

"Hey, Mom, Dr. Hubbard told us beforehand there was a chance that the kidney wouldn't work right away," Scott recalled.

"Right, and a ninety-five percent chance that it will kick in eventually," Sarah responded optimistically. Ken offered a reluctant nod of agreement, realizing that Scott was looking for one.

At 7 AM, an ultrasound technician arrived at Scott's bedside and announced that she would be performing the Doppler ultrasound on Scott's kidney, first explaining the procedure. "Don't worry, no needles – just some cold jelly down here over your new kidney and a little gentle pressure from the ultrasound transducer."

"Wow, you're here earlier than we expected," commented Sarah.

"Yeah, this place has been hopping recently. There was a second transplant last night – and he also needs a Doppler study," said the technician, tilting her head in the direction of another bed at the other end of the ICU. "So, I thought I'd get an early start. They asked me to do your son first."

Sarah looked towards the other end of the intensive care unit and noticed an elderly black woman sitting next to an elderly black man, presumably her husband, resting comfortably in his ICU bed. Like Scott, the man was attached to several IV lines and beeping monitors. A plastic bag at his bedside was filled with urine draining from a catheter. Sarah saw a similar catheter and bag at Scott's bedside, but the bag was empty. She returned her attention to the ultrasound technician who seemed to be applying more than "gentle" pressure over Scott's brand new incision, causing him to wince with pain periodically.

"How does it look?" asked Ken, wondering why the previously talkative technician suddenly clammed up after starting the procedure.

"I'm really not allowed to comment on my findings until a radiologist makes an official reading," she answered in a serious tone and without taking her eyes off the monitor.

Before Ken was able to object, Mark Hubbard arrived with his team of residents and nurses – about seven people in all, entering the ICU looking like a human train. Hubbard was the locomotive, tall and thin with shortly cropped brown hair and a perfectly trimmed moustache. He was wearing a white shirt and red necktie with a clean and starched white lab coat. A scruffy short male intern wearing horn-rimmed glasses was the caboose – the same intern who had wearily stapled together Scott's skin incision six hours earlier. He was dressed in a green scrub suit and a white lab coat with three or four prominent coffee stains and a large ink stain under the coat's upper pocket.

"Good morning, Scott, how are you feeling?" asked Mark, also acknowledging Ken and Sarah's presence with a polite nod.

"Not bad. A little nauseated. And my lower belly feels like it's been hit by a truck."

Mark smiled and pretended to pay attention but was quickly scanning the flowsheets at the bedside and querying his team.

"Any urine output in the past three hours?"

"Only bladder sweat. I tried IV Lasix twice – no response," offered the scruffy intern. "But his CVP is 12," he added, proud that he kept the patient hemodynamically stable over night.

"And no blood pressure drops. One-forty over eighty most of the night," he said, stifling another yawn.

"Good work...Doctor," said Hubbard, embarrassed that he couldn't remember the intern's name. "Did you irrigate the Foley catheter?" he asked further, challenging the intern, in part to test his competency.

"Three times, Dr. Hubbard, and still nothing but bladder sweat. The Foley catheter is *not* obstructed, sir," said the intern, emphatically.

"Okay, good job," Mark said softly, perhaps not appreciating how even a short, but positive comment of that kind could bolster the confidence of a young doctor in training.

Mark turned his attention to the ultrasound images being displayed on the Doppler monitor next to Scott's bed. "Go back to the lower pole," he instructed the technician. "Okay, now scan back up. Okay, now back down."

He shuffled over to the other side of the bed to address Scott and his parents.

"I'll need the official interpretation from radiology, but I don't see any blood flow to the lower pole of the kidney and I think it's infarcted. The good news is that the infarction appears to affect less than a third of the whole kidney. There is good blood flow to the upper pole, but there's no urine output – so we're dealing with delayed graft function as we discussed yesterday...or earlier this morning. There is no reason to re-operate – I'm sure that the lower pole can't be salvaged. We'll have to wait for the upper pole to recover. We'll just have to wait and see."

Waiting. Waiting rooms. Waiting lists. During the past five years, the Andersons had become accustomed to waiting. They would just have to wait a bit longer for Scott's new kidney to start working.

The urgent dialysis was successful in correcting Scott's high potassium level. He was otherwise stable and plans were made for his transfer to a regular floor. Ken and Sarah told Scott that they needed to return home for a few hours. They would come back to visit him later that evening. Ken was a tax accountant and needed to check in at his office in Lima to reschedule some meetings with clients. He was also dying for a cigarette, having been trapped in the smoke-free confines of the OMC for more than half a day. Sarah needed a shower, a change of clothes, and some time to update family and friends about the exciting events of the past twenty-four hours. As they were exiting the ICU, Sarah spotted the elderly black woman, presumably the wife of the man who received the other kidney transplant, in the adjacent waiting area. She was wearing a pink suit and a matching pillbox hat – suitable for a Sunday morning at church. Sarah asked Ken to stop for a minute to say hello.

"Hi there, I hope I'm not being too nosey, but is that a relative of yours who got a kidney transplant last night?" Sarah asked.

"Why yes and it's a miracle!" the woman answered. "My husband, Warren, waited for six years for a kidney and has been on dialysis for eight years. He was so excited when we got the call. It's a miracle, and the doctors say the kidney is working beautifully. Warren hasn't made any urine for several years. To see it pouring out now – well it's simply a miracle! They tell me the donor was a young man – a perfect donor. But I feel so badly about that young man's family. They must be in an awful way."

"We know exactly how you feel. And we know all about dialysis. Our son also received a kidney transplant late last night. This is my husband, Ken. I'm Sarah Anderson. Nice to meet you."

"I'm Cora Mitchell, and nice to meet both of you both as well. I'm sure you are as thrilled as I am."

"Yes, we are," said Sarah, half-lying and not keen on divulging the details of Scott's case. "But we've been here all night and are heading home for a rest. Best of luck to you and Warren."

As they were driving home, Sarah said to Ken, "It must have been the same donor. Dr. Hubbard said the donor was a young man in his early twenties."

"Well, honey, most human beings have two kidneys, so you are probably right. And Hubbard *did* say that there were two kidneys and several other organs taken from the same donor in this case."

"You're missing the point. Cora said her husband's kidney was working beautifully – lots of urine flowing. Heck, I could see the urine in his catheter bag from a hundred feet away in the ICU."

Ken paused to think and then responded, "Okay, okay...and Scott's kidney is *not* working...but you're forgetting the whole story about the arterial stamatosis, or whatever Hubbard called it."

"It's called an *anastamosis*," she retorted. Sarah loved learning medical terminology and was always astounded by her husband's opposite unwillingness to expand his vocabulary. "Sure...yeah, just our luck," she went on. "Great kidney, but a faulty anastamosis. *Seems like good news is always accompanied by some bad news.* God, Kenneth Anderson, are we going to live under a black cloud forever?"

Ken didn't answer. They were silent for much of the remainder of the trip back to Lima, each internally recounting the events of the day and the events of the past five years. Sarah's thoughts once again drifted to a common one that had plagued her for eighteen years. *I should never have agreed to that tubal ligation. Ken talked me into it. We should have had more children.*

As they were pulling into their driveway, Sarah broke the silence with another thought, speaking mostly to herself, "Cora and Warren must be in their upper sixties or early seventies. Why do you think they would transplant a kidney from a twenty-something-year-old person into a man close to seventy?"

18

Chapter Two

Elroy Kirk's Overdose
May 7, 2008

Jason Heeger flicked on the siren and grabbed the two-way radio, preparing to call the Emergency Room physician at Wright State County Hospital. Sitting to his left was Jeff, his partner and driver, in the midst of an adrenaline surge, busily maneuvering the ambulance through intersections and red traffic lights.

"Finally a little excitement!" Jeff exclaimed to Jason, summarizing the sentiments of the entire four-man crew of emergency medical technicians who had grown accustomed to a relatively humdrum life in the Emergency Medical Service of Dayton, Ohio. *Hours of boredom and minutes of excitement.* Jason swiveled around to assess the scene in the rear cabin of the ambulance. There was none of the usual flailing and screaming that was typical of patients having heart attacks or of those with bone fractures or other traumatic injuries. Jason's two partners in the rear of the ambulance were busy securing the "client's" intravenous line and checking vital signs, but the client himself was motionless. A faint fecal odor permeated the rear cabin and was slowly making its way to the front of the vehicle.

Jason swiveled back to the street view and clicked on the radio. "Man found down at the site of a police drug raid. Young black male – early-twenties, mid-twenties maybe," he yelled over the screeching sounds of the siren overhead. "Witnesses described what sounds like seizure activity – including urinary incontinence. Patient is currently unresponsive. Blood pressure 220 over 130. Repeat, 220 over 130. Heart rate 110. No spontaneous movements. There's evidence of both urinary *and* fecal incontinence. We've got IV normal saline running at one hundred an hour. Maintaining airway and ventilating with an

Ambu bag. ETA four to five minutes. Do you read me?"

"Yes, sir, we read you loud and clear. Any ongoing seizure activity?" asked Ken Sanchez, the Emergency Room physician, on the other end of the two-way radio. He was finishing the last morsels of a gigantic slice of meat-lover's pizza delivered to the ER by a mom-and-pop shop down the street.

"None. There's no motor activity at all, sir. In fact, he seems...paralyzed." He looked to Jeff, who shrugged his shoulders and frowned in a sign that basically agreed with Jason's assessment.

Jason looked toward the rear cabin once again, feeling uneasy. *I'd rather have flailing and screaming. I hope this isn't just another expensive taxi ride to the morgue.*

"Okay. Maintain the IV fluids and keep bagging him," said Sanchez, wiping his mouth clean of any remnants of tomato sauce. "We'll have anesthesiology ready here to intubate the patient on arrival."

When the ambulance arrived, the Wright State Emergency Room team jumped into action as the EMS squad whisked the patient's cart into the "Code Room." After a day filled with sore throats, sprained ankles, and a urethral drip or two, the ER staff also craved this kind of action.

Sanchez systematically barked out orders, questions, and commands. "No spontaneous respirations. Please go ahead and intubate," nodding to the anesthesiologist. "I need an arterial blood gas please – STAT. One amp of bicarbonate now – IV push. I need a twelve-lead EKG. STAT portable chest x-ray. Vital signs please?"

"BP 230 over 135...pulse 120 and regular," responded a nurse.

"Thank you. Update in two minutes please. "

Sanchez proceeded to do a quick neurologic examination.

"I get some response to deep pain on the left side. Flaccid paralysis and no response to deep pain, entire right side." He grabbed an ophthalmoscope and pried open the patient's eyes to view each retina for any signs of hemorrhage or swelling. "Papilledema...bilaterally. Sounds like malignant hypertension with cerebral edema and papilledema. Labetalol 10 mg IV now and let's get a nitroprusside drip going. Any family?" Sanchez asked looking toward the EMS team.

"Girlfriend should be here shortly," Jason Heeger responded. "She was at the scene and was being escorted behind us by the Dayton PD."

Sanchez leaned toward Jim Augustine, a senior resident rotating in the ER. "Get out there and get some history from the girlfriend. I'll call the Medical ICU for a bed." Augustine, who was preparing to start a second IV line in the patient's left arm, reluctantly dropped his instruments to follow Sanchez's orders. *I'm a frickin' senior resident! Any medical student can get a history from a girlfriend.*

Augustine was unsure what to make of this girlfriend. She came stumbling into the ER waiting room, sobbing and barely able to keep up with the two brutish Dayton PD officers who were flanking her, each holding one of her arms. *Is she a friend of the patient or a criminal?* She was a young, attractive, dark-skinned, black woman who appeared to be in her mid-twenties. Her long glistening black hair was combed back into a tight pony tail. But she was wearing a red mini-skirt, a low-cut white blouse, a yellow silk scarf, and a shaggy gray sweater – a misfit of apparel that broadcast an aura of "criminal" more than "family friend."

Augustine approached the girlfriend and introduced himself, feeling more like a law enforcement officer than a doctor. "Hello, Ma'am. I'm Dr. Augustine. I need to ask you a few questions about Mr. Kirk," he said, suddenly realizing that he had not prepared any specific questions. He finally offered, somewhat clumsily, "Can you tell me your name? Can you tell me what happened? "

The girlfriend interrupted her sobs and returned a look of suspicion toward the young doctor. *Is this guy a doctor or some kind of student?*

"My name is Tanya Stenfield," she managed. "Is Elroy gonna be okay? When the cops arrived, he fell to the floor and I thought he was faking something. But then his body started shaking and twitching and he started foaming at the mouth – you know like my brother used to do when he had fits."

"Hold on. Back up a little. Where did this happen, and why were the cops there?" Augustine asked, trying to regain his investigative composure.

"We was all at a house in north Dayton. Elroy's been dealing for more than a year. I told him to stop. God knows I aksed him to stop. It was supposed to be a meeting of friends, you know…buyers. Somebody called the cops. We all heard sirens, first of all far away. When the sirens got closer, everyone scattered – mostly out the back door. Elroy didn't run, but he swallowed a bag of dope."

"What kind of dope?"

"Cocaine."

"Was it powder? Crack? How much?"

"I have no idea, man. I don't use that shit. Honest."

Tanya turned away from Augustine momentarily, continuing to sob off and on. As she surveyed the ER waiting room with its assortment of accident victims and sick people, she thought about Elroy and the promise of a better life – now all going downhill fast. She was in trouble most of her life before Elroy. She never knew her father. When she was four years old, her mother suddenly moved to Florida and left Tanya to be raised by her Auntie Esther, who lived on welfare checks. Tanya never made it through high school. By the age of eighteen she already had three abortions and six boyfriends – all dope dealers, two in prison for life. She earned some money as a stripper and rented a small apartment in downtown Dayton. Elroy Kirk seemed to have more promise than any of her previous boyfriends. He talked a lot about giving up drug dealing and going back to school. Tanya dreamed of a normal life with him some day. *Maybe even move to Cleveland or Cincinnati and raise a family.* But she knew Elroy was in big trouble when he hit the floor twitching, shaking, and foaming at the mouth. She had a bad feeling about all of this. *Please, Elroy, don't die and make me go back to strippin'.*

"Is Elroy gonna live?" she asked the student-doctor.

"His blood pressure is extremely elevated and he may have had a stroke of some kind, but he's alive. We're gonna admit him to the Intensive Care Unit. That means it's very serious – he's in *critical* condition. He'll need intravenous medications to get his blood pressure down. Does Mr. Kirk have a history of high blood pressure? Or any other medical problems?

"Nothing that I know about. Far's I know, he ain't never had high blood pressure before. He sure don't take no blood pressure pills, far's I know. But you can aks his Momma. That's his only relative, far's I know."

"And until he swallowed the bag of dope, he had been in good health?

"Just a cold past few days – you know, sore throat and some chills and aches. Somethin's goin' around. Otherwise, he's been ok, far's I know. Never told me about no high blood pressure."

"Thanks, Ms. Stenfield. Please stay here for the time being in case we have any other questions for you."

"Can I see Elroy now?"

"No. As soon as he's stabilized we will be transporting him to the ICU on the second floor. You'll be able to visit him there when he's stable. Someone will come out and let you know when we're ready to transport him upstairs."

When Dr. Augustine returned to the Code Room, the team was performing full-blown cardiopulmonary resuscitation on Elroy.

"What the hell's going on?" he asked. "Why the CPR?"

"Ventricular fibrillation. First, a couple of PVCs, then a long string of V-tach, then rapid deterioration to V-fib," Sanchez answered without taking his eyes off the cardiac monitor. "Let's clear the cart for cardioversion folks."

The Code Room team stepped back, allowing Sanchez to attempt the cardioversion. Elroy's body jolted with the electrical clap of the paddles applied to his chest. All eyes moved to the monitor above his head.

"Still in V-fib. Step back!"

Sanchez applied the paddles to Elroy's chest a second time and fired another jolt.

"We're back in sinus rhythm!" Sanchez announced euphorically, eyeing the monitor at the head of the bed. He always experienced a rush when a patient was successfully defibrillated. It was literally like bringing a dead person back to life.

"MICU has a bed. Let's stabilize him and get him transported as soon as possible. I want normal saline at 150 an hour. Let's give one more amp of bicarbonate now. Any history from the girlfriend?" asked Sanchez.

"Yeah," Augustine responded. "He swallowed a bag full of cocaine a few hours ago at a crack house in north Dayton – probably tried to hide the evidence when he heard the cops coming. Then he had what sounds like a grand mal seizure. The girlfriend was at the scene and witnessed everything. Sounds like the bag of dope broke after he swallowed it. Even orally, that's a lot of cocaine."

"Makes sense," said Sanchez. "Malignant hypertension and ventricular arrhythmias from an inadvertent massive cocaine overdose. Call back the radiology tech and ask for a KUB and upright film of the abdomen. Maybe we can spot the bag of dope and have it retrieved endoscopically."

Sanchez stepped back and watched his team in action. After pondering the situation, he offered a final comment as the patient was being rushed to the ICU. "It may be too late to retrieve the bag of cocaine. This young chap may have already fried his brain. Page the MICU resident on-call and tell them they'll need to order a stat head CT scan."

Chapter Three

A Graduation Party
May 23, 2008

"Dude, it's not just your graduation. It's your frickin' nineteenth birthday too! You gotta get rid of the old folks, dude. We're all gonna get wa...wa...wasted tonight!" It was Scott's friend Brian. He and about a dozen of Scott's senior classmates were invited to the Andersons' Friday night backyard party that began with a mixture of his school friends and members of the Anderson family – aunts, uncles, and cousins – most of whom were born and raised in mid-western Ohio.

"Yeah sure, Brian, sounds awesome," Scott whispered under his breath, spotting his mother a few yards away. "Just cool it a little. My aunts and uncles usually leave by 10 PM. We'll have plenty of time to party after they leave."

"Have you asked them yet?" Brian asked.

"No, but you know my parents are pretty cool about our parties," Scott answered.

The idea of getting a buzz on was suddenly appealing to Scott. *God knows I deserve it.* He hadn't completely recovered from his transplant surgery two weeks earlier and he still had some dull pain over the incision site. Plus, it seemed like he was catching a cold during the past day or so. But he didn't want to miss his one-and-only high-school graduation party. Dr. Hubbard told him he could attend the party so long as he promised to take it easy – no heavy lifting, no athletic activity. *He didn't say anything about getting buzzed.* His urine output was still minimal, so the kidney had not yet "kicked in". He could tell that his doctors and his parents were concerned that the kidney might *never* work. *Might as well get wasted.*

Scott continued on with Brian, "If the weather holds up, my

folks will probably let us crash in the carriage house, but I gotta mingle with my family some before I ask them."

"No problem, dude. You got some cool aunts and uncles."

As if on cue, Aunt Heather, Ken's oldest sister, walked up – a three-olive vodka martini in hand – to chat with her nephew. She looked exactly like Ken, but Scott recalled that she was about ten years older than his father. Scott had a total of five aunts, three on his father's side and two on his mother's. There was also Uncle Rick, Ken's younger brother. The whole clan was here tonight, together with spouses and a truck load of cousins, some older and also married or attached.

"Hello, Scott, isn't this big tent festive?" Heather asked, visually scanning the large outdoor tent that Ken and Sarah had rented in case of inclement weather.

"Yeah, it's pretty neat. And it looks like it's not gonna rain after all, but everybody seems to be having a good time, inside or outside of the tent," Scott responded.

"So how are you feeling, Scott?"

"Not bad, Aunt Heather. I'd feel a whole lot better if this kidney would start working. Plus I've been fighting a cold for the past couple of days."

"It's the Gift of Life – that's what we used to call it," said Heather, ignoring Scott's comments about his cold. "Did you know I used to work for the Ohio Organ Bank?"

"I thought you were a nurse at Lima General before you retired?"

"I was, but before retiring completely, I spent two years working for the regional branch of the OOB. I helped with donor evaluations in hospitals between Dayton and Toledo. It was an interesting job, but sometimes pretty challenging – asking families and friends to consider organ donation just when they were grieving about the loss of their loved ones. In the end, I think it mostly made them feel better – you know, knowing that the organs helped others to survive and lead normal lives."

"I gotta admit, I hadn't thought about it that way Aunt Heather – but I'm sure you're right," Scott responded. "The doctors were pretty secretive about my donor. I think they have a rule against providing too much personal information. All they told Mom and Dad is that he was a young man."

"Those are the hardest cases. I'm sure the donor's family is still upset and grieving. It's tough to lose a young family member, no matter what the circumstances. Did you know that you can write an anonymous letter to thank the family? Just send it to the OOB and they will get it to the donor's family."

"Great idea, Aunt Heather." *Maybe I'll wait until this damned kidney starts working before thanking the family or anyone else.* "I'll talk to Mom and Dad about sending a letter. Hey, I'm ready to try some of that apple pie you brought for dessert," he said, anxious for the first phase of this party to come to an end.

On the way to the dessert stand, Scott ran into Uncle Rick.

"Looks like your Dad is becoming more of a farmer than an accountant these days, Scott," said Uncle Rick, pointing to the newly planted garden occupying the space between the main house and the carriage house on the other side of the party tent.

The Andersons lived on four acres of land wedged between several farms in western Ohio. Although they were not professional farmers themselves, Ken Anderson did maintain a small field for planting vegetables. It was a relaxing hobby and the produce from the property clearly saved a few dollars at the grocery store, especially when the vegetables were harvested in late summer.

"Yeah, this year he's planning on corn, tomatoes, I think peppers, and even some pumpkins. And he's already planted the herb garden there next to the house," Scott said, pointing to a patch of thyme, rosemary and chive plants. "Plus, we still have the chicken shed out there near the carriage house. I don't think Mom has ever bought eggs from a store since Dad started raising the chickens a few years back."

The Anderson "farm", as it came to be known, was a favorite spot for teen gatherings. The property included a creek surrounded by dense woods, so there were plenty of hidden enclaves perfect for late night bonfires – and for drinking beer safely out of the view of Scott's parents or any other neighbors. Many high school social affairs – dances, football or basketball games, car rallies – ended with after parties at the popular Anderson farm and carriage house.

It was approaching 10 PM. The sun went down quite late at this time of year in western Ohio and there was still some faint light in the western sky, but it was fading rapidly. Scott found his mother to ask if a few friends could stay for an after party. "It'll just be me, Brian, Missy, and maybe six or seven other friends from school," said Scott.

"Fine with me, Scott, but I know what you guys will be doing down by the creek and I don't want your friends driving back home later if they've been drinking, okay?"

Scott had heard the lecture before. *"We know you guys are gonna drink,"* Sarah preached to her son often during the past couple of years. *"But no driving drunk. No way. Either pick a designated driver or arrange a sleepover."*

"And just remember, we gotta leave for dialysis at 9:30 in the morning," Sarah continued. "If you want, I can talk to Marilyn Lander to make sure it's okay if Missy stays over."

Sarah loved Missy Lander and often wondered why she and Scott were never anything more than "just good friends." In fact, she was amazed at generational differences in dating habits and relationships. Although Scott had a number of friends – both boys and girls – who were in "relationships," Sarah couldn't remember hearing about any one-on-one dates like those she remembered from her own years in high school and college. Instead, in Scott's generation, dating seemed to happen in groups. Sarah realized that today's kids must have venues for sexual experimentation *(it's just part of growing up)*, but she was oblivious to when and where that kind of activity happened. With virtual certainty, it didn't occur during the group "sleep-overs" that were commonplace during Scott's junior and senior high school years. Scott reassured his mother on several occasions that the sleepovers were intended for one thing only...sleep.

"No, no. Mrs. Lander is used to the gang staying over," Scott responded. "There's no need to call her. And I didn't forget about dialysis. Thanks, Mom. And thanks for this great party. Everybody loved the tent! I'll be ready to go at 9:30. Promise. I have a bit of a cold so I'm not in the mood for a late-night party anyhow."

"Okay," said Sarah, never fully understanding what the truth was when talking to older teenagers.

The crowd surrounding the bonfire was larger than Scott had been expecting, and he was a bit upset that there were a number of people that he didn't recognize. *Whose party is this anyhow?* Missy Lander walked up to Scott, gave him a kiss on the cheek, and handed him a Natural Light. "Happy graduation *and* happy birthday! Look, I saved the comfiest lawn chair for you," she said, pointing to a cushioned lawn chair next to the roaring bonfire.

There were a dozen lawn chairs surrounding the fire together with two coolers filled with beer. A portable iPod player was parked against a tree, booming out hip-hop music.

"Thanks, Missy," said Scott. Then, whispering into her ear, asked, "Who are all of these people?"

"I think they are mostly Brian's cousins who are in town for Brian's own graduation party and family reunion tomorrow," Missy answered. Scott surveyed the crowd suspiciously. Three of the 'cousins' were clearly older than the rest of the party-goers – maybe in their upper twenties. One of them was wearing a wedding ring but didn't appear to have an accompanying spouse.

Missy regained Scott's attention, "We're all excited about your new kidney transplant!"

Scott took a sip of his beer and savored it. He loved Missy but their relationship had always been strictly Platonic. He was about to embark upon a long explanation about how and why his kidney transplant was not yet working. *It's called delayed graft function.* But he changed his mind, deciding not to put a damper on the party with a discussion about his medical problems.

"Thanks, Missy," said Scott. "You're the best. Gonna miss you when you head off to Indiana U." Much of the talk that night would center on college plans. Scott intended to go to college eventually, but decided to postpone plans until he got his kidney transplant. He reached for the second beer that Missy was handing him as he thought once again about his new kidney that was still in a "state of shock".

"I gotta be careful with my beer consumption or I'll go into fluid overload," he said to Missy, again whispering because he did not want to divulge details about the status of his transplanted kidney to the strangers at the party. Scott was a seasoned dialysis patient and had learned his lessons about fluid restriction the hard way. With little or no production of urine, he needed to limit his consumption of liquids between treatments. The dialysis procedure could remove excessive fluid, but in between treatments, there was essentially no way of eliminating bodily fluids aside from sweat, and evaporation through the lungs. If he drank more than two quarts of fluid a day, his lungs would begin to fill with water after about two days, and he'd start feeling short of breath before his next dialysis treatment…a very unpleasant sense of suffocation.

Brian walked over and handed Scott a freshly lit joint. A big fat blunt. Scott was no stranger to marijuana, but he was certainly not a "stoner". His high school crowd consisted more of jocks than stoners, but weed was readily available to almost all of the social circles at Lima High School. In his own circle of friends, it was saved for special occasions while cheap beer was more often the party staple. Considering his fluid restriction, a couple of tokes seemed like an attractive idea tonight as an alternative to drinking beer and worrying about getting fluid overloaded.

"Really good shit," Brian said smiling. "My cousin bought it in Texas – Aguas Caliente Gold...or Red...or something like that....maybe that was Aculpoco Red...whatever...really good shit."

Scott inhaled his third hit *(I think it's my third hit)* and suddenly had difficulty remembering his name. *Might as well get wasted.* "Yeah good stuff Brian," he said, passing the joint inadvertently to Missy. She also was not a complete stranger to the herb, but wasn't in the mood tonight and passed it off as she did at most parties. Scott reached over and returned her earlier kiss on the cheek. He was suddenly experiencing more than the usual giggly space-time disorientation he recognized from smoking weed. He felt numbness in his arms and legs, then felt like his mind was being separated from his body. He looked at Missy and had the feeling that he was looking at himself in another body – a young woman's body. *Really weird.* Suddenly he was concerned that the crowd around him was watching his ego leaving his body and moving into Missy's body. He was losing his sense of being an individual person.

He turned back to Brian who was still sporting a wide grin, appearing flushed and high as a kite. He scanned the rest of the crowd, trying to determine if they were behaving normally or whether they were experiencing the same sensation of body separating from mind. There was a slight sense of nausea. He turned again to Brian, hoping for some explanation.

"Angel dust, baby," said Brian. "Really good shit." It was the last thing Scott remembered, aside from a transient sense of insurmountable mental and physical strength. He wanted to crush something – anything. Brian's cousins from Texas had spiked the joints with PCP.

Chapter Four

Preliminary Consent
May 7, 2008

Lance Turner was driving his 2007 Honda Civic west on route 70, on the way from his office in Columbus to evaluate a potential deceased donor at Wright Sate County Hospital, just north of Dayton. In this part of the country, the four seasons could best be defined by the state of the corn crop surrounding the interstate highways: early corn, knee-high corn ("knee-high by the fourth of July"), harvest corn, and winter (no corn at all). Surveying the columns and rows of seedling plants to his left and right, Lance recognized early corn – a sure sign of spring in central Ohio.

Normally, a collection of Bob Marley tunes would be blaring on the car stereo – fifteen songs basically covered the trip from Columbus to Dayton. But today he was driving with a guest – Frank Orlowski from the Action 9 News Team in Columbus. The TV station was planning a series of reports on organ donation and transplantation, and Orlowski was assigned to shadow Lance Turner during this donor evaluation. Lance was nervous about the arrangement. Orlowski headed a team of investigative reporters that more often exposed shady business practices and other forms of fraud in and around Columbus. Lance's boss, Bob Briggs, assured him that this coverage was intended to put a positive spin on organ transplantation in Ohio. Lance went along with it. He had no choice. But he felt uncomfortable traveling without Bob Marley.

"So, Mr. Turner, how long have you been working for the Ohio Organ Bank?" Frank asked, as Lance's Honda sped beyond the Columbus city limits.

"Please, call me Lance. I've been working as a transplant donor coordinator for the OOB Ohio for just over a year. I like my job. In fact I *love* my job."

"That's great. So what's your background? What kind of training did you have before joining the OOB?"

"I graduated from Cleveland State and worked as a dialysis technician for three years, but ultimately found that job to be tedious and boring. I mean, I liked working with patients and the professional staff, but it was basically the same routine day in and day out – inserting dialysis needles to get patients hooked up to the dialysis circuit, monitoring vital signs and the dialysis machines during the treatment, then removing the needles and moving on to the next patient. Pretty much the same thing every day, day in and day out."

Lance paused. "Do you mind if I turn on a little background music?" he inquired as he turned on the Bob Marley CD at a low volume, without getting Orlowski's permission. "We can still talk," said Lance, with Marley's *'Get Up, Stand Up'* playing quietly in the background. He somehow felt more comfortable talking to this stranger with Marley singing in the background.

"At the OOB, every day brings something new," Lance went on. "The job involves a lot of regional travel, visiting dozens of different hospitals, and meeting lots of new and interesting people. Each organ donor has a unique medical history, although almost all of them have some cause for brain death. Brain dead donors account for the vast majority of deceased organ donors."

As part of his training as a donor coordinator, Lance became intimately familiar with the definition and medical criteria for determining brain death. He also learned about the history behind these definitions, including the 1968 report of a special committee assembled by Harvard Medical School to define *irreversible coma*, the impact of the Karen Quinlan case in 1976, and the landmark 1981 report of a presidential commission entitled *Defining Death: Medical, Legal, and Ethical Issues in the Determination of Death*. That report ultimately led to the *Uniform Determination of Death Act* that was translated into law in almost all of the fifty states, including Ohio, and subsequently used to define brain death in many other countries around the world as well.

Lance glanced over to see that Orlowski was taking written notes. *'Stir It Up'* was now playing on the car stereo. Lance was still not completely relaxed. He realized that some of his comments sounded more like lecture material than a casual conversation, but if Orlowski was going to run a special on transplantation, Lance wanted to be sure that he got his facts straight.

"Nowadays, transplant centers also are accepting more and more organs from donors after cardiac death," Lance went on. "We call them 'DCDs'. These are terminally-ill patients who retain some brain functions but whose families agree to allow organ donation once the patient's heart stops beating. From a coordinator's perspective, these cases are even more intriguing and challenging because decisions have to be made very quickly as the organs need to be surgically harvested within a short period of time – literally minutes – after the heart stops beating. Hospitals that are serious about supporting organ donation often have a functional operating room immediately adjacent to the ICU to facilitate rapid removal of DCD organs. You'll see one of those at Wright State, although the donor we're evaluating will probably turn out to be a more traditional brain dead donor."

"So, do you deal directly with the families of these donors?" Orlowski asked.

"It's a *major* part of my job. I discovered early on that donor families have a wide variety of attitudes and opinions about organ donation, ranging from complete ignorance about the issues to absolute refusal to provide consent for donation, even after we do our best to educate them. Most families fall somewhere in between, and that's when we donor coordinators come in to play. My previous job…working with dialysis patients suffering from kidney failure…has been a big plus when it comes to talking to families about kidney transplantation. But I also now know quite a bit about the transplantation of solid organs other than kidneys, and about transplantation of corneas and other tissues. So, we coordinators are responsible for educating families about the process of organ donation, and ultimately for obtaining consent to procure some or all of the deceased donor's organs. Unless the donor had expressed wishes to donate organs prior to death, consent for donation falls into the hands of the immediate family members. In Ohio, that signature or stamp on the back of a driver's license is very helpful...and technically legally binding. But if families adamantly refuse to allow organ donation, we tend to back off to keep the situation civil."

"I didn't realize any of that," said Orlowski, fumbling to remove the driver's license from his own wallet to check out his organ donor status.

For Lance, working as a donor coordinator was a great opportunity to work with families, doctors and nurses, and hospital administrators. He spent a lot of time in his car traveling to more than twenty hospitals in western Ohio, covering the triangle between Bowling Green, Columbus, and Dayton. The travel provided quiet time for thought and contemplation – mostly thinking about his future. He was engaged to be married. His fiancée, Debbie, was a technician at a dialysis unit in Columbus. With their savings and combined incomes, they were prepared to make a down payment on a house before the wedding. Lance was attending business school at nights and on weekends at Ohio State. Ultimately, he hoped to work in hospital administration – or maybe in the administration of dialysis units. It would take three years to earn his MBA degree. In the mean time, the job at OOB was providing excellent on-the-job training. At the age of twenty-six, the future looked bright.

Lance glanced over to Orlowski, who was still examining his driver's license.

"So, are you signed up?"

"I guess not," Orlowski said, somewhat embarrassed. "But

I'm gonna change that as soon as I get back home."

"Okay, it never hurts to sign up. But remember, it's your family who may ultimately decide for you, so you should let them know of your wishes," Lance said, then picking up on the earlier discussion. "Where were we? So, the only down side of my job is the work schedule. We need to be onsite or nearby to deal with any abrupt changes in the status of the potential donor, so we typically work twenty-four to thirty-six-hour shifts in order to minimize travel time. We're not expected to be in the ICU for that entire time. We get breaks for sleeping and meals. But it's imperative for us to be nearby so we can return to the ICU when the medical status of a donor changes. I typically check into a nearby hotel or motel whenever my assignment is more than an hour away from home. Of course, the OOB's budget doesn't allow for five star hotels. That's why you and I will be checking into a Fairfield Inn, Mr. Orlowski," Lance said smiling.

"You can call me Frank. Hey, there's nothing wrong with Fairfield Inns. What do we need from a hotel room aside from a bed, a toilet, a shower and access to the internet? And maybe some fast food restaurants nearby."

Lance and Frank checked into separate rooms at the Fairfield Inn in North Dayton, quickly dropped off their bags, and headed out to Wright State. Arriving at the hospital's parking garage, Lance filled Frank in on some details about the facility. "I think this may be about my twentieth trip to Wright State County Hospital in the past year. It's nice because I've gotten to know the place and several members of the staff. This hospital has a *level one* trauma center so it attracts accident victims from a large region of Ohio surrounding interstate route 75. On top of the brain injuries suffered by victims of motor vehicle accidents, Wright State also sees its fair share of gunshot wounds to the head and other forms of head trauma. And of course, there are always plenty of patients with the most common brain injury – stroke. Right there, you pretty much cover the gamut of maladies that potentially lead to brain death. So, Wright State is a common source of business for the OOB...and for me."

Of his twenty-or-so assignments to this hospital, however, only four resulted in organ donations. Sometimes the OOB coordinators were called in to evaluate *potential* donors who ultimately died without meeting the criteria for brain death or donation after cardiac death. In other cases, families refused to allow donation from otherwise suitable donors, despite intense efforts to educate them and to change their minds. Then there were cases in which the fully consented donor was taken to the operating team for surgical removal of organs, only to have the procuring surgeons find that the organs were too badly damaged by those terminal processes that characterize all human death, i.e., a fall in cardiac output, low blood pressure, and decreased delivery of oxygen to vital tissues. Sometimes there were unexpected findings, like cancer spread throughout the body. When trauma was the cause of death, the surgeons might find that organs were lacerated, perforated or otherwise damaged beyond repair.

Lance explained all of this to Orlowski as they approached the main entrance of the County Hospital. "Four successful organ donations out of twenty trips to Wright State is not a bad ratio, and those four donors yielded a total of seventeen organs that saved the lives of as many individuals with end-stage organ diseases. To be honest Frank, this is not a bad track record at all for a first year donor coordinator. Not bad at all."

Orlowski already knew all of this. Bob Briggs told him that the OOB was delighted with Mr. Turner's work performance. He was their rising star and would be a great coordinator to feature in the TV series.

Lance was happy to see Nikki manning the reception desk in the lobby of Wright State's main entrance. She was a very attractive light-skinned African American woman, *maybe mixed African and Puerto Rican?* – probably his age plus or minus a year.

Her shoulder-length hair was dyed a dark shade of red with yellow highlights. She was always friendly.

"Good morning, Mr. Turner. Need an ICU pass?" asked Nikki, understanding his mission. She also found Lance to be friendly and attractive. He was lanky and tall, once a small forward for the Cleveland State Vikings basketball team. He had facial features that resembled those of Denzel Washington, complemented by a perfectly trimmed goatee.

"Yes ma'am. I'm here to see a patient – a Mr. Elroy Kirk – in your Medical Intensive Care Unit. All on behalf of the Ohio Organ Bank," he said, while flipping open his wallet with an OOB identification card – all a formality, as Nikki was now very familiar with Lance and the OOB. "And this is Mr. Frank Orlowski from Action 9 News in Columbus," Lance went on, introducing his guest. "He'll need a pass too. Channel 9 is gonna run a special series on organ transplantation," he went on, seeing that Nikki was impressed. "Maybe they can mention my favorite hospital receptionist!"

"Oh sure, that would be great," she responded. "Hey, have you dumped that girlfriend of yours in Columbus yet?" Nikki asked half-jokingly as she prepared the visitor passes.

"No, no. In fact, we got a wedding planned for September. If I come down this way much more often, I'm gonna have to invite you to the wedding, girl!"

Entering the ICU with Frank, Lance also recognized the older receptionist in the ICU but couldn't quite remember her name. *I gotta work on my name recall skills if I'm ever gonna be a successful administrator.* However, she remembered Lance, understood his purpose, and immediately welcomed him back, somewhat oblivious to his guest who she presumed to be a partner. "Hello Mr. Turner. The nursing staff has been waiting for you. Have a seat in the back conference room and I'll have the head nurse and Mr. Kirk's primary nurse join you two right away."

Lance was pouring himself and Frank two cups of muddy

39

coffee when Kathy Briggs, the head nurse, and another unfamiliar male nurse walked in, exchanging cordial introductions. Kathy had been through this process many times and also had come to know Lance and some of the other coordinators from the OOB. But it was Kurt, the primary nurse, who presented the case of Mr. Elroy Kirk to Lance.

"The patient is a young African American male with a large intracranial bleed that developed after an accidental oral ingestion of a large amount of cocaine. The cerebral hemorrhage was precipitated by severe hypertension that was initially controlled with intravenous nitroprusside. The tox screen was positive for cocaine only, although there is a history of recreational use of marijuana. Looks like Mr. Kirk herniated his brainstem even prior to admission from the ER. Pupils are fixed and dilated with no spontaneous movements or respirations, but he was on propofol for sedation and that was weaned off four hours ago to assess for underlying brain activity. The EEG tech is on her way. Despite the hypertension, his urine output and kidney function have been normal...so far."

"Thanks Kurt," said Lance, recognizing that Kurt had probably never been involved with the management of a potential donor. He was impressed by Kurt's poised presentation. Lance explained to Frank that the EEG would be performed to determine whether the donor had any detectable brain wave activity. A diagnosis of brain death could not be made if the patient was receiving a strong sedative, such as propofol. Discontinuation of such drugs was mandatory before proceeding with an EEG for the sake of assessing brain death.

"Does the poor guy have any relatives?" asked Lance.

"A girlfriend has been here since admission. She's not handling this well. I think she's still out in the ICU waiting room. Her name is....Ms. Stenfield – Tanya, I think."

The waiting room was filled with a dozen family members either waiting to see their loved ones in the ICU or resting and waiting for updates from the medical staff. Lance took Frank with him and visually sorted through the small group of people and spotted a young black woman most likely to be the girlfriend as she appeared to be alone and teary-eyed. He approached her and asked, "Are you Ms. Tanya Stenfield?"

"Yeah. Are you Elroy's doctor?"

"No, my name is Lance Turner. I'm from the Ohio Organ Bank. Can I have a word with you? There's an empty consultation room around the corner. This is Mr. Orlowski from Channel 9 in Columbus. I hope you don't mind if he joins us."

Tanya ignored the introduction to Orlowski but stared at Lance for a few moments before asking, "Did you play for Cleveland State? 2004 or 2005?" she asked, revealing her avid interest in Ohio college basketball.

"Yep...well, close. Started as a senior in the 2002-2003 season. We were nineteen and seven and went to the NIT that year...Do I know you?"

"I seen you play back then. Maybe it was the NIT tournament. Elroy played college ball for Wright State but dropped out after his sophomore year."

Lance motioned for Tanya to move to the consultation room and then continued the conversation.

"So how do you know Mr. Kirk?" he asked, carefully avoiding use of the past tense.

"We been together since he was playin' in college and I was dancin' or tendin' bar in Dayton. Goin' on three years now we've been livin' together."

"Are you his closest kin?"

"Well we've been livin' together for all this time now. So, far's I know, that's like common law. But we ain't officially married. Elroy's got no brothers or sisters. He had one brother but he got shot and killed in Cleveland. Stupid bar fight. Far as I know, his Momma's now his only other relative and she's laid up in Dayton with both legs cut off – you know, *amputations*."

The last word rolled off Tanya's tongue as though she had looked it up on Wikipedia and studied its meaning. *Check that, I'm sure that she has never heard of Wikipedia or any other -pedia.* "Have the doctors or nurses explained to you what's going on with Elroy? Have they talked to you about his prognosis?" *Check that.* "Have they told you if he's gonna live?"

"Yeah, he ain't gonna make it, far's I know. From what they told me, they think he had a bad stroke that's put him into a coma – maybe a *permanent* coma," she said rolling her eyes upward.

"Ms. Stenfield, in the next hour or so, the ICU doctors and nurses will be running some tests to determine whether Elroy has any brain function. Right now, he still has a heartbeat, but the doctors think that his brain is dead. They'll only know for sure when they run an electro-encephalogram to see if he has any brain activity. That's also known as an EEG." He looked to her for some sign of insight, but Tanya's expression remained blank. In the mean time, Frank Orlowski was taking notes furiously.

With each new experience dealing with donor families, Lance worried increasingly about the concept of *informed* consent. He dealt with family members and friends with a wide range of intelligence, knowledge, and insight. *Just how much do they comprehend? Just how much do we need to tell them? How much of what we tell them do they really understand? Do they really understand the importance of their decisions? Should we disallow organ donation when we feel that the family is not truly informed, or not intelligent enough to comprehend?* He thought of sharing these concerns with Frank Orlowski, but was concerned that a positive spin on transplantation could quickly turn negative if he ventured too far into these ethical issues.

He continued his conversation with Tanya. "If his brain is dead, Elroy is officially dead even if his heart is still beating. If he is brain dead, Ms. Stenfield, he may be a candidate for donating organs to other people. Do you understand? Have you ever heard about organ donation?"

"Far's I know, yeah, I've heard about it. I figure if Elroy's gonna die, he might as well give his organs to other folks. I'm okay with that. But the problem is, his Momma raised him a strict Baptist."

"Organ donation is approved by the Baptist Church, and by Catholics, Muslims, Jews and almost all other religions," answered Lance, a bit methodically for the sake of his TV guest. "So, would you say that Elroy's mother is his closest next-of-kin?"

"Either her or me. But she ain't coming down here with her *amputations.*" She glanced at Lance, as if she wondered whether he knew the meaning of the word. "She's too sick to be coming down here." Lance was secretly hoping that the mother would be more insightful than Tanya, but he wasn't sure whether common-law marriage trumped direct kinship when it came to providing consent. He would need to check with his supervisors back at the OOB. He liked that he learned something new about the rules and regulations of organ donation with every new case.

"That's okay Tanya. I'll need an opinion from my office about who's got power of attorney in this case, but until Elroy has been declared brain dead, I can't officially ask either of you for consent for the organ donation. In the mean time, do you mind if I ask you some questions that might seem very personal?"

"Go ahead. Makes no difference now, far's I know."

"OK. Please understand that these questions are simply intended to determine whether your Elroy was...umm, whether Elroy *is* at high risk for being infected with the AIDS virus or other infections. If so, we might need to turn him down as a potential organ donor. You understand?"

"Sure," said Tanya, pretending to comprehend what Lance was saying. "He ain't ever had AIDS, far's I know." *Perhaps she doesn't realize that if Mr. Kirk had...umm, has AIDS, she most likely has it too! Or maybe she thinks that AIDS comes and goes like the common cold.*

43

"I understand but I still need to ask these questions. Okay. First, has Elroy had sex with another man in the past five years?"

"What the hell?"

"Please Ms. Stenfield. I technically gotta ask these questions."

"Okay. No," she blurted out, now embarrassed that she was answering a question like this in front of two males. "Elroy may be stupid some times, but he ain't no queer."

"Alright, here's a more important question. Has Elroy used intravenous drugs in the past five years?"

"He ain't never done any intravenous shit, far's I know. He smokes some reefer now and then but not on no regular basis. And he loves Hennessy, but I never seen or heard about him shooting up any kind of dope."

"Wasn't he using cocaine?"

"No sir. Far's I know. He was sellin' the shit, but wasn't usin' it, except for that bag he swallowed."

"OK. Does Elroy have any medical conditions? Does he have any history of blood transfusions or any blood disorders like sickle cell anemia or hemophilia?"

"No sir, far's I know," she said, having no clue what she was being asked.

"Again, please don't take this personally, but, *far's you know*, has he paid for sex…you know, paid for a prostitute…any time in the past year?"

"As I says, we been tight for three or four years now. These questions are really bullshit."

"Okay sorry. Please, one final question. Has Elroy been an inmate at a correctional facility any time in the past year?"

Tanya paused and stared out the window for a few seconds before answering, appearing a bit angry about the previous question. "What? You mean prison?"

"Correct."

"No sir."

"Thank you, Ms. Stenfield. Listen, I know the last several

hours have been rough on you. And I'm sorry about those last questions – its part of my job. I'll be in and out of the ICU for the next several hours. If you have any questions for me, just ask Elroy's nurse to call me, and here is my card. In the mean time, do you have a phone number for Elroy's mother?"

Lance returned to the ICU conference room and called Mrs. Vivian Kirk. Tanya had previously talked to her and provided all the gory details about her son's recent escapades and hospitalization, including the dope deal that went sour. Over the phone, Lance could sense a mixture of grief and anger. Frank Orlowski was frustrated because there was no speaker phone and he could hear only Lance's half of the conversation.

"Stupid! Stupid! Stupid!" she screamed, then pausing to sob. "The boy had a future. He was strong and good lookin' and talkin' about goin' back to school. I knew he was dealing dope, but he promised me he was gonna stop and that he was goin' back to school. Could have gone to Ohio State or better. Could have been a doctor or maybe even a lawyer. And now they tell me he's probably gonna die. How could he be so stupid?" she asked rhetorically.

Lance did not respond immediately, understanding from over a year of training and experience that it was best to let family members vent their emotions before proceeding to any earnest conversation about donation of organs. Opening up with a discussion about brain death and organ donation was likely to yield a grief-stricken, immediate refusal to allow donation. Lance also learned something from his own mother about interacting with other people – whether professionally or socially. *"Always start off talking about them, not you. Folks relax when they can start off talking about themselves."*

"Tanya tells me that you are disabled, ma'am?" Lance inquired. Indeed, Vivian had suffered from diabetes for more than twenty years, was insulin-dependent, legally blind, and had not only bilateral below-the-knee amputations but three finger amputations as well. More importantly, she had kidney failure and required treatment with hemodialysis for more than two years. She immediately bonded with Lance when he told her about his previous job as a dialysis technician. After fifteen minutes, Lance had succeeded in quelling her grief and anger and was able to move on to the more important discussion about brain death and organ donation.

Mrs. Kirk was reasonably familiar with at least kidney transplantation. She herself had been evaluated for a kidney transplant at the Ohio Medical Center, but was turned down because of her diabetes, severe vascular disease, and heart failure. The OMC told her that she was free to get another opinion at another transplant center, but she knew the decision would likely be the same, and she couldn't afford the trips that would have been necessary to get second opinions in Cleveland, Cincinnati, or Toledo. She had two "man friends" from her dialysis unit who received kidney transplants within the past year. They often visited the unit to see their old friend, Vivian, and to show off for the other patients and staff. After listening to Lance's very sincere rendering of organ donation and its benefits to society, Vivian was quite convinced that providing consent to donate Elroy's organs was the right thing to do. But she still had a number of reservations.

"If Elroy's gonna die, I want him to have a regular decent wake and funeral. I can't have his body all torn up for the casket if they take out his organs."

"I assure you, Mrs. Kirk, the surgical procedures performed to remove Elroy's organs do not disfigure Elroy's body in any way. He will look entirely normal for the wake." He was being totally honest. Although multiorgan procurements required large incisions extending from the upper chest to the lower abdomen, the open cavity left behind after removal of the organs could be filled at the funeral home with artificial materials – like ping-pong balls – to maintain the body's normal configuration. The incisions were sewn closed, and morticians craftily re-clothed the corpse to look completely normal in a casket. Families could never tell that the corpse had been eviscerated.

"Well then, Mr. Turner, I believes in God and I believes that if Elroy's gonna die that God would want him to donate his kidneys so others may live without dialysis."

"There are other people who might benefit from transplanting his liver, his heart and his other organs. God willing, Mrs. Kirk, would you be okay with allowing those organs to be donated as well?"

"So long as my boy looks normal in the casket, I believes that it's God's will. I believes that we should give Elroy's organs to all those people who need them. And Mr. Turner, you have a blessed day," she concluded, quietly hanging up the phone and feeling sad but content.

Lance put the phone down and smiled. *Another job well done. I love this job!*

It had been a long day and Frank Orlowski was tired but impressed by Lance and by the entire organ procurement process. "Mr. Turner, this has been a helluva day," he said to Lance. "You know, you are really good at what you do."

Lance and Frank returned to the Fairfield Inn for a dinner break. Lance turned up the volume on his car stereo during the drive back to the hotel. Bob Marley and the Wailers were singing 'Jammin' as Orlowski quietly reviewed his notes and the events of the day.

Chapter Five

Seizures
May 24, 2008

Sarah Anderson woke up at 7:15 AM and peeked through the curtains of her first-floor master bedroom to find the sun shining brightly. *Not a cloud in the sky. Should be a nice weekend.* The large patches of grass surrounding the house were covered with dew. Two weeks earlier, Ken had planted about three dozen tomato plants in the section of the garden most easily visible from her bedroom and there was a fine misty fog hovering over the budding plants that appeared anxious to soak up the morning sun. Being careful not to wake her husband, Sarah ambled quietly to the kitchen and prepared a pot of coffee for her and Ken. In the spring, summer, and fall, he would typically sleep in till after 8 AM on Saturday mornings before heading out to play golf.

Sitting in the kitchen, Sarah could view the carriage house about fifty yards away from the main house. She saw no signs of life. *God, I remember my high school graduation party. We drank 3.2 beer and stayed up till five in the morning.* Strangely, the carriage house door was wide open. Usually when the high school gang crashed there, the door would be closed to preserve warmth on cool spring nights. *Strange. Maybe the kids camped out down by the creek. Or maybe the party ended early?*

She walked upstairs to Scott's second-floor bedroom and was surprised to find that Scott's bedroom door was closed but slightly ajar. She quietly cracked open the door, peeked in, and found Scott sound asleep on his bed. *Dead to the world, probably hung over – ah youth! I hope the other kids didn't drive home drunk. I hope that Scott arranged for designated drivers. I'll let him sleep. We can still make his dialysis appointment if we leave by 9:45. Traffic will be light on a Saturday morning.*

When she returned to the kitchen, Sarah heard her cell phone vibrating on the counter. It was Ken's sister Heather, who often called at this time. Over the years, they had become close friends and Sarah appreciated Heather's experience as a nurse when it came to discussing the family's many medical problems.

"Hi, Sarah. I just wanted to say thanks for the party last night. The food was awesome and Scott looked great!"

Sarah recounted what she could make of the post-party events. "You know, Heather, I really want Scott to live as normal a life as possible, but it's tough with dialysis treatments looming almost every other day. I even wonder whether Scott's kidney failure and dialysis somehow prevent him from having normal relationships with girls. You know, social *or* physical relationships." She peered down the hallway to be sure Ken was wasn't yet awake before going on. "I hate to say this, but I don't feel comfortable discussing this kind of stuff with Scott or even with Ken."

"Give it some time, Sarah. Scott is a nice young man. And good looking too – takes after you. Once his kidney transplant starts working, his life will begin to normalize. You'll be chasing his girlfriends away!"

Ken joined Sarah for coffee at 8:45, already showered and ready to head out for eighteen holes of golf with three business clients at the Shawnee Country Club. They were established clients – not new ones – but these outings helped to solidify Ken's business relationships. Sarah knew that Ken's Saturday golf outings were intended more for pleasure than business, but it was an essential part of his life from April to October. He was a good man, a good father, and a good husband. She was more than happy to let him golf on Saturday mornings. *He can golf all day, every day, so long as he brings home the bacon.*

"Are the kids sleeping in the carriage house?" he asked while sipping his coffee and scanning the morning newspaper.

"I haven't been out there, but they left the door wide open

and Scott's sound asleep in his room. Ken, I hope his dialysis treatment schedule didn't wreck the party plans. On the other hand, he knows he's got a fluid restriction…he shouldn't have had more than two or three beers."

"Who can figure kids?" said Ken, as he finished the last sip of his coffee. "Listen, I should be back from Shawnee around the time you guys get back from dialysis. Looks like it's going to be a beautiful day. Why don't we get some steaks for tonight and let Scott cheat on his renal diet? Maybe he can invite Missy Lander over. She seems like a sweetie-pie. I chatted with her at the party last night and we actually had an intelligent conversation about the economy. Imagine that, an intelligent conversation with a teenager!"

"Okay, I'll get some sirloins in town while Scott is on dialysis." Sarah was delighted to find things to do *during* Scott's four-hour hemodialysis sessions. When he first started dialysis, Sarah would sit at his bedside for the entire session – four hours of dialysis. But that didn't include the start-up time and the end of the treatment when the technicians often had to hold pressure on Scott's AV fistula for up to thirty minutes to stop any bleeding after the needles were pulled out. For Sarah, it was very boring. Scott usually tried to sleep during the dialysis session. Moreover, at his age, he really didn't want his *Mom* hanging around constantly. Between the drive times to and back from the Lima dialysis unit, staying with Scott during dialysis amounted to the commitment of a part-time job for Sarah. And she certainly wasn't being paid for her efforts. In fact, she had to quit her part-time job as a librarian in the Lima Public Library when Scott started dialysis treatments. Even when she was able to do some shopping or otherwise occupy her time while Scott sat attached to the machine, the dialysis treatments dramatically influenced her weekly schedule. Having a son with kidney failure requiring chronic dialysis treatments influenced not only Scott's life, but the life of the entire family.

"I would love to have Scott invite Missy for dinner tonight. I think he likes her," said Sarah looking to her husband for a response that might trigger a discussion about the effects of dialysis on their son's love life. There was no response. Ken was busy checking baseball scores in the Sports section. *Men!*

Ken was preparing to tee off on the fourth hole at the Shawnee Country Club when his cell phone went off. His ring tone was the voice of George Harrison singing *'Tax Man'*. The clients were amused.

It was Sarah on the phone. *She never calls me when I'm playing golf.* She sounded panic-stricken.

"Ken, Listen, I'm on my way to Lima General. I couldn't wake up Scott. He was face down in his bed – in a pool of frothy blood. His arms and legs were twitching. I thought maybe he was just drunk or hung over but I couldn't wake him up. I called 911 and the ambulance has already left with Scott. Can you meet me at the Lima General Emergency Room? I'll be there in a few minutes. Ken, I'm scared to death!"

By the time Ken arrived at the hospital, the Emergency Room team was already preparing to life flight Scott by helicopter to the OMC in Columbus.

"What the hell happened?" Ken asked Sarah after letting her sob in his arms for several minutes in the ER waiting room.

"They think he's having seizures. They're not sure why. He's not awake...he's in a coma of some kind. He's getting a head CT scan right now and then they want to life flight him to the Ohio Medical Center in Columbus. I'm waiting here for the Emergency Room doctor to come out with an update."

"Maybe it's one of his medications," offered Ken. "His medications are all different since the kidney transplant."

Before Sarah had a chance to respond, a young prematurely balding doctor wearing a blue scrub suit and a white smock walked through the double doors between the waiting room and the ER. He looked like a young and thin version of Telly Savalas. Nodding to Ken, he provided a quick update.

"Hi, I'm Pat McIntyre."

Hmm, Irish, not Greek!

"Scott is pretty sick. We think he was in status epilepticus when he arrived – continuous grand mal seizures. We needed to intubate him and put him on a ventilator because people stop breathing during a seizure, and with *continuous* seizures you don't last very long without breathing. We think we have the seizures under control with medication – in this case, intravenous Dilantin and Valium. He's not awake but it's hard to tell if that's from the sedative effects of the anti-seizure drugs or whether he's just post-ictal."

"Post-ictal?" Ken asked, hearing yet another unfamiliar medical term.

"A state of unconsciousness or semi-consciousness that sometimes occurs after a grand mal seizure...can last for over an hour, even longer sometimes. Anyhow, the preliminary read on the head CT scan shows no space occupying lesions...umm, sorry...no masses, tumors, or obvious signs of a stroke. So the seizures may be toxic-metabolic in origin."

"What does that mean? Is it because he needs dialysis? He was supposed to have dialysis this morning back in Lima. Is it an elevated potassium level? Could one of his transplant medications do it?" asked Sarah, suddenly realizing that she was asking several questions at the same time.

"Well he *is* taking tacrolimus as an anti-rejection drug and I've heard that it can cause seizures when the blood levels are very high," McIntyre responded. "But that's why we need to get him to the transplant center at OMC. We don't even have the capability of measuring tacrolimus blood levels here. His renal function panel is not too terrible – his potassium is 4.9 and his other electrolytes are pretty normal, but they will probably want to give him a dialysis treatment as soon as he arrives at the OMC.

By the way folks, I hate to ask this, but is there any chance that your son uses drugs? I mean *illegal* drugs?"

Sarah paused before answering, a little flabbergasted by the question, but recalling the hints suggesting that last night's after party ended in some unusually early manner. "No, not that we know of, although I'm pretty sure that Scott and his friends were drinking some beer last night at a graduation party. Just normal high school seniors, you know?"

"Alright, but just so you know, we did send off a standard toxic screen for illegal drugs. These days you never know, and we've seen seizures with cocaine or crystal meth overdoses. Maybe you don't know this, but the crystal meth thing has gotten out of control in the Lima area. We'll send all the lab reports over to Columbus when they become available. It's too risky to send Scott by ambulance, so he'll go by helicopter to get him there as quickly as possible. I've already talked to the OMC transplant resident, and their team is expecting him. If you guys take off now by car, they should have Scott stabilized by the time you get there."

Ken and Sarah decided to drive directly to Columbus in Ken's Explorer, leaving her car behind at the Lima General parking garage. On the way, Sarah cell-phoned the Landers.

"Hi, Marilyn. It's Sarah Anderson. Did Missy get in okay last night?"

"Hello, Sarah. Yeah...actually Missy got in before Jim and I went to bed. She said Scott wasn't feeling well and the party ended early. It was well before midnight. In fact, we were still watching the 11 o'clock news."

"Hmm. Is Missy awake? Can I speak to her?"

"Sure. Hang on."

"Hi, Mrs. Anderson, is something wrong?" Missy asked nervously.

"Scott is sick and on his way back to the Medical Center in Columbus. Can you tell me what happened last night? And,

Missy...please be very honest with me, because it's very important for the doctors...were there any drugs at the party last night?"

There was a pause and Sarah could tell that Missy was moving out of earshot of her mother. With a lower voice, she responded, "There were a couple of older guys there – Brian's friends or cousins. They were passing around a marijuana joint, but I don't think Scott smoked it," she lied. "Well, I just don't recall for sure. He drank two beers, maybe three, and said he wasn't feeling well, so I walked him back to the house and the party sort of fizzled. You and Mr. Anderson were already sleeping when I left Scott."

"Missy, was anybody using crystal meth at the after-party get-together last night?" Sarah asked.

"We all know about crystal meth, Mrs. Anderson. It's all over the place. But trust me, its bad stuff and the kids in our group will have nothing to do with it."

Missy had been within earshot when Brian mentioned angel dust the night before. She was only vaguely familiar with the drug and now was horrified that Scott might have overdosed on it. *I thought he took only two hits.* "Is Scott going to be okay, Mrs. Anderson? What's wrong?"

"He had a seizure and the doctors aren't sure why. We're half way to Columbus and we'll keep you posted. And Missy...*thank you* for being honest with me. We were all young once, understand?"

"Yes...I understand...Thanks, Mrs. Anderson. God, I hope Scott is okay," said Missy, hanging up the phone, but wondering if she should call back and tell Mrs. Anderson about the two hits. *Or was it three?*

"Does she have any clues?" asked Ken, after Sarah hung up.

"Not really. Sounds like some kids were smoking pot at the after party, but marijuana is not a common cause of status epilepticus as far as I know."

"Not from the stuff we smoked when we were in college," Ken

replied, fondly recalling the days when he and Sarah first met at Ohio State.

"Indiana Gold? Now Kenneth Anderson, you know I never inhaled that stuff," Sarah responded, struggling to lighten up their serious predicament. "Besides, I think *that* pot was mostly oregano."

They arrived at the OMC and, presuming that Scott would be in the ICU, quickly made their way through the familiar hallways of the hospital to get to the ICU reception area. Between Sam and Scott, they had spent a good chunk of their lives in the OMC. It was like a second home, but not a comfortable one. It was now early Saturday afternoon and they were surprised when Mark Hubbard walked up to address them, even before they announced their arrival to the receptionist. *Do these guys ever take a day off?*

"Hello, folks," Hubbard said seriously. "Lima General called us and we've been expecting you. Scott is stable but he is still on a respirator and barely conscious. Our nephrologists want him to have routine dialysis this afternoon, but they don't think his seizures are the result of kidney failure. His potassium and other electrolytes are only moderately abnormal. I need to tell you...we just got the tox screen results from Lima General. The results are positive for cannabinoids...umm...marijuana – and also for phencyclidine. Phencyclidine is a sedative and hallucinogen that's sometimes added to marijuana."

"PCP right? Damn kids. Is that the cause of the seizures?" Ken asked. "If so, I'll head back to Lima and start busting some serious asses."

"I'm not so sure. It's my understanding that seizures are rare with PCP, even with much higher blood levels than reported form the Lima lab. But the combination of kidney failure, uremia, a little PCP, a little of this, a little of that – could explain things. The neurologists call it 'toxic-metabolic'."

"Yeah. We've heard the term before. Is there any specific treatment?" asked Sarah.

"We'll do the dialysis and hopefully all of this will resolve on its own. By the way, the Lima team put a bladder catheter in Scott before his transfer and he's made five hundred ccs of urine since he was transferred here. Did he tell you that his urine output was picking up? That's a good sign that the kidney may finally be kicking in. He might not need any further dialysis after today's treatment."

"Fantastic. At this point, we can use some good news," Ken responded.

Sarah and Ken decided to stay at the OMC for at least another few hours to see if Scott would wake up after dialysis. While waiting, they also decided to take a break for lunch in the hospital cafeteria. As they walked into the cafeteria, Sarah recognized a familiar face. It was Cora Mitchell, sipping on a cup of tea. She was wearing the same pink suit and pink pillbox hat that she had on when they first met her the day after her husband's and Scott's kidney transplants. Sarah immediately motioned to Ken to move towards her table.

"Mrs. Mitchell? Cora? We met you the day after your husband had his kidney transplant. Remember? Sarah and Ken Anderson. What are you doing here now?" asked Sarah.

"Yes, I remember meeting you. Well, I'm afraid Warren had a stroke two days ago. He got up in the middle of the night to go to the bathroom – he's been doing plenty of that since the kidney transplant because he's been making so much urine. Doctors said his bladder needed to stretch out after being lazy for all those years on dialysis with no urine. Anyways, then all of a sudden, I heard a big *thump* and found him on the bathroom floor. I had to call 911. He's paralyzed on the right side and he can't talk. Well, he talks, but its gibberish – like he can't get his words out. The doctors say only time will tell, and they're hopeful for some recovery. But this morning he had a seizure. I was here when it happened. Scared the heck out of me. That set him back some. I saw it happen. I've never seen a person have a seizure like that. Only lasted a few minutes, but it scared me to the bone – looked like a man possessed by the devil. And frothing at the mouth! And now he's hardly talking at all – not even gibberish. Doctors said not to worry – it was just a seizure."

Sarah looked at her husband and found the same look of astonishment that she knew she was wearing. *Complete coincidence. Old men on dialysis have strokes all the time. Just a coincidence. The seizures are just a coincidence.*

"And why are you all here? Did your son never go home? Is his new kidney working?" asked Cora.

Ken peered at Sarah intensely with a look that said...*let me handle this and we'll talk it over later*...before answering, "He went home for a few days but is back now for some routine tests. Just this morning, Scott's doctor told us there were signs that the kidney is beginning to work. He's beginning to make more urine and may not need any more dialysis."

"Well, praise the Lord, I am sure the doctor is right," said Cora. "Praise the Lord."

"Give our regards to Warren, Cora, and we'll say a prayer for his recovery from the stroke," said Sarah. "He'll be fine I'm sure!"

"Why did you lie to her?" Sarah asked her husband over lunch.

"I just thought she might become panicky if we told her that two recent kidney transplant recipients – probably getting their kidneys from the same donor – were readmitted within twenty-four hours of each other with seizures. It sounds spooky."

"Well it *is* spooky, Ken. I *am* spooked, aren't you?" Sarah asked.

"A little. But reason tells me that it's just a coincidence. Besides, you heard Cora – her husband had a stroke. Scott didn't.

So the seizures *are* a coincidence. Let's discuss it with Dr. Hubbard before we start jumping to conclusions about medical stuff that we don't understand. It's all probably a *complete* coincidence."

Chapter Six

Declaration of Brain Death
May 8 - 9, 2008

Lance Turner was in his Fairfield Inn room for his dinner break, feasting on a double whopper with cheese, fries, and a Diet Coke. The Diet Coke always eased his guilt about consuming fast foods. *Bad diet, but I'll go out for a long jog when I get back home after this shift.* He felt particularly guilty because Frank Orlowski headed to the fitness room to get some exercise during their break, promising to get a bite to eat later. Lance was blankly staring at the TV screen, watching something on the Food Network of all things, but mentally creating a checklist of things to do on the return trip to the ICU at Wright State.

On the way back to the hospital later that evening, Lance provided Frank with some further details about his responsibilities. "As you saw earlier today, we are responsible for counseling family members and friends in an effort to obtain consent for procuring organs from their deceased loved ones. It's important that families are not coerced – they need to understand the concept of brain death and willingly agree to organ donation after fully understanding the benefits to other people. On this follow-up trip, you'll likely get a feel for my second set of responsibilities. I'll be calling my central office in Columbus to initiate a series of communications between the organ procurement organization, multiple transplant centers in the region, and the physicians and nurses who ultimately will perform the transplant surgery and follow the transplant recipients. We take these responsibilities very seriously because, when successful, the process ultimately can provide organs and tissues from a single donor that could save or help as many as fifty people."

"Fifty?" asked Frank. "I didn't know there were that many organs in a human body!"

"We're talking about organs *and* tissues. When families agree to what we call a 'multi-organ procurement', the surgeons also obtain tissues and parts of blood vessels that can be used as jump grafts. And you've heard about corneal transplants I'm sure. So yes, in some cases, up to fifty people can receive either organs, blood vessels, tissues, or corneas from one donor. On the other hand, some families refuse to allow donation and it's important that we respect their decisions."

Long before brain death was officially declared, Lance made several calls to the central office, asking his colleagues to notify personnel from the transplant centers about a potential donor. He would run several checklists to be sure that all of the essential clinical and laboratory data was available for the transplant teams to make decisions about accepting or turning down the organs. Frank Orlowski kept a tally of all the phone calls and scribbled a diagram on his notepad, illustrating the complex network of institutions and individuals involved with this one donor. The diagram would ultimately serve as a graphic in the TV series. In between his many phone calls, Lance would meet with Tanya Stenfield or call Vivian Kirk with updates and additional counseling.

Like many African Americans, Tanya had a great deal of mistrust for the medical system and expressed a concern that Elroy's organs would be removed before he was truly dead. Although Lance was informed by his supervisors at the OOB that Elroy's mother had power of attorney and would need to provide the final consent for donation, he thought it was important for Tanya, the girlfriend/common-law wife, to understand that the entire process was legal, ethical, and beneficial to others.

"Being an African American myself, I feel particularly obliged to guide ethnic minority families through the organ donation process as a form of public education," Lance explained to Frank.

"My own family has a long history of mistrust and misunder-standing of the medical system. I grew up with seven brothers and sisters in the Glenville section of Cleveland in the late 1980s. You familiar with the neighborhood?"

"Well, I spent a week in Cleveland one day, but I don't recall Glenville. I gather it's not the Polish section of town?"

"No...not exactly, at least it wasn't in the 1980s," said Lance, chuckling. "Anyhow, believe it or not, all eight of us Turner kids were raised by our real mother and father – we all lived together in a four bedroom house with a basement that was finished to make an extra bedroom for my two youngest sisters. Both of my parents worked, but neither of them had health insurance. Their collective income disqualified them from Medicaid coverage, like many of our unemployed neighbors had. So, for my parents, any need for medical care was perceived as costly and there was always the suspicion that rich doctors were taking advantage of uninsured poor people. When my Dad developed kidney failure, he qualified for Medicare coverage before the age of sixty-five. That's when I first began to appreciate the complexity of the American medical system and resolved that I would make an effort to understand it and to demystify it for the sake of my family."

"Or for anybody else's sake," added Frank, now impressed with Lance's fund of knowledge. "How about Lance Turner for President?"

Lance was getting to like Frank. Their conversation ended as they pulled into parking lot at Wright State. Lance needed an update from the ICU staff and he wanted to renew his discussions with Tanya Stenfield.

"In a few minutes, the ICU team will perform an apnea test," Lance explained to Tanya in the ICU waiting area with Frank in attendance and taking more notes. "Earlier, they did the electroencephalogram or EEG – the brain wave test – and it showed no signs of brain activity. With the apnea test, they will take Elroy off the respirator for a few minutes to determine if there are any spontaneous breathing efforts. If not, he will be declared brain dead. As we discussed earlier, if he is brain dead...he is legally dead, even if his heart is still beating. At that point, I will call Mrs. Kirk for final consent to donate organs. Do you understand?"

"Yes," Tanya responded. "Far's I know. And thanks for explaining all of this to me, Mr. Turner. I just want all of this to be over so Elroy can rest in peace."

Brain death was officially declared at 10:20 PM, May 8, 2008. Mrs. Kirk provided the final consent over the telephone shortly thereafter – with Kurt, the primary nurse, serving as a third party witness. A team of surgeons would be on their way soon to procure the organs from the donor. Legally, those surgeons were not allowed to participate in the terminal care of the potential donor, and they could do nothing but wait until brain death was declared by the ICU team. In this case, because the family agreed to donate all organs, there was not just a single team of procuring surgeons, but multiple teams – each with the intent of removing specific organs.

Frank Orlowski turned down an invitation from the ICU staff to observe the organ procurement in the OR, citing his tendency to faint at the sight of blood as a good excuse. Instead, Lance filled him in on the general procedure. "The organs are removed in a standard order: first the heart, then the lungs, then the liver and pancreas and intestines, and finally the kidneys. This order is based largely on a well-known hierarchy of organ survival with out-of-body preservation. Kidneys can be preserved for the longest period of time, the heart the shortest. Generally, the hearts have to be transplanted in eight hours or less. Kidneys can be preserved for more than twenty hours and still function, but most kidney transplant surgeons try to get kidneys sewn into the recipients with less than twenty hours of preservation time."

"So what happens after the organs are harvested?" asked

Frank.

Lance cringed. "First, the politically correct term is *procurement*. *Harvesting* is for corn and other vegetables."

"Got it," responded Frank, blushing some.

Lance went on. "The procurement teams usually don't know in advance whether the organs will be allocated to patients at their own center or to one of the many other transplant centers in the region. Those decisions are made behind the scenes by computers, using complex allocation schemes that vary depending on the organ."

Elroy Kirk was now officially UNOS donor # OH7450. Lance got on the phone with the central office to review the checklist items needed to create the official donor data for UNOS – the United Network for Organ Sharing – the regulatory agency that was responsible for organ allocation in the United States. He had already entered his data electronically, but the OOB insisted upon oral verification in order to assure complete accuracy of the data. He was speaking to Linda Mayes, one of the newer donor coordinators who had been working for the OOB for just three months. Bob Briggs, whose title was "Administrative Director" of the OOB, often gave the junior coordinators "home office" duties before sending them on the road to deal with hospitals and donor families. It gave them some basic training in the language and logistics of organ donation.

"OK Linda, let's go down the list for donor #OH7450:

Age – 23,

Gender – male,

Race – black,

Blood type – B positive,

Time of brain death – 10:20 PM, May 8, 2008,

Cause of death – cerebrovascular accident,

Past history of hypertension? – negative,

HIV antibody – negative,

Cytomegalovirus antibody – negative,

Epstein Barr Virus antibody – positive,

Varicella antibody – positive,

Hepatitis C antibody – negative,

Hepatitis B surface antigen – negative,

Hepatitis B core antibody – negative,

Terminal serum creatinine concentration – 1.1 mg/dl,

Pressors at the time of death? – none,

CDC high risk? – negative,

Expanded criteria donor? – negative.

Do you copy?"

"Copy and it all verifies your earlier electronic entry," Linda responded. She was still a little green and didn't fully understand the importance of some items on the checklist. Earlier in the week she attended a training session to learn more about expanded criteria donors or "ECDs." It was all a bit confusing. ECD donors were basically older donors who sometimes had a history of high blood pressure or impaired kidney function at the time of death. Kidneys from ECDs did not survive as long as those from younger, healthier donors. But patients who were transplanted with such kidneys lived longer than if they stayed on dialysis.

Promising herself to review all this and to understand it better, Linda completed the checklist and continued on. "Sounds like we're good to go. We'll initiate the list run. Good work, Lance. I'll run the list from here."

It was now well past midnight and Lance and Frank were wrapping up at Wright State. Both men had been energized by the events of the night, but now their brains and bodies were becoming aware of the late hour and the length of the preceding work day. They would catch a few hours of sleep at the Fairfield Inn, then head back to Columbus early in the morning.

On the way back to the hotel, Lance tried to explain the complex UNOS system for organ allocation. "Transplanted hearts, lungs, and livers are allocated to potential recipients based on computerized scoring systems that determine which recipient is the sickest and in the greatest need of a life-saving transplant. That's not so for kidneys – in large part because patients with kidney failure usually can be kept alive indefinitely on dialysis. There's no equivalent of dialysis for patients with heart, lung, or liver failure. The allocation system for kidneys is based on a complicated 'point system' that awards points for time spent on the waiting list but also for the degree of tissue type matching between the recipient and donor. Whenever a kidney becomes available, the UNOS computers generate a list of all waitlisted patients with the same blood type as the donor. For any donor, the recipient with the most points is at the top of the list. The one with the fewest points is at the bottom – and everyone else is somewhere in between. The lists are long. For practical purposes, the transplant teams focus only on the top ten or twenty potential recipients. The point system doesn't include age matching, so occasionally there are crazy pairings like a 20-year-old recipient matching with a 65-year-old donor, or vice versa."

"Sounds like a less than perfect system," offered Frank, stifling a yawn. It was an interesting day, but his energy was fading fast.

"My friend, you are beginning to see that there are many less than perfect things in this world of organ transplantation," Lance concluded.

At 1:10 AM, Andrew Siegel, a kidney transplant surgeon at the Ohio Medical Center, was awakened at home by his beeping pager and a text message from the OOB. When he took "kidney call", he typically received two to three calls per night about potential donors, and so never planned to get a full night's worth of sleep. Many donor candidates – perhaps as many as three-quarters of them – were clear-cut turndowns. They were either too old, too sick prior to death, or had kidney function that was too abnormal. This was his first call of the night and Siegel was happily surprised to find that the Wright State donor sounded very acceptable.

Siegel called the OOB to speak directly with the coordinator who had sent the text message. "Yes, we're interested in the donor from Wright State. Please give the on-call OMC kidney transplant coordinator a call with the results of the list run – it's Kristy Young tonight. Have her call me when the list is available."

Andrew realized that he would sleep only intermittently for the remainder of the night. *Might as well not sleep at all.* Running the list would now involve a series of calls between him, his on-call residents, the operating room, Kristy, and potential recipients. His phone rang again at 2:05 AM.

"Hi, Andy, it's Kristy. Good news, looks like we'll get *both* kidneys from this Wright State donor. First up is Warren Mitchell. 72-year-old black man. Last annual review was just two months ago and Nephrology said he was okay, even at his age. He's been on the waiting list since 2002. No previous anti-HLA antibodies. Next on the list is a Cleveland Medical Center patient, but she is highly sensitized and has antigens to avoid, so probably is a no-go. Next is a Cincinnati patient who just had a myocardial infarction last week, so another no-go. We're up next with Scott Anderson. 18-year-old white male, in good shape, no previous antibodies and no antigens to avoid."

"I know Hubbard just saw the Anderson kid in Pretransplant Clinic recently, so he should be all set. But, Jesus, isn't the donor in his early twenties? I can't believe the system would assign a kidney from such a young donor to a 72-year-old man. Just doesn't seem right to me. I guess we have no choice. Go ahead and call in the two patients. Let me know if either of them need dialysis before going to the OR so I can contact Nephrology sooner than later. Do you know if the organs have been procured yet?" asked Siegel.

"Apparently they're just finishing up. We should have final

crossmatches back by 8 AM," Kristy replied.

"Alright. If we get both kidneys and neither patient needs dialysis, I'll do the old man first and ask Hubbard to do the Anderson boy later in the day since he knows him. No reason to wake up Mark at this hour. I know he has only a hernia repair scheduled for tomorrow, so I'll let him know about the transplant first thing in the morning."

"Okay. Hope you can sleep some…I'll bug you only if either of the patients has a medical issue or needs dialysis." Kristy would be on the phone for the rest of the night, talking to doctors, patients, and the OOB. It was just part of the job of being a transplant coordinator.

The OMC was lucky to be getting both kidneys from this ideal donor because they shared kidneys with four other centers in Ohio. More often than not, they would get only a single kidney per donor – or sometimes neither of the kidneys if they were both assigned to the other centers. The other non-kidney organs were allocated throughout a broader multi-state geographic region, again based on the severity of illness of the potential recipients. As was true in many cases, donor #OH7450's small intestines, being highly susceptible to the effects of low blood flow, showed signs of ischemic injury and were discarded without being offered to any of the regional small bowel transplant centers. However, all of the other organs were successfully procured and allocated. In this case, the heart was allocated to the Cleveland Medical Center. The liver and one of the lungs went to Cincinnati General. The other lung went to Pittsburgh State. The pancreas went to Michigan University Hospital in Detroit.

From Detroit to Pittsburgh – with three Ohio cities in between – there were dozens of phone calls going on in the middle of the night as each transplant center ran their lists to match the donated organs with needy recipients…seven Gifts of Life.

PART II

Chapter Seven

A Deposition
January 2010

Dr. Dan Ulek took his seat in one of the plush leather swivel chairs in the Division of Cardiology's conference room. From this eleventh-floor location, Dan looked out the window and could view rush-hour traffic converging at the intersection of Euclid and Chester Avenues in the heart of University Circle. The oak-paneled conference room was most often used for faculty meetings or educational lectures. However, today the room was reserved for a legal deposition. Dan was preparing himself for an uncomfortable and long day. Bill Matthews, the lawyer representing Dan and the Cleveland Medical Center, took his seat to Dan's right. The only other people in the room were the court stenographer – a modestly overweight and busty bleached blonde woman in her mid-fifties – to Dan's left, and two prosecuting attorneys – William Hackett and Jim Gannon – sitting directly across from Ulek and Matthews. Behind Hackett and Gannon was a wall covered with portraits of past Chairmen of the CMCs Division of Cardiology – seven in all, dating back to the 1930s.

William Hackett was the senior prosecutor, appearing tall and thin with an angular nose and wiry gray hair – probably over seventy years old – and weighing no more than a hundred and sixty pounds. He was wearing a woolen black suit, a starched monogrammed white shirt with ruby cuff links, and a red paisley tie. His younger partner, Gannon, was in his late twenties or early thirties, wore gray slacks, black loafers, a blue blazer and a plain yellow tie. He would have little to say during the deposition and was clearly present mostly to observe his senior colleague in action.

Like Hackett, Gannon lived in Cincinnati. Unlike Hackett, however, he had no familiarity with the medical community in Cleveland. Prior to the deposition, Hackett provided Gannon with some background information. "This Dr. Ulek is a transplant cardiologist here at the Cleveland Medical Center which has one of the largest heart transplant programs in the country. He is internationally recognized for his research. I think some of it is basic science, but he's also been a major player in virtually every important clinical trial in heart transplantation in the past two decades – owing to the size of his program and his outstanding reputation. He's also a bit of a Renaissance Man...he's written several novels...and has some water colors on show in major metropolitan art galleries. That's as much as you need to know. From our point of view, he's just another doctor who made a medical mistake."

Ulek was being sued for malpractice in the case of Mr. Fred Jackson who, in May 2008, received a heart transplant at the CMC. His postoperative course was complicated by seizures and a prolonged vegetative state. Dan was tremendously upset by the outcome of the case, but he was even more disturbed by the looming meetings with lawyers. For all intents and purposes, he needed to take an entire vacation day for today's deposition – clearing his busy schedule to meet with Bill Matthews in the morning for a review of the medical records and a "rehearsal" of the deposition, and then in the entire afternoon for the actual interview with the prosecuting attorneys. Matthews figured that the deposition would take anywhere from one to four hours. *Can't wait.*

During the morning rehearsal, Matthews offered some advice. "I realize that you've been through this kind of thing before, Dan. And I honestly think they are going more after the organ procurement organization than the individual doctors in this case. But we want to be prepared. This law firm is based in Cincinnati, so I've had no first-hand interactions with this guy

Hackett. His team has a state-wide reputation and they've won some big medical malpractice cases in recent years. In fact, they are also heading up the prosecution for two other patients who received organ transplants from the same donor, one in Columbus and the other in Cincinnati. The word from my friends in Columbus and Dayton is that Hackett is hard core. He'll try to get you upset and to cough up comments that will come back to hurt you. They would just love to drag a doctor into the fray if they get an opening. Just remember...whenever he ruffles your feathers, count to ten and look to me for some helpful body language. You have nothing to confess."

For Dan, the entire process evoked a state of anxiety and disgust. Over the years, he had been involved in numerous malpractice cases – both as a defendant and as an expert witness. He served as an expert mostly for defense attorneys, but sometimes on the plaintiff side. His overriding impression was that doctors were trained to do something good for their stake-holders, while lawyers most often were on a mission to do something bad for somebody. *"Injured on the job or by a doctor's mistake? Call us. We'll make them pay"..."Serious attorneys for serious accidents"..."Have you experienced headaches after taking Tylenol? Call 1-800...We'll get you the money you deserve."* Even civil suits and simple divorce cases were designed to hurt individuals and to make *someone* pay a price.

Dan spouted off to his attorney, "Bill, in American medicine, it seems increasingly true that if a patient has a bad outcome, *someone* must be responsible and *someone* – the patient or family – always needs to be compensated." Dan worried that the entire process was kindled and promulgated by the testimonies of doctors against other doctors. *If we all just agreed to stop offering opinions, the entire problem with malpractice suits might come to an end.* Unfortunately, the use of doctors as expert witnesses was a big business. Ulek was aware of some doctors who virtually made a career out of expert witness gigs. For other doctors, serving as an expert did not constitute an entire career, but the available dollars provided a nice supplement to their income. On the other side of the coin, the constant threat of malpractice suits certainly formed the basis for *defensive medicine* – the ordering of diagnostic tests and treatments that weren't necessarily in the patient's best interest, but performed in anticipation of answering to lawyers in a deposition or in a courtroom. *Doctor, you didn't order an abdominal CT scan in this unfortunate patient with a belly ache??* Defensive medicine clearly added enormously to the cost of healthcare in America. Dan felt that, as a leader in academic medicine, he had some obligation to help defend good doctors against frivolous allegations that often were rooted in defensive medical practices.

"Bill, I know I did nothing wrong in this case," Dan went on. But somehow you lawyers have a way of making doctors feel guilty until proven innocent. I've known about this lawsuit for almost a year. It's been rare for me to sleep through a night without waking up thinking about Mr. Jackson's prolonged vegetative state and worrying about this lawsuit. The whole process stinks."

Matthews nodded but offered no verbal response. He was too busy reviewing the pre-deposition notes that he had written on his oversized yellow legal pad.

"Remind me again about the difference between organ procurement and acceptance?" he asked Dan, anticipating a question that the prosecuting attorneys might ask.

"Technically, it's the organ procurement organization or OPO – in this case the Ohio Organ Bank in Columbus – that makes the decision to *procure* organs. But they almost always contact a transplant surgeon at the closest center – in this case the Ohio Medical Center in Columbus – for an opinion about proceeding with the procurement, at least in marginal cases. It would be foolish for them to procure organs that *no one* would accept. After all, the OPOs are graded on their conversion rates. You know – the number of actual donors per the number of potential donors. If there is no *potential* for obtaining organs because the person is too sick or too far gone, it would be a waste of the OPO's time to pursue donation at all. Now, it is the local transplant center that makes the final decision to *accept* an organ for a particular recipient following procurement of the organ, *if* the organ is offered to that center based on the allocation rules," Dan explained.

"So then who *accepts* the organ at the transplant center? Is that a nurse-coordinator, a physician, or must it be the actual transplanting surgeon that makes that decision?" asked Bill.

"I'm not aware of any transplant center that allows a coordinator to accept an organ. Whether it's a physician or surgeon, however, varies from one center to another. When we hired Sharon Costanzo to replace Jack Hurtuk to be the new surgical director of heart transplantation here at the CMC in 2006, she and I developed a new on-call system in which the surgeons and transplant cardiologists rotate donor call. So, I or one of my cardiology colleagues takes call on a regular basis, usually for a block of a week or so at a time, alternating with the surgeons. It's really just a way of sharing the burden of those middle-of-the-night phone calls. Let me tell you, Bill, those blocks of time on donor call are grueling. You get very little sleep and need to make some serious decisions – day or night. Yes, we cardiologists make decisions to accept organs. However, I have personally never accepted a heart transplant without first running it by Sharon or one of her surgical colleagues who is actually on-call to perform the surgery."

"So then, who officially accepted Fred Jackson's heart transplant for the CMC in May 2008?" Bill asked.

"I was on-call and technically accepted the organ...*after* notifying Sharon Costanzo about the likelihood of doing the transplant."

"Hmmm. It sounds complicated, Dan. I think Hackett will try

to beat you up on this issue so be careful with your explanation. To date they've elected not to depose Costanzo, even though she performed the surgery on Mr. Jackson. But they would love an opportunity to pull her in. Surgeons pay big malpractice premiums for a reason. It's strange, because in the Columbus case, they are targeting the surgeon and not the medical doctors. Not yet at least."

"The OMC kidney transplant program is dominated by their surgeons. The medical guys – the nephrologists – play a relatively minor role in managing the transplant patients there. Our heart transplant program here in Cleveland is different – the medical and surgical teams have equal responsibilities. It's just a different model for managing transplant patients. Neither model is better than the other. The lawyers are just targeting the doctors with primary responsibility for care of the patients. But what the hell, why not pull Sharon Costanzo into the Jackson case? Another layer of legal fees," said Dan, his sarcasm mounting. "What do you guys make anyhow, two hundred, two-fifty an hour?"

Matthews didn't answer, presuming the question was rhetorical and also that Dan was joking about the wage estimate. Most attorneys were charging at least two to three times that amount.

The morning rehearsal session ended with Matthews suggesting a ninety-minute lunch break for Dan to 'cool off' before the afternoon deposition. "The last thing I need is for you to be in anger mode for this. Remember Dan...no wrong-doing...nothing to confess."

Dan stuck an index finger in an imaginary dimple of his right cheek and offered a fake smile. "Don't worry counselor, I'll be a pillar of reason and good humor!"

The deposition started promptly at 1 PM. After the swearing in, Hackett asked Dan about the correct him pronunciation of his name.

"It's Daniel H. Ulek, as in 'U-Lick'. The 'H' is silent," Dan responded, happy to get his little inside joke into the legal record. In reality, he had no middle name or initial. But two generations ago, the family name was actually Huleshvsky. Long after the name was Americanized by his great grandparents, Dan's father always joked about the "silent H" in the family name. Hackett of course was oblivious to the pun and the joke, but thanked Dan for the correct pronunciation.

After twenty minutes of mandatory identifications and a review of personal history (name, date and location of birth, educational history, etc.), Mr. Hackett went to work. "So Dr. Ulek, you have an impressive academic portfolio – lots of research and publications – but I see you are also no stranger to malpractice lawsuits."

Dan did not respond, following Matthews' suggestion to speak only when asked a specific question.

"Most recently…2001…the case of Samuel Bennings versus Daniel Ulek and the Cleveland Medical Center."

Dan could not resist interrupting, "That case was dropped and never went to court. The patient was noncompliant and…"

Hackett interrupted, "Oh yes, the record is perfectly clear….and earlier…1999…we see Sylvia Goldenstein versus the CMC, Daniel Ulek, and Jack Hurtuk," Hackett retorted.

"That was a frivolous case that was dismissed before I was even deposed! The patient had a minor complication of a cardiac catheterization that I didn't even perform!" Dan turned to Bill Matthews who was holding up ten fingers. *Count to ten for Christ sake.*

"And four other cases between 1987 and 1996," Hackett went on.

"Objection. Question the relevance?" bellowed Matthews.

"Establishing background." Hackett retorted unemotionally and stone-faced.

Matthews and Ulek both knew that Dan had never been found

guilty of malpractice, despite being named in a number of suits – none of which ever went to trial or even resulted in an out-of-court settlement. Each case was dropped. Hackett knew this too, of course. But he also knew that this deposition would be read and reviewed by a number of lawyers and expert witnesses in the next several months. Even the hint that this doctor had a tainted track record could establish a subconscious bias that would ultimately help his case. *Makes no difference if the allegations were frivolous.* And for Hackett, there was nothing more pleasurable than questioning an angry defendant.

At the very least, Bill Matthews' objection succeeded in changing the direction of the deposition and Hackett's questions.

"Alright then, Dr. Ulek. Tell me, were you involved in the care of Mr. Fred Jackson in May of 2008?" asked Hackett.

"Yes." *Remember Dan, just answer the question....yes or no, whenever possible...don't give information he hasn't asked for.*

"And can you tell me how you were involved in his care?"

"I was the transplant cardiologist on the inpatient transplant team at the time of Mr. Jackson's cardiac transplant. Before his transplant I cared for this patient for about two months while he was hospitalized for severe heart failure and maintained on medical therapy and a ventricular assist device. We call them 'VADs'. After the transplant, I served as a consultant to the surgical team, helping with Mr. Jackson's medical management."

"And what do you mean by medical management?" asked Hackett.

"Management of immunosuppressive drugs, cardiac medications...that sort of thing."

"I see. I am reviewing the hospital chart and focusing on the events of May 22, 2008. There is a progress note signed by you. My goodness, it's so hard to read a doctor's handwriting some times. Could you read this for me?"

Dan took the copied notes, recognized his own hand-writing, and read, "Two grand mal seizures last night. Neurology on board. Etiology unclear. Head CT without contrast – unremarkable. Now on phenytoin. Need to watch for interaction with tacrolimus. Phenytoin may decrease tacro levels. Suggest continued daily tacro levels."

"And that is your note? Your signature?" Hackett asked.

"Yes."

"Dr. Ulek, did Mr. Jackson have a problem with seizures before his transplant?" Hackett inquired.

"Not to my knowledge. He was certainly not taking anticonvulsant medications at the time of his transplant," Dan responded.

"Good enough. And where is Mr. Jackson now? Do you still care for him?"

"Mr. Jackson developed irreversible brain damage and, as far as I know, remains in a persistent vegetative state in a nursing home. I last saw him about two months ago. His heart transplant was still functioning well at that time."

"I see, and was he in a vegetative state prior to the heart transplant?" asked Hackett.

"Of course not," Dan responded, after counting to five or six, but not to ten. The room was warm and he realized that some beads of sweat were forming on his forehead. Pulling out a tissue or handkerchief to dry his sweating forehead would be like an admission of guilt. Besides, he never carried a tissue or a handkerchief on his person. He just took some deep breaths, hoping the room would cool down and that his perspiration would dry up. *Never let 'em see you sweat.*

Hackett decided to change the direction of his attack, seeing that Dan looked a bit frazzled. *Make 'em sweat and then go for the kill.*

"Dr. Ulek, who accepted the heart from the Ohio Organ Bank for Mr. Fred Jackson on May 8, 2008?"

"I was on donor call and accepted the organ after a discussion with Sh...with our transplant surgeon," Dan responded.

Shit. Dan looked nervously at Matthews...T...M...I...too much information! He felt a drop of perspiration dripping down from his forehead to his left cheek.

Surprisingly, Hackett did not go on to ask for the name of the surgeon.

"I see," said Hackett, then pausing for what seemed like five minutes, flipping through copies of the hospital records, then through his notes, then back through the records. He almost seemed flustered. *Or maybe it was an act of some kind?* Dan took advantage of the pause to innocently wipe his forehead with the back of his hand. No one seemed to notice save for the busty stenographer who offered Dan a tiny smile. Hackett pulled a handkerchief from his pants pocket and dried his own face and neck – as though *he* was the person breaking out in a sweat. A crafty move – Hackett was handling it comfortably while Dan was trying to hide it.

Hackett finally continued. "Dr. Ulek, are you familiar with the Centers for Disease Control's criteria for high risk donors?"

Dan again glanced over to Matthews who had a quizzically concerned look on his face. *Where in the hell did that question come from?*

After a long pause, Dan reluctantly replied, "Yes, I am familiar with those criteria."

"Can you list them for me?"

"List them? Not verbatim," Dan responded nervously. "They are criteria for identifying patients at high risk for sexually transmitted diseases like HIV."

Hackett leaned over to his briefcase and removed a new folder.

"Yes I know that," Hackett said. "I happen to have a copy of the CDC high risk criteria right here."

Matthews motioned to the stenographer. "We're going off the record now."

She immediately stopped typing.

Twenty seconds of silence and staring ensued.

Peering at Hackett, Matthews finally ranted, "What the hell is this all about? There was no mention of any high risk criteria in the original allegations. This is foul play."

"We recently deposed Ms. Tanya Stenfield, the donor's girlfriend, and yes we have some new information. May I suggest a thirty minute recess?" asked Hackett, realizing that technically, he was out of order. *Who cares? This is going to blow open the entire case... Maybe dozens of cases!*

Matthews demanded more than thirty minutes – he demanded a postponement. After less than an hour, the Ulek deposition came to a grinding halt. It was 1:50 PM. After a brief post-mortem with Matthews, Dan returned to his office to ruminate. Having cleared his calendar for the day, he had nothing else to do but mull over the deposition...and to get on the CDC's website to review their criteria for high risk donors.

Chapter Eight

An Investigation
May 25, 2008

Mark Hubbard was concerned and very puzzled as he reviewed the flowsheets at Scott Anderson's bedside during morning rounds. He was not on donor call the night before, but he slept fitfully worrying about Scott's condition. The good news was that Scott made more than a liter of urine overnight. *More than a quart! Really, close to what an average normal person makes in an entire day.* So, the transplanted kidney was beginning to show signs of life. Hubbard was even hopeful that Scott might not require any further dialysis treatments.

The bad news was that Scott was unarousable and had another seizure in the early hours of the morning – despite treatment with the anticonvulsant drugs recommended by the Neurology Service. He was still intubated and on a ventilator. And now he had a fever. With his kidney now showing some signs of function, and with yesterday's dialysis treatment, the blood chemistries listed on his bedside flow sheet were close to normal. *So much for the toxic-metabolic theory.* He started firing off comments and questions for his team of interns and residents.

"The white blood cell count looks a little low at 3,400 – but remember that some of his immunosuppressive drugs can suppress the white count. Tell me what the WBC was at his last office visit."

An attentive intern quickly worked with the bedside computer to find the data in the electronic medical record. "The white count was 5,300 on May 19, so we're seeing a *relative* decrease, Dr. Hubbard. A *relative* leukopenia."

"Yep. Got it. Do we have the lumbar puncture results?" asked Mark, referring to the spinal tap that had been recommended by

Neurology.

One of senior residents chimed in, "It was a traumatic LP, and so there were some red blood cells in all four tubes...hard to interpret. The spinal fluid white count is slightly abnormal with 10-20 cells...all lymphocytes, in the third and fourth tubes. Total protein is just above the normal limit. Gram stain is negative. Doesn't sound like bacterial meningitis. Special stains and cultures are still pending, Dr. Hubbard."

"Does the Neurology Service want an MRI of the brain?" asked Mark, wondering why that service was so sluggish in expressing interest in this case.

"They haven't seen him yet this morning. So far, they're still sticking with the PCP, toxic metabolic theory."

"I'm not so sure about that theory any more. Remember guys, consultants offer advice. As the primary team, we have no obligation to follow their recommendations or to agree with their opinions. I think we should just go ahead and order the MRI. By the way, what antibiotics is he on right now?" Mark asked.

"Piperacillin, vancomycin and, after curbsiding the Infectious Disease fellow last night, we added ampicillin to cover for a possible Listeria meningitis, even though the spinal fluid is not typical for Listeria."

"Yeah, good idea. Listeria is pretty common in kidney transplant patients. I've seen a half dozen cases over the years. And right now we need to cover *broadly* until we figure out what's going on. Let's get ID *formally* on board. See if Bob Avery is attending this month. It's a little early in the course, but this could be something opportunistic – viral, fungal, who knows? Does anyone know if the parents are around?" asked Mark.

"The mother was in the ICU waiting room earlier," the resident replied.

Mark interrupted rounds to speak with Mrs. Anderson. He had previously found Sarah to be an attractive woman in her mid- to late forties – medium-length brunette hair and an athletic, slim figure – quite the opposite of her overweight husband. But right now her eyes were puffy and she looked weary. The calm and collected woman he met just prior to Scott's kidney transplant had been transformed into an emotional wreck.

Hubbard initiated the conversation. "Scott has had a series of seizures and we're still not sure of the cause. Our Neurology consultants think that phencyclidine is the culprit, but I'm not so sure about that considering the relatively low levels found on the tox screen. We may be dealing with an infection of some kind – maybe even meningitis or encephalitis – but we don't have anything pinned down. The spinal tap results are nonspecific and inconclusive at this point. It all depends on the cultures, and it usually takes a couple of days for those culture results to come back. In the mean time, we have Scott on broad spectrum antibiotics and I've asked our Transplant Infectious Disease consultants to see him today."

Fighting back some tears, Sarah asked, "If he has a serious infection, is it safe to continue him on the anti-rejection drugs? I thought those drugs promoted infections. We learned that when Scott was taking high doses of prednisone years ago, and I remember hearing about it in all of those pretransplant classes."

"Good question and something we always need to consider if we find an infection. Mrs. Anderson, the damned thing is, he's starting to make urine in the middle of all this – the kidney is beginning to work. That makes it tough to give up on his immunosuppression too hastily. But it's a day-to-day decision, maybe even hour-to-hour depending on what we learn from the cultures and other tests. Unless you have any other questions, Mrs. Anderson, I need to get back to rounds."

"No. We'll just keep praying. Ken will be here in an hour. Can we call you if he has any other questions?"

"Of course, just call my office and ask my secretary to have me paged."

As Mark was walking back towards his house staff team,

Sarah remembered one more thing.

"Oh, Dr. Hubbard," she called out. "I know it's probably none of my business, but do you happen to know a patient named Warren Mitchell?"

Retracing his steps, Mark answered, "Sure I do. My partner did a kidney transplant on him same day as Scott's. Same donor, as a matter of fact."

"Yeah, we wondered if it was the same donor. Did you know that Mr. Mitchell is here in the hospital with a stroke?"

"Oh, no. I had no idea. He must be on the Neurology Ward, otherwise he would be on my morning rounding schedule. Maybe they called Dr. Siegel directly about him, but I wasn't aware. I'll look into it right away."

"His wife told us he had a seizure," Sarah noted.

Mark paused and found himself staring blankly into space for several seconds. *Must be a coincidence. Lots of reasons for seizures. The old man had a stroke. That's what old people do. It's still possible, even probable, that Scott's seizures are related to an illegal drug. That's what young people do. It must be a coincidence.*

"That's a strange coincidence. We'll stop in on the Neurology floor during rounds and find out what's going on. Meanwhile, I am hopeful that Scott will wake up soon," Hubbard said, suddenly feeling a little nervous about the sequence of events and embarrassed that his patient's family was telling *him* about the coincidental seizures instead of him telling *them*.

After finishing rounds on the kidney transplant patients, Mark left his house staff team and went by himself to the Neuro ICU to find the Neurology house staff team taking care of Warren Mitchell.

The receptionist overhead paged the responsible resident to the front desk.

"Hey, did you guys call Transplant about Warren Mitchell?" Mark inquired a bit angrily of the resident, a young woman who appeared intimidated, knowing of Hubbard's senior stature at the OMC. "He's a fresh transplant from just a couple of weeks ago," Mark went on. "The Transplant Service needs to be involved with these kinds of readmissions."

"Yes, Dr. Hubbard. We actually called Dr. Andrew Siegel because he was listed as the surgeon who performed the transplant surgery. He said he would stop by later this morning. He had any early case in the OR. I'm sorry, were we supposed to page the on-call team?" she asked apprehensively.

"No that's okay. I didn't realize that Siegel was aware. Just tell me what's going on with Mr. Mitchell."

"He presented with a dense right hemiplegia and aphasia – kind of a classic left middle cerebral artery occlusion with paralysis of the right side and speech problems both suggesting a lesion in the left side of the brain. The head CT on admission was negative – I was kind of surprised – but as you know it can take a day or two for even a large infarction to show up on a CT scan. At least we're confident that the stroke was not hemorrhagic – no signs of a bleed in the brain. However, he had a grand mal seizure yesterday, so he's now on phenytoin. Dr Siegel said he'd make some recommendations about immunosuppression. The serum creatinine concentration is 1.1 so his kidney transplant is working fine. He's making plenty of urine. More than two liters in the past twenty-four hours."

"Any fever or white count?" Mark asked.

"Not on admission. Morning labs should be back by now – let me check quickly," she said while furiously typing at the computer terminal in the center of the unit. "Hmm. WBC is actually *down* to 2,800 today. It was normal on admission. Let me see...yes, 7,400 on the day of admission and 3,700 yesterday. Looks like he's gradually becoming leukopenic."

"I'll talk with Dr. Siegel but I suggest you get an ID consult. In fact, never mind. I'll call Bob Avery myself and ask him to see Mr. Mitchell today. I'm sure Siegel will agree."

"Okay, thank you, Dr. Hubbard. Should we transfer him to

the Transplant Service?" asked the resident, eager to offload this complicated case.

"That's up to Dr Siegel, but I think maybe that Mr. Mitchell would be better off staying on the Neurology Service for now. The man *did* have a stroke after all. We can follow him as consultants." *Everyone is afraid of immunosuppressed organ transplant patients. Nobody wants to take care of them, afraid that they may have unique complications related to their transplanted organ or to their immunosuppressive drug treatment. For crying out loud, this patient has had a stroke – I'm a surgeon, not a goddamned neurologist!*

As he was walking back to his office, Mark ran into his chief resident and told him about Mr. Mitchell. "I want you guys to keep an eye on him from a distance. I don't trust the neurologists to understand or manage his immunosuppression. Just so you know, I'm now seriously concerned about the possibility of a donor-transmitted disease."

"Really? You think it's an infection of some kind?" the chief resident asked.

As Mark recalled, the Anderson donor died after an accidental ingestion of cocaine, but he didn't satisfy the CDC's criteria for high risk behavior because there was no history of intravenous drug use. Mark also knew full well that the absence of those formal criteria did not rule out the possibility of a transmittable disease.

Mark continued on for the sake of his chief resident. "Tests for HIV are now very sensitive, but there is still the small chance that a donor can die during that short period of time between acquisition of the virus and the development of detectable HIV using even the most sensitive of assays. So, when the OPO obtains a history of behavior that might increase the risk of HIV – intravenous drug abuse, promiscuous sexual behavior, etc. – many transplant centers will turn down the organs even if the HIV tests are negative. But HIV isn't the issue in Scott Anderson's case anyhow. It would take weeks or months for an HIV infection to cause problems with opportunistic infections, and HIV would not cause seizures this soon after exposure. But there are a number of rarer infections that can be transmitted to transplant recipients by organ donors. The problem is, in most cases, there are no adequate tests to detect many of these infections in the donor. In other cases, the diagnostic tests can be performed, but the results aren't available for days or weeks, long beyond the short window of time available for procuring organs after declaration of brain death."

"Well, I'm glad they leave these decisions to the attendings and not to house staff," the chief resident responded. "I guess that's why they pay you guys the big bucks!" he added, sensing Hubbard's concern.

Mark returned to his office with the intent of calling Bob Avery and Andy Siegel. However, when he arrived at his office, there was a written message from his secretary to call Lance Turner at the Ohio Organ Bank. He had dealt with Lance on several occasions during the past year. *Nice guy, very dedicated and competent.* Calls from the OOB were common when he was on donor call, but he wasn't on call today. Besides, it had recently become customary for the donor coordinators to initiate donor queries by way of text messages, not telephone calls, so the written message to call Lance Turner was unusual.

He called the OOB and asked for Mr. Turner, using his first name. "Hi, Lance. What's up? Did you realize Andy Siegel was on donor call for OMC this week?"

"This is not about a new donor, Dr. Hubbard. Do you know Dr. Dan Ulek up in Cleveland at the Cleveland Medical Center?"

"Sure. He runs the heart transplant program up at CMC. First-class cardiologist. Why?"

"He called me this morning to inquire about the status of the two patients who received kidney transplants from donor #OH7450 on May 9th. You may recall that the donor was from Wright State County Hospital. It seems the recipient of the heart from the same donor is not doing well and he just wanted to be sure the other organ recipients were okay. As you probably recall, it was a multiorgan donor."

"Yeah, that's what I remember. We got both kidneys from that donor. So what's wrong with Ulek's patient in Cleveland?"

"He was doing well initially and had excellent function of his cardiac allograft, but it seems that he went into a coma about three days ago and they're not sure why. Obviously they're running a number of tests. But they're still not sure what's going on."

"Jesus. Lance…did Ulek say anything about seizures?"

There was a long pause. A number of thoughts were running through Mark's head. Lance Turner was now distraught and also temporarily lost in thought.

"Lance, are you still there?"

"Uncanny, Dr. Hubbard. I was just about to tell you that the Cleveland patient's coma started after he had a seizure."

"Alright, Lance, I think we may have a problem. Our two kidney transplant recipients are *both* back in the hospital here at OMC with neurologic symptoms. And I didn't even know about this until one of the family members made the discovery! Both of our patients have had seizures. One of them had a stroke. I need to call Dan Ulek in Cleveland and also need to talk to our Infectious Disease guys here. In the mean time, find out where the other organs from this donor went and call me back as soon as you have the list. If possible, I need a list of the transplant surgeons or physicians caring for these patients at their respective centers. Also, can you fax me all of the donor information right now? I need to review the medical history in more detail as soon as possible."

"Will do, Dr. Hubbard. I'll fax the stuff right now and call you back with the other information shortly," said Lance.

But Lance really didn't need to look up the information. He knew exactly where the organs from donor # OH7450, otherwise known as Elroy Kirk, were transplanted on May 9th. For any individual donor coordinator, "converting" donor *candidates* into actual multiorgan *donors* was a tremendous feat – a very *big* deal – and the details remained vivid in the mind of the coordinator for some time. The Wright State multiorgan donor was one of Lance's most memorable conversions, especially because it was featured on Frank Orlowski's three-part TV series on Channel 9. After the series aired, Frank called Lance and told him that the program might qualify for an Emmy award – the feedback was *that* good. The fact that Hubbard was now calling in his Infectious Disease consultants suddenly made Lance feel ill. Hubbard was implying that three patients may have acquired a disease transmitted by the donor from Wright State...the donor that Lance had so proudly evaluated. *Must be a coincidence. Please God, let it be a coincidence. My reputation and my job may be at stake.*

Chapter Nine

Hepatic Coma
May 15, 2008

Dr. Steven Fung walked into the consultation room outside of the surgical intensive care unit at Cincinnati General Hospital to meet with the family of Henry George. Fung was accompanied by Sharyn Penko, a new inpatient transplant coordinator on the Liver Transplant Service. She was no stranger to patients with liver disease, having worked in the General Hepatology Clinic for three years before taking on her new inpatient job. The family consisted of Mrs. Shirley George, a black woman in her late-fifties, and her two adult sons. All parties knew in advance that the discussion would focus on withdrawal of life support from Mr. George and provision of comfort measures only.

Sharyn had not been involved previously in Mr. George's case. All she knew was that he was a 55-year-old African American man with cirrhosis caused by a combination of infection with hepatitis C and alcohol abuse. To prepare for this family meeting, she met earlier that morning to meet with Shirley George to get a more complete medical history.

Shirley was happy to review the details. "As a young man, my husband Henry used and abused a number of drugs, including crack cocaine and IV heroin. After we met and ultimately got married, he gave up those drugs but eventually turned to alcohol. In his mid-forties, he was drinking one to two fifths of vodka daily, but somehow managed to hold down a job at Proctor and Gamble and to help me raise our two boys. We really didn't have a clue how much alcohol Henry was consuming in recent years."

Sharyn never ceased to be amazed by the number of alcoholics who could drink incredibly large amounts of alcohol and still lead essentially normal lives. Mr. George was first diagnosed with cirrhosis two years earlier, when he developed jaundice and swelling of his legs and abdomen. His family was incredulous, thinking that Henry was a "social drinker" and not appreciating his massive daily consumption of vodka. *He would have one glass of vodka on the rocks before dinner every night – rarely two. That was it!* When the truth came out, Henry admitted to drinking every day, all day – when he woke up in the morning (vodka and milk) – and throughout his workdays (vodka and juice), using secret stashes of Smirnoff's in his car and at the P&G plant. The pre-dinner cocktails were just for show, and enough to get him through the dinner hour with his wife and family.

Shirley George went on with her story. "After Henry was diagnosed with cirrhosis, he was hospitalized several times, most often for bleeding from the stomach. The doctors explained that he had ruptures of *esophageal varices*...big ugly veins in the lining of the stomach – just like these varicose veins on the back of my legs," she said, briefly exposing the back of her right leg to reveal an enlarged and tortuous vein, but not realizing that Sharyn was already completely familiar with the concept.

"So, the big stomach veins ruptured because of the high pressures in the veins resulting from the back-up of the sick liver, right?" asked Sharyn, trying to convince Shirley that she was actually knowledgeable about liver disease. "They call that back-up pressure *portal hypertension* – is that what they told you?"

"Yes, exactly. Well, on three occasions, Henry almost bled to death at home before being rescued by emergency squads. He's probably received fifty blood transfusions over a period of two years. Henry's liver doctor referred him to the Cincinnati General Transplant service to be evaluated for a liver transplant, but the transplant team demanded that he quit drinking alcohol for six months before putting him on the waiting list. For the first time in his adult life, my husband was completely sober, but we were all afraid that he might bleed to death before completing his required time of abstinence. Well, he didn't bleed to death. But shortly after he was put on the waiting list, he developed severe confusion and was admitted to the hospital again. They called it *encephalitis* or something like that."

"You mean hepatic *encephalopathy?*" asked Sharyn, referring to a form of severe confusion associated with end-stage liver disease.

"That's it," Shirley responded, now impressed that Sharyn was no novice. She went on, "And then, miraculously, just when Henry seemed to be on death's doorstep, our family was notified that a liver had become available for a life-saving liver transplant."

Praise the Lord. A Gift of Life.

Dr. Fung started the family meeting with introductions around the room. The two sons, probably in their mid-twenties, appeared anxious and suspicious – and *very large*, each standing well over six feet tall and weighing well over two hundred and fifty pounds. Shirley George, much smaller in stature, appeared sad but relaxed. She had already come to a decision about withdrawal of care. From her point of view, this family meeting was a formality.

"Henry continues to do poorly," said Fung. "His transplanted liver is actually functioning reasonably well. But the coma that he developed prior to the liver transplant has persisted, somewhat unexpectedly. We really thought we could turn things around with a liver transplant, but in this case we were wrong."

Sharyn Penko, now quite familiar with the Henry George case, spoke next – mostly for the sake of the two sons – and almost as though her tandem presentation with Fung had been rehearsed. "Your father received his liver transplant on May 9th from a donor at Wright State County Hospital up near Dayton. Previously he had been here in Cincinnati General for almost two weeks and he developed something called hepatic encephalopathy that progressed to a state of severe confusion and then to a frank coma. Your father's case became extremely severe when he developed swelling of the brain. Our Neurosurgical Service was consulted and treated this intracranial hypertension by surgical placement of a 'bolt' – a valve-like device inserted through the bony cranium to relieve pressure around the brain," she said, pointing a finger to the top of her own head to demonstrate the location of the bolt. She noticed the older son wincing, but went on. "Based on this sequence of life-threatening events, his transplant status became 'status 1', making him the sickest of the sick patients with liver failure in this region. Status 1 patients often receive livers for transplantation within hours or days – and that's exactly what happened in the case of your dad…Mr. George."

Fung took over, "In most cases, hepatic coma will resolve with transplantation of a healthy liver that is capable of removing some of the toxins that are thought to cause the encephalopathy in the first place. In Henry's case, it appears that he may have had irreversible brain damage even prior to the transplant. There was no way of our knowing that without trying the transplant as a desperate measure to save him. At this point, our neurologists believe that his chances of any meaningful neurological recovery are minimal."

The younger of the two sons nervously spoke up while looking at his tearful mother, then back at Fung. "But you're sayin' he can still recover, right?" He looked back at his mother. "Momma, he's gonna get better."

Am I not making myself perfectly clear?? Speaking more slowly, Fung tried again to make his points. "The neurologists believe that, *at best*, your father will remain in a coma *permanently*…a persistent vegetative state," Fung said. "He will likely need to stay on a respirator, *permanently*. He will remain hospitalized…he will *never* return home…he will *never* have any quality of life…he will *never* wake up and talk to you."

The older son still looked suspicious and confused and started clenching his fists. *What does this doctor know about my father's quality of life? A Chinese doctor to boot.* His younger brother stood up and started pacing back and forth in the small consultation room, occasionally exhaling deep breaths. However, neither of the sons had anything further to say. Sharyn suddenly had a real concern that one or both of the sons could become violent and leaned backward toward the door of the consultation room to open it slightly, in case she needed a quick getaway.

Shirley George finally spoke and broke the tension.

"I know what Henry would want, and I sure know what I want. I don't want Henry in no persistent coma with no quality of life. Dr. Fung, you and your team have tried your best. God love ya'll. You tried to give Henry life when he spent so many years abusing his body and destroying it with drugs and alcohol. We almost made it. We thanked God for this liver transplant and we almost made it. But God has decided, and Henry is in God's hands now. Dr. Fung, please give me a few minutes alone with my sons."

That afternoon, Shirley sat at her husband's side as the tubing connecting him to the respirator was disconnected by a respiratory therapist with the ICU staff standing by. Her sons refused to be in the room and stayed outside in the ICU waiting room. Shirley kissed her husband on the cheek and forehead. Five minutes later, he was pronounced dead.

Chapter Ten

A Lung Transplant
May 23, 2008

Dr. Mahboob Kumar had been living in Pittsburgh for only eight months. He was recruited to the Pittsburgh State Transplant Institute from his previous job at St. Louis University to serve as Medical Director of the PSTI's Lung Transplant Program. PSTI was not the biggest lung transplant program in the country, but it was certainly one of the most innovative when it came to novel immunosuppressive protocols. Together with the opportunity for a leadership position, the pioneering spirit of the PSTI was a key factor in Kumar's decision to move his family to western Pennsylvania. It was also helpful that a large Indian population had accrued in the Pittsburgh area over the years during which the rapidly growing PSTI attracted hundreds of medical professionals with a variety of ethnic backgrounds. On top of all that, the Institute provided him with start-up funds to begin his own clinical research program, and gave him a large office with a lovely view of the Pittsburgh skyline. Kumar was happy he made the move.

During his short time at PSTI, the center had performed twenty new lung transplants. Twenty lung transplants in eight months, each treated with a revolutionary protocol that involved the use of a new monoclonal antibody and infusion of donor-derived bone marrow cells at the time of the lung transplantation – it was novel and exciting. The protocol was designed to create a state of immune tolerance that would allow gradual elimination of maintenance immunosuppressive drugs. No one had ever tried this in lung transplant recipients before. Care of the lung transplant patients at PSTI was just as challenging as it had been during Kumar's ten years in St. Louis, but now he enjoyed almost constant interactions with immunologists and other scientists who were performing adjunctive immunologic studies behind the scenes.

To date, his first twenty patients were all success stories. Of course, there were rejection episodes, infectious diseases, and all of the usual psychosocial issues that characterized management of these complicated patients. However, until now, his personal patient survival rate at the PSTI was one hundred percent. *One hundred percent patient survival!*

Linda Skaper was lung transplant recipient number twenty-one for Kumar. He was about to see her on his daily rounds, but first needed to provide a medical history to two new residents who had just joined the inpatient Lung Transplant Service that morning.

"Ms. Skaper is a 48-year-old woman with end-stage lung disease resulting from idiopathic pulmonary fibrosis. She received a single lung transplant on May 9th from a young multi-organ donor in Ohio. Her course has been complicated by a minor dehiscence of her tracheal anastamosis. This now seems to be healing well. It's important to remember that immunosuppressive drugs can impair the healing of wounds, including tracheal wounds. Anyways, Ms. Skaper received two doses of alemtuzumab at the time of transplantation, together with an infusion of bone marrow obtained from the donor. Right now she is on maintenance treatment with tacrolimus and prednisone and we plan to wean her off prednisone within three months, so long as her immune tests show no activity against donor cells that were collected and stored at the time of the transplant."

Kumar was in the mood to do some teaching. Under normal circumstances, it was a trainee who presented a case history to the attending physician, but Kumar enjoyed this opportunity for a little role reversal: a short, concise presentation containing all of the essential facts. *Now that's how you present a case!* After quickly scanning the name badges of the new residents, he went on,

"Now, Dr…Young, can you tell me what alemtuzumab is and how it works?"

Young was miffed at getting such a tough question on his first day of the rotation. He was a second-year resident but this was his first rotation on the infamous PSTI Lung Transplant Service and he didn't have much time to review the immunosuppressive drugs that he would be prescribing to patients during the next month. "I believe that's the generic name for Campath, Dr. Kumar, and it works as an antibody."

Kumar chuckled, "You mean, like an antibody against gonorrhea? Yes, it's an antibody – a *monoclonal* antibody, in this case directed against a lymphocyte surface antigen called CD52. Now, I won't embarrass you by asking about the distribution of CD52 in the human body. Suffice it to say, a single dose of the anti-CD52 antibody causes a prolonged and profound reduction in circulating lymphocytes, thus preventing rejection of a transplanted organ. We give *two* doses – one in the operating room, during the surgery, and the second on posttransplant day number three. We are one of only a handful of centers using alemtuzumab in lung transplant recipients. Anyways, Ms. Skaper has done quite well aside from the tracheal breakdown. She would have been ready for discharge but she developed a low-grade fever about five days ago and we're not sure of the origin. All cultures have been negative so far."

Dr. Young spoke up, "Dr. Kumar, just before rounds, the patient's nurse called me and was concerned that the patient was hallucinating – talking to imaginary people who weren't in the room, apparently seeing things too. This just happened and I didn't have time to assess the patient."

Now Kumar was a bit miffed, hearing about a new adverse event for the first time, but he was still in bedside teaching mode. "OK, so if she's hallucinating, what is your differential diagnosis?"

"It could be a primary psychiatric problem, but I'd guess it's more likely drug-induced. My guess is that prednisone is the culprit," Young responded.

"Possibly the right answer, but probably the wrong drug," Kumar quipped. "Remember, she's on low doses of prednisone. Only high doses of steroids are associated with hallucinations or other psychiatric symptoms. But we've seen hallucinations and other neuro-psychiatric symptoms with tacrolimus, and that's the more likely cause – especially since her levels have been running a little high the past few days. So let's have a look-see," said Kumar as he directed his team into Skaper's private room.

The patient's hospital gown was pulled up to her neck and she was lying on the bed, virtually naked and spread eagled, generously exposing her chest wound, her abdomen, and her genitalia. She was staring at the ceiling and trembling. Kumar quickly covered Skaper's torso with her bed sheets. "Good morning, Linda, how are you feeling today?"

"Bugs. Watch out for the bugs!" she responded.

Delirium tremens! That was the first thought entering Kumar's mind as he tried to remember if Skaper had a history of drinking alcohol.

"What are her vital signs this morning?" Kumar asked of Dr. Young.

Young checked his notes, "Temperature 38.1, Blood pressure 110 over 70, heart rate 72, respirations 18."

Nope, delirium tremens is usually associated with hypertension and tachycardia. Her blood pressure and heart rate are normal.

Kumar proceeded to do a crude neurologic examination first assessing the patient's orientation to time, place, and person. She flunked: "1961", "Mom's place", and Kumar was not her doctor but the "blessed virgin, Mary". *Wild hallucinations!* He continued his neurologic examination and found no focal motor deficits – no obvious weakness or inability to move her extremities.

Kumar escorted the team of residents back out into the hallway. "Call her husband immediately and notify him that there has been a change in his wife's mental status. Have Neurology and Psychiatry see her as soon as possible. And call me when this morning's tacrolimus level gets back. We will likely need to reduce the dose. Oh, and she still has a fever, so I want a complete new set of blood and urine cultures and an ID consult too. See if they want a lumbar puncture."

Kumar had a bad feeling about Ms. Skaper. *My perfect track record in Pittsburgh may be coming to an end.*

Chapter Eleven

Conference Call
May 26, 2008

After apprising Bob Avery of his concerns about the two recent kidney transplant recipients, Mark Hubbard arranged a morning conference call with Dan Ulek in Cleveland.

"Good morning, Dan, I've got Bob Avery here. He's the Chief of our Transplant Infectious Disease Service," Mark started.

"Hi Mark. Hi Bob. How's the weather down south?" asked Dan.

"Unseasonably cool and dreary for May, but at least there's no lake effect snow today," Mark joked before getting on with the serious matter at hand.

"Lance Turner from the OOB called me yesterday and informed me that your heart transplant recipient from May 9th has had seizures and is now comatose," Mark reviewed. "We recently readmitted two patients who got the kidneys from the same donor. Both have had seizures and both are comatose. What's going on with your patient, Dan?"

"Jesus. Similar story here in Cleveland. Our guy was doing okay until about four days ago when he had two seizures. Now he's hardly arousable. His head CT scan was normal. He had high tacrolimus levels at the time and that was our first thought. You know, tacrolimus neurotoxicity," said Dan.

Mark responded, "Yeah we've seen that with tacro...but more often with liver recipients. Our two kidney patients have had mostly therapeutic tacrolimus levels, so we don't think that's the problem. One of our patients has a fever. Neither of them has an elevated white blood count...in fact, just the opposite...both have a mild leukopenia – low total white blood cell counts and low counts of both lymphocytes and granulocytes."

"So are you thinking of some kind of donor-transmitted infection or malignancy?" asked Dan.

"Hey, Dan, Bob Avery here," interjected Bob, leaning toward the speaker phone. "We are sort of in the middle of our consultations on these two patients at the OMC. I can tell you that all of the standard cultures are negative, but hearing your story definitely makes me very worried about a donor-transmitted disease. It's a little too early to be a transmitted malignancy – and there are no masses on the CT scans or MRIs done on our pair of patients. I'd be more worried about a viral disease...the low white blood cell counts are compatible with something viral. Given the central nervous system involvement, it could be a herpes virus...a little early for cytomegalovirus, and rare for CMV to cause this kind of neurologic disease anyhow...West Nile virus comes to mind...there was even that case of rabies a few years ago. Did your patient in Cleveland have a lumbar puncture?"

"Yes. Pretty bland. Modestly elevated protein. Just a few white cells...five to ten lymphocytes as I recall. Cultures are negative and so are the special stains, including the India ink stain for cryptococcus."

"A bit too early for cryptococcus and pretty rare to be transmitted through a common donor, although possible I suppose," offered Bob. "Jesus, we need to consider *all* possibilities at this point. The spinal fluid samples from our two patients were similar to yours. A virus makes the most sense. Of course it's still possible that this is all a complete coincidence. Our elderly man presented with a stroke after all. So that's different than the other two. We may still be looking at horses and not zebras."

"I hope you're right," Dan responded. "Still, it's pretty horrific that we have three sick patients on our hands. By the way, I'm here flipping through my patient's electronic records...his white blood cell count has been steadily drifting downwards, actually down to 1,800 today."

"Jees, this is getting a little scary," said Hubbard.

"I am going to get the CDC in Atlanta involved sooner than later," said Bob.

"Centers for Disease Control? Good idea. Do you guys know the whereabouts of the other organs that came from this donor?" asked Dan.

Mark spoke up, "A lung and liver went to Cincinnati – two separate recipients, the other lung went to Pittsburgh, and the pancreas went to Detroit – Michigan U. There were also multiple blood vessels procured and preserved for jump grafts, but none have been used to date and remain in cold storage, according to our friends down here at the OOB. I'm going to call Steve Fung in Cincinnati when we get off the phone. My secretary is trying to find out who is caring for the lung recipient at the Pittsburgh State Institute."

Dan responded, "I know the pancreas team in Michigan and can give one of their docs a call. I've got a hairy schedule today, but this is serious stuff and I think we should reconvene at the end of the day."

"Okay with me, preferably after 5 PM – I also have a full afternoon clinic," said Bob, looking at Mark who nodded in agreement. "In the mean time, I would call your laboratory at the CMC and ask them to save any serum, urine, or spinal fluid specimens from your patient. I'm sure the CDC will want as many samples as we can supply. You also might ask the lab to freeze any available cells from blood or tissue specimens just in case the CDC needs viable cells for PCR testing or other DNA analyses. We'll all talk later then."

"OK, later," Dan responded. "I hope we can get to the bottom of all this as quickly as possible."

Chapter Twelve

Another Deposition – Part 1
March 2010

Lance Turner woke up with a sense of dread worse than any he had ever experienced before. Worse even than the day his mother called to tell him that his father had died. Today was the day he was finally being deposed in what had become known within the regional transplantation community as "the Anderson Case".

Not even Frank Orlowski's phone call the evening before could lift Lance's spirits. Frank and Lance had become close friends after their original meeting in May 2008. They dined out with their wives a number of times, went to a few Ohio State football games, and played racquetball or pick-up basketball on a regular basis. One week after the infamous donor from Wright State was declared dead, Action 9 News ran the three part series, interviewing Lance, Bob Briggs, personnel at the OMC, Ken Anderson, and Warren Mitchell. The series included video images of the ICU at Wright State, the transplant ward at OMC, and the homes of the new kidney transplant recipients. Frank's report highlighted the dedication and hard work of transplantation professionals and focused on the happiness of two families from the region who had been blessed with Gifts of Life. A few weeks later, when the two kidney transplant recipients became ill, Frank's program manager wanted to run a follow-up investigative report. Frank refused, telling his boss that he had nothing negative he wanted to say about the OOB or the OMC. He had spent four consecutive days with the personnel involved in procuring, accepting and transplanting organs from the Wright State donor and was truly uplifted by the experience.

"Lance, listen, I've never been in a deposition, but I'm sure you'll do fine," said Frank on yesterday's call. "You and I both know you did nothing wrong. Just don't let those lawyers sway you away from the facts. You'll be fine."

Lance wasn't so sure. He had been worrying about today's deposition ever since receiving a letter delivered by certified mail more than a year ago. It was a summons to appear in court on an unspecified date in the case of Kenneth and Sarah Anderson versus Robert Briggs, Lance Turner, Mark Hubbard MD, Fred Nochomovitz, the Ohio Organ Bank, and the Ohio Medical Center. He had never seen a letter or summons of this kind. *I think I'm being sued!* He immediately took the letter to Bob Briggs who had already received and opened his own copy of the letter earlier in the day.

"Yes, it's a lawsuit alright," said Briggs. "A wrongful death lawsuit. Hubbard is the surgeon who did a kidney transplant on the Andersons' son. Nochomovitz is the overall administrative director of the OMC Transplant Center. They always name more people than they are really after and then whittle it down to key defendants. They'll always keep the hospitals and doctors in the lawsuit because they have the big insurance dollars."

As Briggs was talking, Lance was scrolling through the pages of the lawsuit – about fifteen pages in all with lots of legal jargon. He got stuck on comments like "willingly and knowingly accepted," and "intentionally and knowingly transplanted," and worst of all..."fell short of the standard of practice in coercing the Kirk family to donate infected organs."

"Coercing? Bob, this is such bullshit. We all know what happened. Nobody feels worse than I do. But there was *never* coercion. There was no evidence for an infectious disease at the time that donor died. I feel badly about what happened to the Anderson son and to all of the other organ recipients, but at the time I had all of the best intentions."

"I think all of that will all come out in the end," said Briggs. "Unfortunately, we still have to deal with the lawsuit. You and I will both need to meet with our legal staff as soon as possible."

It would be the first of dozens of meetings with lawyers during the next year. During each meeting, Lance would be asked to review depositions and testimonies from family members and "expert" witnesses. The OOB lawyers were resting their case on the lack of any data suggesting an infectious disease in the donor prior to the declaration of brain death. Moreover, testing for a number of unusual pathogens was impossible in the short time frame between a donor's death and transplantation of the organs. The prosecutors' experts mostly focused on the donor's death from a cocaine overdose as a sign of high-risk behavior, and on the girlfriend's testimony that the donor had symptoms of an upper respiratory tract infection during the week prior to death. Lance felt that the case of the prosecution was very weak. He was very familiar with the CDC's high risk criteria, and the overdose from oral ingestion of cocaine did not qualify.

He was convinced that he would be acquitted. But that didn't help him sleep at night. More importantly, he found it extremely difficult to do his job without being paranoid about additional lawsuits. He had previously enjoyed interacting with donor families. Now he viewed even the kindest of grieving family members as litigious conspirators, out to sue him, the doctors and the hospitals in order to get a huge financial award. Recognizing Lance's state of mind, Bob Briggs began assigning him easy cases – potential donors who were over eighty years old…one with metastatic cancer…another being treated for active tuberculosis. All of these would be automatic turndowns – no contentious issues, but also no *potential* for donation, and no personal satisfaction for a donor coordinator. Lance could see what Briggs was doing. This was not turning out to be the challenging job that he initially signed up for, and he seriously considered resigning. But right now that would appear suspicious to the prosecuting lawyers and might look like an admission of guilt. Plus, he needed his job and the income now that he had a family and a monthly mortgage payment. The job he once loved had become an unpleasant chore. He was close to completing courses for his business degree, but what hospital or dialysis company would hire him to an administrative position with a record previously tainted by a lawsuit?

Lance's wife, Debbie, was concerned about her husband's physical and mental health. The couple had a 14-month-old daughter and Debbie was pregnant again, due in about three months. Lance was eating and sleeping poorly. He was losing weight from an already thin and lanky frame. For several months, he had literally stopped exercising – once a daily passion. She could tell he had become emotionally disturbed. "Baby, maybe you should get back into the dialysis business," she suggested on the evening before the Anderson deposition. "You have the right background and dialysis has become a big business these days. With your new degree you can probably get an administrative job with one of the big dialysis chains, like Davita or Fresenius."

Debbie and Lance actually met working together as dialysis technicians at a Fresenius dialysis unit in Cleveland. Unlike Lance, Debbie and most of their fellow dialysis techs were not college graduates. Lance became interested in dialysis mostly because his father had been on hemodialysis for three years before dying of a massive heart attack during Lance's sophomore year at Cleveland State. He would sometimes visit his father during his outpatient dialysis treatments and was amazed by the life-sustaining technology that so many patients took for granted. Outside of his college classes, he spent time reading about the history, technology, and economics of hemodialysis. At that time, the population of hemodialysis patients was growing by five to ten per cent yearly in the United States. It was all medically interesting, but more importantly for a business major like Lance, dialysis was a business with opportunities for further growth. Working as a dialysis technician would be a stepping stone.

"Might be reasonable, Hon," Lance responded to his wife. "But the timing isn't right for a career move. And I'm not going back to work as a dialysis technician...that would be a giant step backwards. Besides, I can't be thinking much about the future right now. I gotta get through this deposition and get it out of my system."

To make things worse, the deposition in the Anderson case was only the tip of the iceberg. Lance recently was named also in the cases of Fred Jackson versus the OOB and the Cleveland Medical Center and in the case of the Estate of Henry George versus the OOB and Cincinnati General Hospital. Each of those lawsuits included the names of several doctors, hospital administrators, and OOB employees. Each of the suits would spawn dozens of depositions and collectively would solicit hundreds of opinions from experts earning thousands of dollars for their services. In addition, there were teams of lawyers representing each of the institutions and individuals named in each suit. Lance realized that the amount of time, effort, and money being spent on his case alone was enormous. Multiply the cost of one case by the number of other parties involved in the same process and the cost was astounding. From the perspective of the attorneys, it was all worthwhile if it ended with a large award. For the multiple defendants, many of whom would either be acquitted or dropped from the suits, there was no compensation – just lost time and a great deal of mental anguish.

Lance's own anxiety had been increased and prolonged by two postponements of today's deposition, originally scheduled almost two months earlier. His attorney, assigned by the OOB's insurance company, was a young preppie-looking red-haired fellow named James Kennedy. Initially suspicious because of his youthful appearance, Lance ultimately became friendly with James who seemed truly empathetic as well as knowledgeable about medical malpractice. He also played guard for Ohio University basketball team in the late 90s, so there was room for social bonding when their many conversations drifted from lawsuits to sports.

After the most recent postponement of the Anderson deposition, Kennedy explained to Lance that the prosecution had come up with some new testimony from the donor's girlfriend and that they needed another month to reassemble their case. In their communications with Kennedy, the prosecuting attorneys were being intentionally fuzzy on details, but Kennedy at least learned that girlfriend's testimony revolved around the donor being in the county jail just prior to his death.

"Do you recall any discussion about a prior incarceration when you talked to Kirk's girlfriend?" James asked during their pre-deposition meeting.

"Yes, I recall a discussion. In fact I specifically asked her. It is part of the checklist...standard questions based on the CDC's criteria for high risk behavior," responded Lance, now worried that something serious was missed during the evaluation of the donor. "And she specifically told me that the donor had not recently been incarcerated." He paused to think and then added, "And Frank Orlowski from Channel 9 was there as a witness."

"Okay. I'm not sure where they are taking this. We'll just have to see," said Kennedy. He stood up. "Ready to rock and roll?"

They walked down the hall to a conference room where the stenographer, Hackett, and two other lawyers were already set up for the deposition. After the traditional swearing in, Mr. Hackett began the series of questions.

"Could you please state your name, your date of birth, and your current address?"

Lance answered the questions.

"Mr. Turner, can you now please tell us about your educational background, beginning with grade school?"

It was 10:05 AM. *This is going to be a long day.*

Chapter Thirteen

Follow-up Conference Call
May 26, 2008

Mark Hubbard clicked on the speaker phone and dialed up Dan Ulek's number in Cleveland.

"Hi, Dan," said Mark. "Hope you got through your hairy schedule today. Bob Avery is here with me once again. Can you start and tell us if you were able to talk to the folks at Michigan University?"

"I did. Their patient is doing well. She's a 30-year-old woman with a history of juvenile diabetes. She had a kidney transplant from her mother about two years ago. On May 9th she got the pancreas transplant from the Wright State donor. The pancreas is functioning well...her blood sugars are normal and she is no longer taking insulin. The only problem has been an intestinal leak at the junction of the donor duodenum and the recipient jejunum, but this is being managed with a drain and octeotride injections. The patient was discharged from the hospital on May 17th and has been seen twice in outpatient clinic since that time. She's had no fever, no leukopenia...no neurologic symptoms of any kind."

Mark responded, "Interesting. And good news. Not so good with the other five recipients. You already know the stories in Cleveland and here in Columbus. In Cincinnati, the lung recipient died in the operating room...she precipitously dropped her blood pressure towards the end of the case...the lung had already been transplanted...cardiac enzymes were positive and they think she had a massive myocardial infarction on the operating room table. So much for pretransplant cardiac evaluations. Our guess is that this had nothing to do with the donor. The family agreed to an autopsy so there are blood and tissue specimens available."

Andy Siegel's attention drifted away from his partner's presentation as he pondered his own experience with every surgeon's nightmare – an intraoperative death. He wasn't familiar with members of the Cincinnati lung transplant team, but his heart went out to them, especially the surgeons. Doctors dealt with death on a regular basis. However, an intraoperative death created a pervasive sense of loss and personal failure for the responsible surgeon. It took Andy several days to get over the emotional trauma generated by the loss of a patient in the OR.

Andy regained his attention and Mark went on. "The liver recipient is more interesting, but unfortunately, he's also dead. The transplant was performed urgently when the patient developed hepatic coma with intracranial hypertension requiring a bolt. The liver functioned well, but the coma persisted and after about a week the family requested withdrawal of life support and comfort care only. The patient died shortly thereafter. There were never any signs of infection. But the patient did have a low white blood cell count on the day before his death...down around 2,300 despite holding a bunch of suspected medications. The family refused an autopsy...but there are plenty of blood and urine specimens in the Cincinnati General's lab."

Mark went on, "I just got off the phone with Mahboob Kumar in Pittsburgh an hour ago. Their lung recipient never left the hospital, mostly because of some breakdown of the tracheal anastamosis. About a week ago she developed fever and flu-like symptoms...achiness and weakness. All routine bacterial and fungal cultures have been negative. Until three days ago, there were no neurologic symptoms...no seizures for sure. But since then she has become agitated and is having some visual and auditory hallucinations. Much as with our other recipients, the Pittsburgh team has been concerned about tacrolimus toxicity, but blood levels have been well within the therapeutic range, or only slightly elevated."

Bob Avery again leaned toward the speaker phone, "So, Dan, to summarize, we have seven patients who received organs from this single donor. Two are dead, one death probably unrelated to donor issues. Three patients have been comatose or have had seizures. Three of the seven patients have had fevers. All the patients, save for the one in Cincinnati who died on the table, have had at least mild leukopenia. One of the seven patients appears to doing well. All things considered, I think we are all concerned about a donor-transmitted neurotropic infection – some infection that targets the central nervous system, albeit with varying clinical manifestations."

Hubbard interjected, "I'm not sure how you explain the outlying case in Detroit. She doesn't have any of the signs or symptoms of the other six."

"Yeah, I've been thinking about that," said Avery. "First of all, the duration of any viral prodrome generally varies substantially from one individual to another, so the Michigan University patient may still be at risk. Second, maybe the size of an organ determines the viral load. The liver is the largest organ and our one liver recipient is dead. I presume, by weight at least, that a pancreas is the smallest of the organs transplanted."

"That's true," said Ulek. "But my guess is that the amount of immunosuppression has something to do with it. The patient in Detroit was already on immunosuppression for her mother's kidney and the team there decided not to use induction antibody therapy after transplantation of the new pancreas. Our patient here in Cleveland received an induction antibody...basiliximab...just like all of our heart transplants. What about the others?"

"We use rabbit antithymoglobulin in all of our deceased donor kidney transplants including Anderson and Mitchell," Hubbard noted. "I forgot to ask Fung and Kumar, but it's a good point and I'll get back to them."

"Excellent point, especially because these antibodies are

potent T-cell inhibitors and are known to promote other viral infections," Avery commented. "I've called the CDC and they have assigned Genevieve Stager to begin an investigation. Dan, I'm not sure if you know Gen. She's an ID specialist and epidemiologist who worked here in Columbus for years before moving to Atlanta to work at the CDC a few years ago. She's excellent. Unfortunately, there was no autopsy on the donor and certainly no brain tissue saved. As a preliminary measure, Gen is requesting blood, urine, and other body fluid specimens on all seven patients as well as tissue specimens from the autopsy on the Cincinnati lung recipient. I will email the shipping instructions and shipping address to you and the folks in Michigan, Cincinnati and Pittsburgh."

Dan Ulek had been listening intently and responded, "Seems reasonable. I also suggest that you notify UNOS immediately. This may qualify as a sentinel adverse event."

Mark Hubbard was concerned. "You think we're ready to go public with this?"

"I would leave that decision to UNOS. Its part of what they do. I just think you need to let them know right away. The one thing no one wants is the appearance of a cover-up."

Chapter Fourteen

May 28, 2010
The Life and Death of Warren Mitchell

Dr. Andrew Siegel met with Cora Mitchell to update her on the latest developments with her husband, Warren. When he was readmitted to the OMC with his stroke, he wasn't breathing adequately and required ventilation with a respirator. During the intubation of his airway, the anesthesiologist noted that some food contents from Warren's stomach had been aspirated into his airway. Despite attempts to suction the material out of his lungs, a follow-up chest x-ray showed an infiltrate or shadow in the right upper lung field, compatible with aspiration pneumonia. He was given appropriate antibiotics, but on each subsequent day thereafter, repeat chest x-rays showed worsening of the infiltrates, eventually involving *both* lungs. In addition, the ventilator readings indicated that the pressures within his pulmonary tree were rising. Even with the help of the mechanical ventilator, it was becoming progressively more difficult to inflate his lungs properly. The ICU specialists believed that Warren had developed the adult respiratory distress syndrome or ARDS – a frequently fatal complication in which the lungs stiffen, become filled with fluid and inflammatory tissue, and fail to provide the oxygen needed by the rest of the body.

"There have been patients who recover from ARDS, but considering Warren's age and his underlying stroke, and the fact that he is on immunosuppression for his kidney transplant – well, this is not a good thing," Siegel explained to Cora, who seemed calm and unfazed. He went on, "We'll take it day by day and continue to change the respirator settings to keep his lungs inflated as best we can. In the mean time the ICU staff asked me to talk to you about Warren's DNR status."

The puzzled look on Cora's face reminded Siegel that he was as guilty as many doctors for occasionally dropping medical abbreviations into discussions with patients and families. "Sorry, DNR stands for *Do Not Resuscitate*. As I said, we will continue to support Warren with the respirator, IV fluids, antibiotics, and so on. However, his prognosis is now poor, and should he have a full cardiopulmonary arrest...that is, if for some reason his heart stops beating, we believe it would do Warren more harm than good to provide aggressive cardiopulmonary resuscitation."

Siegel could not tell if Cora had assimilated all of this. "There is no urgency here, Mrs. Mitchell. Perhaps you would like to discuss this with your family? Do you have children?"

Cora looked up and responded, "Yes, three."

She went on, capitalizing on Siegel's question to share her life story. "Warren and I met in Birmingham, Alabama where many of our relatives still live. We moved to Ohio in the late 1950s, hoping for better job opportunities in the North. Warren worked in the maintenance department of the Anheuser-Busch plant north of Columbus for more than thirty years, doing janitorial work before he retired on disability at the age of sixty-one. I did domestic work – mostly house cleaning – in between raising the three children – now all married adults living either in Columbus or Cleveland. I finished high school in Alabama, but Warren was a high school dropout and lived to regret it. Aside from marrying me and loving his eight grandchildren, his proudest accomplishment in life was to see each of his three kids graduate from college – the oldest two from Columbus State Community College and our youngest from Capital University. And I am just as proud. They all needed financial aid from the schools, but it was still a big step forward to have college-educated children."

"So when did Warren develop kidney failure?" asked Dr. Siegel.

"He had a long history of hypertension and also a strong *family* history of high blood pressure. Both of his parents had it.

His mother and two his uncles died from strokes. Our oldest daughter is now forty-five years old and was just found to have hypertension recently. Despite taking blood pressure pills for more than twenty years, Warren ultimately developed end-stage kidney failure that his doctors attributed to hypertension. He was always perplexed by the fact that he had excellent doctors, took his medications as prescribed, and seemed to have good control of his blood pressure – yet still went on to develop kidney failure. The doctors had no adequate explanation, except to say that the pattern was common in African Americans. Before he started dialysis treatments, Warren had surgery on his left arm for the construction of an arteriovenous *fistula.*"

Siegel was of course familiar with this kind of dialysis history. He knew that the vascular "access" that Cora was describing would be used for placement of needles to provide blood flow to and from the artificial kidney machine. But he decided to let Cora go on with her story.

"The access never developed properly, despite three attempts at revising it with separate operations. So, Warren's vascular surgeons converted the failed fistula to an ateriovenous *graft* – implanting a piece of rubber-like tubing between one of his veins and arteries in his left arm. While he was waiting for all of the surgical wounds to heal, he developed a poor appetite and some nausea. He got this bad taste in his mouth, and itching. Plus, he started to retain fluids and felt short of breath when he walked just a few steps. The doctors said he was developing *uremic poisoning* and that it was time to start dialysis. His first dialysis treatment was very emotional as you can imagine, but insertion of those large dialysis needles into his new graft was also really painful – something he never would get completely accustomed to. But after three or four runs on dialysis, Warren felt much better. His symptoms slowly got better and his fluid retention was controlled by removal of water by the dialysis machine. Dialysis was certainly no fun, but Warren woke up every day realizing that, without dialysis, he would be dead from uremic poisoning. At least he was still alive."

"I forgot if your husband was retired or still working," Siegel interjected

"Warren had every intention of working, at least part-time, while receiving regular hemodialysis treatments. But it proved to be impossible. He required dialysis for four and a half hours three times a week. Together with the drive to and from his dialysis unit, three days of the week were essentially wasted. Moreover, he often felt washed out and fatigued for several hours after each treatment. So, in addition to qualifying for Medicare because of his kidney failure – even before he turned sixty-five, Warren was forced to apply for disability."

Cora paused to think about Warren's life on dialysis and his transition to a kidney transplant. Going to dialysis eventually became something of a social outlet as Warren and Cora befriended other patients and staff members. With time, it became clear to the couple that death rates were high among dialysis patients. When one of his dialysis mates did not show up for a treatment, Warren held his breath when asking a staff member the whereabouts of the missing patient. *Oh, Mr. Simmons was found dead by his wife at home. Mrs. Hudson was hospitalized with an infected leg ulcer and died from sepsis. Mr. Hunt apparently had a massive heart attack and didn't make it.* Among patients in his age group, the yearly death rate was about twenty-five percent. *One out of four!* After a year on dialysis, Cora and Warren realized that those statistics were quite real. The dialysis staff always seemed happy when the missing person was a patient who had been called in for a kidney transplant. It puzzled Warren that the transplanted patients were most often young white people, even though more than three-quarters of the patients in his dialysis unit were older and black.

Cora remembered when Warren asked his nephrologist about kidney transplantation during a routine office visit about a year after starting dialysis. The doctor, Mark Zand, was overtly embarrassed that he had not previously talked to Warren about transplantation as an option for renal replacement therapy. Zand was familiar with the medical literature describing barriers to transplantation. For a number of reasons, black patients were less often referred for transplantation than white patients. When they *were* referred, their evaluations inexplicably took longer than those of referred white patients. And most importantly, when listed for a transplant, black patients waited longer than white patients before receiving a kidney transplant. The latter phenomenon clearly resulted from the UNOS allocation system that awarded points for tissue matching between a deceased donor and the recipient. Because most donors in the United States are Caucasian, their tissue types most often match more closely with Caucasian recipients. But none of that accounted for lower referral rates. Zand, of German and Slovenian heritage, always considered himself to be color blind when it came to his care of patients, but Warren's question reminded him that there were still at least subconscious racial biases that influenced his practice and his referral patterns.

Cora remembered Dr. Zand's comments. "Well Warren, you're now sixty-five years old and not getting any younger," said Dr. Zand while flipping through the medical chart to avoid direct eye contact. "On the other hand, you've done well on dialysis...no heart disease that we know about...no cancer...your blood pressure is well-controlled. If you are interested, I'll be happy to refer you to the Ohio Medical Center and see what they say. They'll want to run a bunch of tests – x-rays, scans, a stress test and other cardiac studies. It's pretty intense, but if you're up for it, I'll make the call today."

The OMC, of course, thought that Warren was a good candidate for a kidney transplant and wondered why he hadn't been referred earlier. His ABO blood type was B+. Before being subjected to the UNOS point system, kidneys from deceased donors were allocated first based on a match between the recipient and donor ABO blood type. For patients with common blood types – type B being the *most* common among African Americans – this implied a long wait because of the large number of kidney patients with the same blood types. The transplant team told Warren that he could expect to wait five to seven years before receiving a kidney. *I may be seventy-two years old before I get a kidney!* The OMC team also strongly recommended a living donor transplant as an alternative to going on the waiting list because living donor transplants could be performed more expeditiously and because the transplants from living people tended to last longer. But Warren adamantly refused to take a kidney from a family member. With his personal and family history, he was very concerned that someone in the family younger than he would themselves ultimately develop end-stage renal disease and require a transplant at a younger age. As Dr. Zand said, he wasn't getting any younger. He would keep his fingers crossed, pray to God for a kidney transplant from a deceased donor, and take his chances on dialysis.

Cora continued her story for Dr. Siegel. "After a few years of dialysis, it became clear to me that my husband's health was slowly deteriorating. The graft in his arm started clotting on a regular basis, requiring surgery for extraction of the clot. On two occasions, the graft became infected and Warren was hospitalized for treatment with antibiotics. During one of those admissions, the infection spread to one of his heart valves resulting in a serious condition called *endocarditis*. The doctors explained to me that when a heart valve became infected, the bacteria could spread throughout the entire body. There was some discussion about surgically removing and replacing the valve, but the cardiothoracic surgeons ultimately recommended against surgery based on Warren's age and underlying kidney failure. They just thought that the risk of death or complications would be too high after major heart surgery. Fortunately, he recovered after getting antibiotics for weeks and weeks."

Siegel glanced at his watch, realizing that this unexpectedly long discourse from Cora was now making him late for a Quality Assurance Committee meeting. He was dealing with a life-and-death issue and felt strongly that this took priority over the QA meeting. *I am about to tell this woman that her husband has no hope of living. She deserves some empathy. I can listen to her story and be late for my meeting. And I don't like those QA meetings anyhow!*

Cora went on. "Eventually, the graft in Warren's left arm clotted off, and he required a second graft in his right arm. I remember him joking, 'There goes my throwing arm!' While he was waiting for the new graft to heal, he dialyzed using a catheter inserted into a large vein through his left upper chest. The line got infected with Staph...another hospitalization... another endocarditis scare. The right arm graft also failed eventually after multiple clotting spells, and a third graft was placed in Warren's left groin area, extending down to the upper thigh. Warren was gradually losing weight. The dietician at his dialysis unit told us that his blood protein levels were low and that his nutrition was poor. Even on his dialysis 'off' days he lost the energy and zest for life that he once had. Only a week before he was called in for the kidney transplant, Warren was joking with me, 'I better get that transplant soon 'cause I'm running out of places on my body for these damned grafts!'"

Cora now could sense that she was spending too much of Dr. Siegel's valuable time. After a short pause, she ended her story and looked up to Siegel. "I have talked to my children at length and there is no need for another meeting. I know that Warren is not going to make it. Dr. Siegel...Warren has been sick for many years. Getting a kidney transplant was a miracle that we honestly thought was never going to happen. He was only out of the hospital for about a week before having the stroke...but Dr. Siegel, that week with Warren at home was probably the happiest week of our married lives. Warren and I both struggled with the idea that his kidney came from a young healthy man. Maybe that kidney should have been assigned to a younger, healthier person – someone with a longer life to look forward to. But Warren's two weeks off of dialysis with a functioning kidney have been like two weeks of...redemption. You doctors are always worried that something has gone wrong and that you are responsible. You doctors all walk around with guilt feelings. But Dr. Siegel...it's all in God's hands. All of us are in God's hands. I only want to thank you and your fellow doctors and nurses for bringing incredible happiness to my husband before his death. I am okay with your...DNR."

As Siegel was preparing to leave the consultation room, Cora stopped to say, "And thank you for listening to me, Dr. Siegel. You are a wonderful doctor."

And ALL I did was listen.

Just before midnight, Warren Mitchell's oxygen levels decreased dramatically. He was already receiving 100% oxygen and his lung pressures reached dangerously high levels. His heart rate slowed to twenty beats per minute, then to ten, then to zero. He expired at 11:55 PM.

Chapter Fifteen

CDC Investigation
June 1, 2008

Genevieve Stager was busy hooking up her laptop to the LCD in the OOB's conference room when the other meeting attendees arrived, each grabbing some morning coffee and muffins provided in the back of the room before getting down to business. The attendees included Bob Briggs, Drs. Mark Hubbard, Andrew Siegel, and Bob Avery from the OMC, Lance Turner and three other donor coordinators from the OOB. Hubbard also invited his boss, Dr. Henry Bolman. He was the Director of the Organ Transplantation Center at the OMC, and was ultimately responsible for all of the clinical activities involving organ transplant recipients at the institution. A conference call device was set up on the middle of the oval conference room table. Drs. Steven Fung from Cincinnati General, Mahboob Kumar from Pittsburgh State, and Millie Punch from Michigan University Hospital were expected to call in at 8 AM.

Conveniently, Bob Briggs was currently a member-at-large on UNOS' Membership and Professional Standards Committee. This committee, composed of transplant physicians, surgeons, OPO executives and a handful of transplant patients from each region of the country, convened on at least a quarterly basis and was responsible for reviewing patient outcomes at transplant centers. In addition to routine reviews of patient and graft survival rates at every transplant center in the US, the MPSC was responsible for initial peer review of "adverse events", including "sentinel events" such as the rare deaths of living donors, misconduct of personnel at transplant centers, and donor-transmitted diseases. The committee would initiate root cause analyses in an effort to determine if such adverse events could have been avoided and whether the adverse event was jeopardizing the safety of other patients transplanted at the involved centers. In cases of suspected misconduct, the MPSC ultimately made recommendations to the UNOS Executive Board regarding sanctions against programs or individuals.

The MPSC meetings usually took place at the Hilton Hotel at O'Hare Airport. Briggs would return from those "Chicago" meetings with stories about allegations of misconduct, threats of sanctions, and resolutions. "It was like being in court!" he would tell his troops back at the OOB. "The transplant center was represented by the hospital president and six lawyers!" His intention was to convince his employees that they were involved in a high-stakes business. However, in his two years on the MPSC, Briggs recalled only two sentinel events that resulted in probationary sanctions. He was hopeful that today's meeting would dispel any concerns about wrongdoing on the part of his organization.

Dr. Stager, an erudite and lovely, gray-haired woman in her sixties, started the meeting once all of the outside callers had joined in on the conference call. She was very business-like, impeccably organized, and gracious. Mark Hubbard thought she had a remarkable resemblance to Katharine Hepburn.

"Let's get started," Gen announced. "For the local folks here in Columbus, I have a few slides depicting data generated by the CDC to date. For the outsiders, I can fax hard copies later. Feel free to interrupt at any time with comments or questions."

She sipped some coffee, turned on her PowerPoint presentation and went on.

"Our investigation began with analysis of blood and tissue specimens from UNOS donor #OH7450, who provided organs for seven organ transplant recipients in your five cities. The available tissues were limited to a number of lymph nodes, the spleen, and several segments of veins and arteries that were removed, preserved and, *fortunately*, never transplanted into patients."

Genevieve's emphasis on the word "fortunately" prompted Bob Briggs to glance over to Lance Turner and the other donor coordinators with a disparaging look. *This doesn't sound good folks.* She went on. "We started with standard serologic studies searching for antibodies to common pathogens in the donor's stored serum. Standard cultures for bacteria and fungi were obtained, and a polymerase chain reaction or PCR was performed on all available specimens to screen for genetic footprints of common and uncommon viruses, focusing on neurotropic viruses that are characterized by their tendency to infect the central nervous system. This first slide depicts the serologic data. As you can see, the data confirmed what was found during the donor evaluation with respect to common pathogens...no antibodies against HIV, cytomegalovirus, or the common forms of hepatitis such as hepatitis B and C. The bottom panel of the slide shows that, like most adults, the donor had antibodies to the Epstein Barr virus and to Varicella...indicating that he had been exposed to mononucleosis and chicken pox, respectively, sometime during his life – as is true of the majority of adults in this country. We detected no antibodies to either West Nile virus, the rabies virus, or to five other viruses known to cause sporadic cases of meningitis or encephalitis."

Genevieve then used her laser pointer to emphasize the bottom line of the slide.

"Interestingly, we detected low titers of antibodies...both IgM and IgG...to the viral agent that causes lymphocytic choriomeningitis, a member of the arenaviridae family of viruses. I'll refer to it subsequently as the lymphocytic choriomeningitis virus, or LCMV for short.

Mark Hubbard quickly scanned the room and was happy to see puzzled looks on the faces of most of the attendees...with the exception of Bob Avery who was nodding with affirmation. Mark leaned over to whisper in Andy Siegel's ear, "Never heard of it, have you?"

Siegel shrugged and offered a "yes/no" look as though he was sifting through memories of microbiology classes in medical school many years ago. *We forget so much of what we learned in school, but fifty percent of what we learned has turned out to be obsolete or incorrect anyhow!*

Genevieve clicked to the next slide. "We next turned our attention to the recipients. None of the standard cultures for bacteria or fungi were revealing, save for two of roughly sixty blood specimens that grew low colony counts of Staph epidermidis. We dismissed these as contaminants. Among four of the six recipients who survived their transplant operations, PCR of blood specimens revealed viral loads for LCMV ranging from 10.5 to 75 million copies – rather overwhelming viremia. PCR on blood samples from the Cincinnati lung recipient who died on the operating room table were negative. However, tissue samples from the transplanted lung, obtained both intraoperatively after revascularization of the allograft and at autopsy, were highly positive for LCMV with viral loads of over 5 million copies."

Lance Turner felt a wave of heartburn. He didn't understand all of the virologic terminology, but it was now abundantly clear that they were dealing with a serious donor-transmitted disease. *What did I miss?*

Dan Ulek chimed in over the speaker phone, "What about the Detroit patient? Millie, is she still doing well?"

"She's doing very well," said Millie. "But now I'm worried as hell. Are all of her studies negative for this virus, Dr. Stager?"

Genevieve responded, "Yes, but if you could see my next slide, you might understand why. This slide shows the serologic data that we have accumulated in each of the recipients to date. In some cases, we have serial measurements. For example, look at recipient SA from here in Columbus. Pretranspant blood specimens showed no antibodies against LCMV. Almost three weeks later, he is beginning to show low IgM titers against

LCMV. I understand that this young man is still in a coma?"

Mark Hubbard frowned and nodded, then realized the outside callers could not see his facial gestures. He spoke up, "Yes, he is doing poorly."

Genevieve went on, "The most recent blood specimens from the Cleveland heart recipient show low titers of antibodies... both IgM and IgG...against LCMV."

One of the younger donor coordinators raised her hand to ask a question. "Sorry, Dr. Stager. For those of us who are relatively new, could you please explain this IgM and IgG business?"

"Sure," Genevieve responded, now moving to a flipchart in the corner of the office to spell out some of the terms she was using. "As the human immune system mounts an attack against a pathogen such as a virus, it produces antibodies against the pathogen. The antibodies, also called 'immunoglobulins or *Ig's*' are normally produced in sequence. IgM is the first antibody produced, followed by IgG. The presence of IgM thus indicates that the infection is of recent onset. Eventually, IgG antibodies against the pathogen appear and the IgM antibodies gradually disappear."

She retuned her attention to the slide presentation. "Unfortunately for those last two patients, the antibodies were generated too late. Their immune systems have been overwhelmed by the high grade viremia," Genevieve surmised. "Now, look at the serial data we have from the patient in Michigan. Even prior to her pancreas transplant and at every time point thereafter, she has high titers of IgG against LCMV. IgM was not detected. It appears that this patient had previously acquired natural immunity to the virus."

Bob Briggs spoke up, "Now just wait a second, Gen. The donor in this case had consumed a huge amount of cocaine...evidenced by witnesses and all confirmed by the toxic screens. The clinical diagnosis was malignant hypertension resulting from an overdose of cocaine, complicated by arrhythmias and a hemorrhagic stroke. Are you trying to tell us now that he actually died of a rare viral infection that caused his stroke and brain death? Are you telling us that the cocaine had nothing to do with his death?"

"Without access to brain tissue from the donor, it is very difficult to answer your question," Genevieve went on. "In normal people, LCMV can cause all of the neurologic symptoms that you have observed in your transplant recipients, but sustained coma and death are extremely rare. So, my guess is that the donor indeed died from a cocaine overdose, and that his LCMV infection may have been coincidental. But we can't be certain. The problem with your patients is that, unlike the donor, they are all being treated with immunosuppressive drugs, suppressing their ability to combat the viral infection. Having said all this, it is quite clear that the LCMV was transmitted from the donor to at least six of the seven recipients. And I must say, it is impossible for me to state that the cocaine ingestion was anything but coincidentally associated with his seizures. It remains possible that the patient's seizures occurred one to four weeks after his exposure to LCMV and were causally related more to the viral infection than to his consumption of cocaine."

Dan Ulek had been listening intently and again spoke up, "So I still don't understand the Michigan patient. How is it that she acquired natural immunity to LCMV?"

Genevieve Stager paused, appearing a little dumfounded that the answer wasn't obvious to these academic physicians, and then said succinctly, "Well, of course she must have been exposed to mice."

Twenty seconds of silence indicated that she had stumped almost all of the meeting participants, save for Bob Avery, who provided a terse clarification, again leaning toward the speaker phone.

"Folks, the disease is transmitted by rodents."

"Mostly by mice, but sometimes by rats or other rodents,"

Genevieve reiterated. "Millie, you might go back and ask your patient if she has been exposed to mice – you know, living on a farm...or even a pet hamster or some other pet rodent."

Millie paused, then over the speaker phone offered, "No need for that...our patient works as a laboratory assistant in a research lab here in Detroit."

She paused again and added, "It's a laboratory that does research with mice."

Genevieve dared not to smile given the gravity of the situation. But she felt a sudden internal satisfaction. *Another epidemiological puzzle solved quickly and efficiently!*

Lance Turner's emotions and thoughts were at the other end of the spectrum. *Elroy Kirk was no farmer and he sure as hell was no research assistant in a mouse laboratory.*

Genevieve was ready for her wrap-up. "So that brings me to my last slide which summarizes the natural history of LCMV. Mice and, less frequently, other rodents such as rats or hamsters, are the natural reservoir for the virus. About five percent of mice in the North American continent carry LCMV and shed it for the duration of their lives, but rarely exhibit any signs of illness. The virus is found in the infected animal's saliva, urine and feces. Humans presumably become infected after exposure to fresh urine, droppings or nesting materials. Transmission can also occur when these materials are introduced through broken skin, including that induced by the bite of infected animal. Person-to-person transmission is thought to be rare, but the CDC is aware of at least two previous cases of *suspected* transmission through organ donation. Infected humans usually display symptoms beginning seven to fifteen days after exposure to the virus. Initial symptoms are variable but can include fever, lack of appetite, headache, muscle aches, sore throat or cough. All pretty nonspecific."

Lance suddenly remembered that the donor had a sore throat and muscle aches prior to his death. *Goddamnit!*

Genevieve went on, "After a few days, some infected humans display a second wave of predominantly neurologic symptoms that can include sensory disturbances, hallucinations, severe confusion, paralysis...or seizures. Complete recovery is the rule and mortality rate is generally less than one percent in previously normal people – that is, people who have no underlying diseases and who have normal immune systems. The previous cases described after organ transplantation suggest that the disease and its neurologic manifestations are more severe and more often fatal when they occur in patients receiving treatment with immunosuppressive drugs. The development of neurologic symptoms two to four weeks after initial exposure to the virus in six of the seven transplant recipients in this case is very compatible with the natural history of LCMV infection in immunosuppressed human subjects."

It was 9 AM. Dr. Bolman had been listening quietly to the hour-long conversation with great interest and concern, but now wanted to bring this intense meeting to a close. Both Hubbard and Siegel needed to get back to the OMC for scheduled surgeries, and Bolman was sure that all of the other conference call participants needed to get on with their daily work schedules as well.

"Well folks, I'd say we have a big problem on our hands," said Bolman. "Two of seven patients are dead already and four of the living patients have serious neurologic impairment. So, Dr. Stager, now that we know what we are dealing with, what's the treatment for this LCMV infection?"

Genevieve glanced over to Bob Avery who was staring blankly at the floor.

Then she said, "There is no known treatment".

Chapter Sixteen

The Case of Anna Korhonen
June, 2008

A team of nursing assistants was busy obtaining vital signs on the first patients appearing for the morning clinic. They were also distributing charts to the examination rooms that would soon be populated by transplant coordinators and physicians. It was the beginning of another busy day in the Transplant Clinic at Michigan University in downtown Detroit. Dr. Millie Punch walked into the clinic and reviewed the list of patients she was scheduled to see that morning. Anna Korhonen's name was at the top of the list – her first appointment at 8 AM. There were two MU medical students assigned to Millie's clinic this morning. She loved teaching, but spending time to teach usually converted her already busy clinic to a very long one.

Millie figured the timing of Anna's office visit was perfect. She was told that UNOS had scheduled a meeting with the press on this very day to discuss the sentinel adverse event involving a donor-transmitted infection from an Ohio donor that resulted in a fatal or near-fatal neurologic disease in six of seven transplant recipients in three Midwestern cities. The news would hit the national wires almost immediately. Millie would use today's office visit with Ms. Korhonen to defuse the situation by being totally honest with her regarding the facts of the case.

Anna was a "Uper" (pronounced *Yooper*), a sometimes derogatory name applied to residents of Michigan's upper peninsula or UP – that section of the state north of the Wisconsin border. It was a huge land mass, but it accounted for less than three percent of the state's population. In recent years, a demise of the upper peninsula's lumbar industry was responsible for a serious decline in the UP population. Anna's Finnish ancestry was certainly typical of "Upers" who were notorious for being politically Democrat (based on election results from the past three decades), but behaviorally and culturally right-wing conservatives.

Like many Upers, Anna left the UP after high school, hoping to find a better life "down south" in the college atmosphere of Michigan University. She landed a job in one of the medical center's research laboratories, initially washing glassware, but ultimately working her way up the ladder to be a certified laboratory technician, a process that took almost six years. She had the dream of returning to college and perhaps getting a college degree. But at this point in her life, she was making good money – at least compared to anything her parents had known in Schoolcraft County up in the UP. She had her own apartment and a steady boyfriend. She had endured her share of medical problems, but she was content.

Dr. Punch reviewed Anna's medical history for the two medical students. "This patient has type 1 juvenile-onset diabetes mellitus. At the age of six, she developed polyuria and polydipsia. And that means what?"

"Excessive thirst associated with excessive urination, probably from severely elevated blood sugar concentrations," offered one of the students.

"Very good. Don't worry, my next questions will get harder!" said Millie. "So, her pediatrician admitted her to the local hospital with 'dehydration'. She required immediate treatment with insulin injections and remained insulin-dependent thereafter. Her parents bore the responsibility for administering daily insulin injections when Anna was a young child but she mastered self-administration of the injections by the end of grade school. As an adolescent, she was rebellious and was not compliant taking her insulin or other medications in any regular fashion – pretty typical behavior for that age. Between the ages of twelve and seventeen, she was admitted to hospitals on eight different occasions for treatment of diabetic ketoacidosis. Which is what?" The second student spoke, "Severely elevated blood sugars, profound dehydration, and acidosis resulting from the lack of insulin and deranged fat metabolism."

"You guys are good. Anyhow, Anna once required a life flight from Schoolcraft County to Detroit for a life-threatening case of ketoacidosis that resulted in a transient coma. Her compliance with medications improved as she got older, but she ended up paying the price for a life of poor blood sugar control – namely the dreaded complications of diabetes: kidney failure from diabetic 'nephropathy', loss of vision from diabetic eye disease or 'retinopathy', loss of sensation in her hands and feet from diabetic nerve disease or 'neuropathy', and chronic nausea and diarrhea from diabetic bowel disease or 'enteropathy'. You guys need to know *all* the '-opathies' associated with diabetes mellitus. Anna had them all. Her kidneys failed at the age of twenty-seven. She needed dialysis and chose peritoneal dialysis for renal replacement therapy. Do you guys know the difference between hemodialysis and peritoneal dialysis?"

The students were stumped, both blaming their ignorance on not having rotated yet on the Nephrology Service.

"In brief *(teaching like this always detracts from my time spent with patients!)*, peritoneal dialysis is a form of dialysis that she could perform at home, mostly at night, so she could continue to work. Fortunately, Anna was only on dialysis for four months because her mother, who was still living in the UP, proved to be a suitable living donor for a kidney transplant. Anna had six siblings, two of whom proved to be 'perfect' tissue matches, but her Mom insisted on donating a kidney for the transplant, concerned that the other siblings were all busy with their jobs and families. At the age of twenty-eight, Anna received the kidney transplant from her mother here at MU. The entire process went very smoothly for both the donor and the recipient. Six weeks after the surgery, Anna was off dialysis and back to work in her research lab which was testing new cancer drugs in mice."

Millie looked at her watch, realizing that her teaching had now consumed ten of the twenty minutes allotted for her office visit with Anna. *Oh what the hell, these kids are learning a lot.*

"A few months later, I encouraged Anna to consider a pancreas transplant. Not only would a pancreas transplant eliminate the need for insulin injections – it might halt the progression of her current diabetic complications and prevent blindness, kidney failure in her mother's kidney, and the other terrible complications of diabetes. Plus, she was already taking immunosuppressive drugs for her kidney transplant, and essentially the same drugs would be used after a pancreas transplant. However, unlike the kidney transplant, she would have to go on a waiting list for a pancreas from a deceased donor and I told her then that the average wait was two to three years."

Anna was transplanted with the pancreas from the Wright State donor on May 9, 2008. It was nice that Dr. Punch was trained to do both kidney and pancreas transplants, so that Anna had no need to switch doctors. The pancreas transplant surgery turned out to be a much bigger deal than the kidney transplant. For the kidney transplant, Anna woke up from surgery – about three hours in duration – with a seven to eight inch incision in her left lower belly – right along the bikini line. The pain was pretty bearable – she got a couple of injections of morphine during the first twenty-four hours, took three or four Percocet tablets on the second day and then needed nothing more than Tylenol for a few additional days. She was able to eat regular food – diabetic diet of course – on the same night of the operation. Millie Punch performed the surgery. She drew some pictures for Anna at the time, and explained that the kidney was placed outside of the peritoneal cavity, so that her bowels were not paralyzed as they often are with other abdominal surgeries. Her mother was discharged from the hospital on the third postoperative day and

Anna on the fourth. Other than a long list of new medications, it all seemed pretty simple.

Readdressing the medical students, Millie contrasted the earlier kidney transplant with Anna's more recent pancreas transplant. "The pancreas transplant is performed through a large vertical midline incision, extending from two inches above the belly button to about seven inches below it," she said, while drawing some rough sketches on the backside side of a blank progress note from the patient's chart. "The pancreas transplant is much more complicated than the kidney transplant owing to the fact that a pancreas has two normal functions: production of insulin and production of digestive juices. Diabetics need only the insulin-producing function of the organ. We surgeons must be creative in dealing with the digestive secretions – sometimes sewing that portion of the pancreas into the bladder, but more often connecting it to the patient's small intestine. It is an *intrabdominal* operation that generally takes about two to four hours."

"Did her pancreas surgery go smoothly?" asked one of the students.

"Well, I remember Anna waking up from the surgery complaining about the uncomfortable nasogastric tube in her right nostril. She forgot that I had explained that she would have an ileus or paralyzed bowel for two to five days after the surgery. The tube was necessary for a day or two to decompress the paralyzed bowels. Otherwise, a build-up of gas in the small intestines could rupture the sutures that connected her new pancreas to her small bowel. Although she received plenty of intravenous fluids, she was unable to eat anything for three days and then consumed only a liquid diet for another four days after the nasogastric tube was removed."

Millie went on to tell the medical students about Anna's postoperative course, falling short of telling them about the viral infection that had affected recipients receiving organs from her donor. "On the day that she began eating solid foods, Anna developed a fever and new pain in her right lower abdomen. We ordered a CT scan of the abdomen and pelvis and it revealed a large fluid collection adjacent to the transplanted pancreas. Interventional Radiology drained the fluid collection using a needle and a drainage catheter poked directly through the skin above the fluid collection. Anna was awake for the procedure and told me that the needle immediately drained over a quart a light brown, foul smelling fluid into a plastic bag connected to the drainage tube. She said it looked gross, but her pain was almost instantly relieved by removal of the ugly fluid. The laboratory analyses suggested gross fecal contamination, so we presume that there is a small leak at the site where the new pancreas was sewn into her own small bowel – basically forming an abscess. The treatment has consisted of multiple antibiotics and continuous drainage from the catheter to the bag. We taught Anna how to empty the bag regularly, measuring the volume and recording the output for me to review at her office visits. And so here we are! I'm sure that it wasn't pleasant for Anna to go home from the hospital with an IV in her upper chest and the drainage bag attached to her lower belly was not very. But at least we got her home. And for the first time since the age of six, she doesn't have to take insulin!"

Today's office visit was pretty routine. One of Dr. Punch's nurses first reviewed all of Anna's medications to make sure the doses were updated and correct. Punch had a few routine questions and briefly examined Anna's belly. She was happy that the amount of fluid draining into the bag was decreasing on a daily basis and told Anna that she would remove the tube in one week if the pattern continued.

"Now, I need to tell you something that we have learned about your donor," Punch said as Anna was re-dressing.

For Anna, this was somewhat unexpected. Until now the only information she had been given about the donor was that he was a young healthy man from Ohio with excellent organs. In fact, she and her family were constantly told that the Transplant Center was not allowed to divulge much information about the donor.

Punch went on, "You were not the only person to receive a transplanted organ from this Ohio donor. In fact, seven patients received organs from the same man. A couple of weeks ago I was called by doctors in Columbus, Ohio. They were concerned that two of their kidney transplant recipients were sick. This led to an investigation and it turns out that the donor had a rare viral disease – one that apparently can be transmitted through transplanted organs."

Punch had a very serious look on her face and Anna started feeling anxious.

"What kind of rare virus? Are the patients in Columbus okay now?" Anna inquired.

"No. One of them was an old man who may have died from a stroke. The other is a young man who has been having seizures. The virus has now been identified. It's a rare virus called LCMV," Punch explained. "It stands for lymphocytic choriomeningitis virus."

"So is that why I have this abscess? It's a viral infection?"

"No, No, No. The abscess is not a viral infection. It's totally unrelated. In fact, you have no signs of the viral infection at all."

Anna was somewhat relieved but still confused.

"But am I going to get sick with the virus, and have a stroke or seizures like those other people?" she asked.

"No, that's highly unlikely. It turns out that you have some natural protection against LCMV. It's a virus that normally lives in mice. Your exposure to mice in the research laboratory apparently has allowed you to build up antibodies against LCMV – so you're protected," Punch explained further.

Anna wasn't satisfied with that answer.

"So are you saying that there is a good chance that I will never get the infection?"

"I learned a long time ago that, as a doctor, one never says 'never', but my understanding is that—"

Anna interrupted Punch, "Won't my anti-rejection drugs lower my antibodies to the virus?"

Millie Punch realized that she was now getting backed into questions that were way beyond her area of expertise.

Then thinking through it, she offered, "Good question, but you had antibodies detectable while you were receiving immuno-suppressive drugs for your kidney transplant so it seems unlikely that the antibodies will be affected by your current drug regimen. Your current anti-rejection drugs are very similar to those you were taking for the kidney transplant."

Seeing that Anna wasn't completely satisfied with her answers, Millie went on. "It might be a good idea for you to see one of our infectious disease experts. They might be better able to answer some of your questions."

"What do I do in the mean time...besides worry? Should I be on an anti-virus drug?" Anna asked.

"We already have you on an anti-viral drug called ganciclovir, but that's to prevent some other more common viral infections that can be problems for transplant recipients. Apparently ganciclovir doesn't work against LCMV. In fact, there is no known treatment," Punch stated, worried that she was maybe providing too much information.

"No treatment! So it's still possible that I can become sick from a virus for which there is no treatment?" asked Anna, now with a slightly raised voice and appearing increasingly upset.

Punch had not expected such a negative, almost hostile, reaction. She hadn't even begun to tell Anna about the UNOS press conference and the news story that would likely break later in the day. The two medical students were now cowering in a corner of the examination room, somewhat stunned by the patient's behavior.

"As I said, I think it's unlikely because in your case..."

Anna interrupted again, "You said that there were *seven* transplant recipients from this one donor?"

Oh crap. I didn't want to get into these details, but she's going to hear about them later anyhow. Punch went on, "Two organs went to Cincinnati. One of the Cincinnati patients died in the operating room and the other may have died from complications of liver failure – so it's not clear to me that the virus..."

Anna interrupted yet another time, exclaiming, "So another two patients from this one donor are dead?"

"Yes, but in those Cincinnati cases..."

Anna was now visibly hyperventilating, and cut off Millie's response once again. "Jees, Dr. Punch...I'm sorry...this is all just a little scary. And unexpected. Why are you telling me all of this if you don't think I'll get the infection?"

Millie went on to tell Anna about today's UNOS press conference. "This will soon be a regional news item – maybe even a national news item. So I thought it was better for me to tell you rather than have you find out on the six o'clock news. Listen, you are doing fine. You're going to be fine."

Anna wasn't so sure. By the end of the day, every Uper in Schoolcraft County was buzzing about Anna's impending death from a rare viral infection that was accidentally transplanted into her body by doctors at Michigan University. As Anna left the office, Millie looked over to the two medical students, still hovering in the corner of the office and each appearing like a deer in the headlights. She checked her watch – 9:00 AM. Between teaching and dealing with an angry patient, her twenty-minute office visit had turned into sixty minutes. Now she would be late for her remaining patients who would also be angry about the prolonged waiting times for their appointments.

Millie smiled at the medical students and asked, "Are you guys having fun yet?"

Chapter Seventeen

Linda Skaper's Angry Husband
June 2008

Frank Skaper was seething as he sipped on his Rolling Rock at the neighborhood pub. His brother, Jim, suggested a couple of beers at the tavern, hoping to cool off Frank – known among family members and friends for his volatile temper. It was now more than seven weeks since Frank's wife, Linda, had her lung transplant. She remained in a coma, on a respirator. Frank had not been able to talk to his wife since the first week after the operation.

Coming from the small town of Johnstown, southeast of Pittsburgh, Frank was intimidated by the big city and by the huge medical center that included the PSTI. He never liked being in any hospital, but this one was overwhelming and gave him the creeps. Beyond the parking garage, the center included a motley collection of dusty old buildings connected to glistening new ones, with complicated signage that seemed intent on confusing visitors. For a visitor like Frank, it was daunting. On top of all of that, it seemed that there was a different team of nurses and doctors taking care of Linda whenever he visited. Frank always seemed to be in the dark about her progress – or lack of it. He was never quite sure who he should approach to ask questions. When he did ask questions, the answers often included medical terminology that he rarely understood. He was embarrassed to admit that he didn't understand half of what he was told. Not to mention that more than half the doctors were Chinese, or Asian, or Indians, or something other than good old-fashioned Americans. Even if he understood the medical terms, he couldn't understand many of the doctors with their foreign accents. *Damned towel-heads. Where the hell are the American doctors? Out playing golf?*

"Everything was going well for the first week and then, baam, Linda went looney-tune just like that," Franked barked to his brother, between chugs from the green bottle of brew. "And they're telling me it's some kind of virus. I never heard of no virus that makes a woman go looney-tune. Colds and flu – those are viruses. And even if it's true, they ain't telling me why there's no signs of improvement. She's in a bad coma, Jim. A real bad coma."

Like his brother, Jim hated hospitals and didn't have the fortitude to visit his sister-in-law, especially knowing that she was hooked up to a machine in an intensive care unit. The Skapers were simple folks – mostly sons and daughters of coal mining families that migrated north from West Virginia into western Pennsylvania and northeastern Ohio in the 1940s and 1950s. Frank managed a hardware store. Jim owned a home security business. They were not savvy when it came to medical issues, and they were intimidated by hospitals and doctors.

Jim ordered another round of beers. "Yeah it sounds bad, Frank. I feel bad for Linda. I feel bad for you and the boys, too."

Frank and Linda had three sons, seventeen, nineteen, and twenty-two years of age, each still living at home, and none educated beyond high school. The oldest boys, Frank Junior and Chris, could find nothing better than part-time jobs after finishing high school, and could not afford to live away from home. The youngest son, Joe, just finished his junior year of high school. Frank was never very good at being a "Mr. Mom", and family life really deteriorated at the Skaper household with Linda's prolonged illness and hospitalization. Fast foods became the dietary staple and the house was a mess, cluttered with dirty dishes, food wrappings, beverage cans, and unwashed clothes.

"And now I find out it's a goddamn cover-up!" Frank exclaimed.

"What the hell are you talking about?" Jim asked.

"Linda's sister, Tricia, called me this morning from New Jersey and read me an article from the New York Times," Frank explained. "It was all about these organ transplants in Ohio and Pennsylvania and about how the patients all got infected from the one dead man who donated all the organs. Tricia thought the Pennsylvania case sounded like Linda, but the article didn't give out the names of any of the people involved. You know, to protect their privacy. I'm sure it's Linda, 'cause the date of the transplant quoted in the story was the same as hers. And I remember they told us that her lung transplant came from a man in Ohio."

"And nobody at the hospital has told you about this?" Jim asked.

"They don't tell me nothin'. They keep telling me Linda's got a virus. But I never heard of no virus that puts you into a coma or makes you a looney-tune. And they sure as hell didn't tell me the virus came from the donor."

"Sounds fishy to me. They should've checked that out better," said Jim.

"Damned straight!" Frank exclaimed, now on his third beer, and pounding his fist on the bar counter hard enough to attract stares from several patrons. "I'll tell you what, if Linda don't get better soon, I'm gonna find me a lawyer."

"Maybe. But why would they hide something like that from you, Frank?" asked Jim, who was suspicious that Frank didn't have all his facts straight.

"I don't know. Doctors wanna protect their hides, I guess. I don't know, but I'm gonna find out and maybe get me a lawyer."

Two days later, Frank arranged to meet with Dr. Kumar at the PSTI. He was the Indian doctor that Frank had seen most often during his daily visits with his wife. He could barely understand him because of his thick Indian accent, but Frank figured he probably knew the most about Linda's case. *And it least this Indian doctor is one who doesn't wear a towel on his head!* On the day Tricia called him, Frank went to a local Starbucks and bought a copy of

the New York Times with the article about infected organ transplants in the Midwest. He intended to confront Kumar with the
article. He intended to get some answers.

In fact, Mahboob Kumar had made efforts to meet with Frank
Skaper and his sons on several occasions following Linda's lung
transplant. Frank always reeked of tobacco and sometimes of
alcohol. The meetings were never pleasant because Kumar felt
that Frank and his family had little insight into the nature of
Linda's underlying problem or her grim prognosis. Most of his
discussions elicited nothing more than angry blank stares.

Real hillbillies. Kumar had not been in western Pennsylvania
for very long, but he already had an appreciation for the term
"hillbilly". Historically, the term was coined to describe poor
Irish immigrants who lived in shanty houses in the hills of
Virginia. At night, they would sing odes to King William. The
more civilized folks in the valleys would thus refer to them as
people who sang of King "Billy" up in the "hills". In the modern
era, the term "hillbilly" was an offensive expression referring to
any uneducated person from a rural area. Johnstown,
Pennsylvania was not exactly in the countryside, but Kumar had
no doubt – the Skapers were hillbillies.

Kumar led off the meeting by pointing out that Ms. Skaper
remained critically ill but was stable. No, there were no signs of
her coming out of the coma. Yes, she still required the ventilator.
No, the transplanted lung was not rejecting. Yes, she still
required a lot of medications.

"And what about that virus?" Frank asked. "Is it gone yet?"

"Mr. Skaper, I've told you before, there is no known treatment
or cure for lymphocytic choriomeningitis. We cannot afford to
reduce immunosuppression any further as it would risk rejection
of the allograft and would only be palliative anyhow. If she were
to reject the transplanted lung it would be equivalent to letting
her die."

Frank did not understand a single word of Dr. Kumar's explanation. *Him and his damned pallating allographs! More Indian doctor double talk. Why can't this guy speak plain English?*

"Well I don't know about *that*. But what can you tell me about *this*?" Frank asked Dr. Kumar, reaching into his back pocket to extract the folded copy of the Times article.

He allowed Kumar a couple of minutes to scan the article before inquiring, "It's a story from a newspaper called the New York Times. Just tell me the truth. Is my wife Linda the lung transplant patient in that article?"

"Yes, of course. The story was also covered in the Pittsburgh Post-Gazette and probably many other newspapers around the country."

Frank was a bit embarrassed as he really didn't keep up with any of the Pittsburgh newspapers, or any other newspaper for that matter. He was also stunned that Kumar wasn't surprised and upset about the newspaper article. So he paused before asking, "And you didn't tell me and my family about this?"

Kumar also paused. *Would I really expect this hillbilly to understand the concept of donor-derived viral infections? About immunosuppression? About allograft rejection? I guess even uneducated people can be litigious in America. This guy actually thinks I've never heard of the New York Times!*

"I have told you about the LCMV viral infection, Mr. Skaper," Kumar said to Frank. "At this point, it makes no difference whether Linda got it from the donor or whether she caught it on her own. There is no treatment or cure. Don't you understand what I am saying?"

"Oh, I understand alright. Sounds like you transplanted Linda with an infected lung and you weren't gonna tell us. All sounds like a big cover-up to me," Frank said in a raised voice. "And now my wife's dyin' and I don't see you interested in doin' anything about it."

"Mr. Skaper, I assure you…"

Frank interrupted, "Sorry, Doctor, I think this meeting is over."

He stood up and abruptly walked out of the room. *Gonna get me a lawyer.*

Chapter Eighteen

Honeymoon in Montego Bay
September 2008

As their 737 jet approached the Montego Bay Sangster International Airport, Lance Turner could see the island mass in the distance and the glistening clear blue and green waters of the Caribbean Sea below. *If only Dad was alive to see me now.* Neither his parents nor any of his siblings had ever traveled out of the country. His marriage and this exotic honeymoon added to the aura of success and promise that Lance was generating among friends and family members.

He and his new wife, Debbie, always wanted to visit Jamaica. They were hardly Rastafarians. For one thing, they did not embrace cannabis as the spiritual foundation of their Christian beliefs. Nor did they reject Western society, as did the true Rastafarians who referred to Western civilization as *Babylon*. However, they did sympathize with some of the other Afro-centric social and political views of the Rastafarian movement, coming just short of calling it a religion. Some day they hoped to travel to *Zion* (i.e. Africa). Jamaica was a stepping stone – and a pleasant place for a honeymoon. And they *did* love reggae music – not just that of Bob Marley – but also the music of less-celebrated early reggae artists such as Peter Tosh, Toots and the Maytals, and Freddie McGregor.

Relying mostly on their cash wedding gifts to pay for the honeymoon, Lance booked a Pineapple Villa Suite at the Round Hill Resort in Montego Bay. He was well-advised to stay away from Kingstown, a city best described as one existing under a state of anarchy. Montego Bay was much more friendly for tourists from the US, Canada, and Europe. The Montego Bay Airport provided convenient access to the northern Jamaican resorts including those in Ochos Rios – a popular area that was a little off-limits for the college spring-break crowds and more appealing to New York socialites. Lance studied the Ochos Rios resorts at length online and found that they were a bit out of his financial reach. Montego Bay seemed nice enough and was a bit more affordable.

The taxi ride from the airport to the Round Hill Resort was disturbing in several ways. First, the "highway" known as "A1" was more of a dirt road than an expressway and was hardly in "A1" condition. In many sections, the road was so badly damaged with erosions created by monsoons and floods that the driver needed to drive *off* the road to prevent damage to his car. *Off* the road meant driving through dense vegetation. Debbie honestly thought that they would get stuck in the middle of a Jamaican jungle. She envisioned large reptiles – lizards and snakes – attacking the taxi. *And maybe lions and tigers and bears, oh my!* The fifteen-mile journey to the resort – a twelve-minute trip on any decent American highway – ended up taking over an hour.

More importantly, Lance and Debbie observed incredible poverty on the way to their resort. Like all Americans, they were accustomed to seeing poverty in the inner cities of the US. But this was a different kind of poverty.

"Oh my God," Debbie exclaimed. "Look at those folks living in shanty houses. It looks like their homes are made of tin and cardboard."

There were hungry children running, literally naked, down the streets of shanty neighborhoods looking for edible foodstuff in garbage cans. Old and young men, presumably unemployed, congregated on neighborhood sidewalks playing board games, smoking, and drinking. Much of the smoking was conventional tobacco in cigarettes, but Lance spotted a number of fat marijuana joints too. Debbie had been to Freeport and Nassau before she met Lance and noted similar impoverished neighborhoods in those Bahaman venues. As relatively affluent Americans, Debbie and Lance needed to crawl over poverty to get to the luxurious seaside resorts of the Caribbean islands. As "people of color", they felt a special sense of shame and guilt.

Any sense of guilt was quickly erased within a few hours after settling in at Round Hill. The Turner's open-air villa had an ocean view and a patio entrance to a semi-private pool. They were a short walk away from the resort's two major restaurants, a larger pool adjacent to the ocean, a small beach, and a sports club that rented kayaks, small sail boats and snorkeling gear. During their honeymoon vacation, they took day trips to the lush tropical forest and its many waterfalls surrounding Mystic Mountain, and to the seven-mile beach stretching down the northwestern edge of Jamaica near the town of Negril. Debbie was an amateur photographer and brought her new Nikon camera – a wedding gift from her parents – focusing on close-up photographs of the floral vegetation surrounding their Jamaican abode. Lance tried snorkeling for the first time but didn't care for the experience. *White men can't jump and black men can't swim or snorkel!* Not once, but twice, he was stung by poisonous sea anemones that he mistook for ocean flora – leaving him with two nasty welts on his right hand.

With ocean breezes cooling the northern shore line of the island, there was no need for air conditioning other than that provided by ceiling fans. There was lots of lovemaking – both day and night, and for the first time in months, Lance slept well with his new wife in his arms. He and Debbie got their fill of Blue Mountain coffee, salt fish, jerk chicken, and rum-based tropical drinks by the side of the pool.

At the end of their week in paradise, Lance and Debbie spent their last evening in the resort's seaside bar, sipping Tia Marias on the rocks. For almost an entire week, Lance was successful in avoiding any discussion about life back in Ohio or about his eventful spring and summer. Debbie realized that this was not just a honeymoon, but a vacation from reality. *What the hell...that's what vacations are for!* But on this night she looked at Lance and noted the serious expression on his face as he stared out at the dark ocean nearby, listening to the shallow waves rumbling against the shore.

She tried to lift his mood. "Did you know that if you spit in the ocean right here in Jamaica, at least one molecule from your saliva will show up in Lake Erie within a year?"

Lance snapped out of his momentary trance. "Girl, do I know you? Where did that come from?" he laughed.

"It just looked like you needed to lighten up some. Lance, this has been a great honeymoon. I can't wait to go on other trips with you. I wanna see the whole world with you! Maybe even Africa some day. Or, better yet, why don't we cancel our airline tickets home and just stay here forever? Same resort, same villa."

"Sounds good, babe," Lance responded wistfully. "I imagine if we pool our life savings, we could probably stay here for another week, maybe two, before going broke," he continued with a sarcastic smile, realizing that the past week had really been one of overindulgence. *Who cares? Life is short. And I am only planning on having one honeymoon!* "I'm afraid it's time to head back to the real world."

"The real world is not so bad, Lance. You have a good family, a loving wife, and a great job."

"Well it *was* a great job," Lance responded.

Debbie looked puzzled. At that time, she was only peripherally aware of a problem with an organ donor several months earlier. There was mention of a transmitted infection from an Ohio organ donor in the national news early in the spring. Debbie read about it on AOL and mentioned it to Lance who just blew it off.

"These things happen all the time," he said at the time.

He didn't mention that he was personally involved. In fact, Lance never liked to discuss his work with Debbie. He seemed to like his job, but he rarely discussed a day's events and did not like to socialize with fellow workers. Even though they were now married, Debbie would be hard pressed to name any of the people he worked with at the organ bank. Among his large group of co-workers, only his boss, Bob Briggs, was invited to their wedding.

Lance, of course, had no intention of bothering his fiancée with details of the Wright State donor during the summer before their wedding. Debbie had lots of other things to worry about, and he didn't want to spoil the fun she was having with her wedding plans. Besides – after a tumultuous spring that included the UNOS announcement of a "Level 1" adverse event, newspaper and television coverage with teams of reporters descending on the OOB, and site visits from UNOS and the CDC – things had actually quieted down during the late summer months. Bob Briggs bore the brunt of the exposure with the media, protecting Lance and other OOB workers who were involved in the case. Briggs seemed to enjoy the publicity. *Fifteen minutes of fame. Or maybe he has plans for a career in politics.* Fortunately, the Membership and Professional Standards Committee of UNOS decided not to recommend probationary sanctions against the OOB, but instead asked only for a detailed action plan to improve their screening procedures for donor-transmitted diseases. *A slap on the hand.* Aside from drafting an action plan, life went on as usual at the OOB...for all except Lance. Briggs had already started the process of protecting Lance by giving him easy cases – no challenges, no controversies. At first, it was not obvious. But as the summer wore on, Lance realized what Briggs was doing.

"*Was* a great job? What are you talking about?" Debbie asked.

Lance ordered another round of Tia Marias before answering. "Bartender, make this round straight up."

He went on to tell Debbie the entire story. One donor. Seven organ transplant recipients. Four deaths. Two patients in prolonged vegetative states. Who ever heard about lymphocytic choriomeningitis? He told her about his interactions with the donor's girlfriend and the donor's mother. He told her everything he knew about the case...the cases...the Anderson case, the Mitchell case, the other cases. He told Debbie everything. By the time he was finished, his second Tia Maria was gone and it was time for another round. He found Debbie to be attentive and mesmerized. This may have been the first time he ever divulged this much information to her about his work and the stresses it provoked. She was seeing a new side of her new husband – a man under covert stress and unwilling to bring his professional problems home.

"You know, Deb, when I was working as a dialysis technician, I felt like I was doing something good, helping sick folks to stay alive. With this job, I really started feeling that I was doing something more than good – it was something *great* – not just keeping people alive but offering new lives to people who were otherwise gonna die. But now I realize that it's a very fragile field. Some donors are better than others and some of the organs from some donors are worse than those procured from others. I know it and the transplant doctors and nurses know it. It's just a fact of life in organ transplantation. So at some time in some place, someone is gonna get an organ from a donor with an unanticipated problem. Maybe the organ won't work. Maybe the donor has an unrecognized cancer or some rare infection. It just seems like something has to go wrong eventually and then – who is to blame? Should we only accept the absolutely perfect donors with perfect organs? If so, are we willing to let people wait longer and longer for those perfect organs, and let them die while waiting? Or maybe we should just stop doing the transplants altogether and let people die from organ failure? I just don't know any more, Deb."

Debbie sipped on her last drink of the evening, loving her husband more than ever, but concerned now about his anguish.

"Baby, it seemed like you did everything right. It seemed like your interests and intentions were all good. Why are you so worried about all of this?"

"All of the inspections and site visits have quieted down, but Briggs thinks that there may be lawsuits."

"You're just a coordinator. Will they sue you?"

"Briggs doesn't think so. They usually go after doctors and hospitals. They have the big insurance policies and the big bucks. That's what drives the entire process – money. But you never know. Yeah, I might get sued. It could happen."

"The entire process sucks I'd say."

"So I *do* know you," Lance quipped.

"Baby, I want you to feel comfortable talking to me about your work. I want to help you through good times and bad – just like the wedding vows said. And right now, I want to take you back to bed," Debbie concluded, giving her husband a kiss on his forehead and gently brushing her hand along his upper inner thigh.

Chapter Nineteen

The Postponed Deposition
February 2010

William Hackett was feeling wonderfully aggressive. Despite Bill Matthews' repeated objections, he once again insisted on reviewing Dan Ulek's track record with malpractice lawsuits, before getting to the meat of the deposition. Dan had mentally prepared himself for this and rolled with Hackett's punches.

"Now Dr. Ulek, I believe we had previously discussed the CDC criteria for high risk behavior?"

Indeed, when the deposition was interrupted in January, Dan seized the opportunity to review the CDC criteria, word for word. At this point he was prepared to recite them verbatim. "Yes, we did."

"Well I won't embarrass you by asking you to list them verbatim," said Hackett.

Ulek was disappointed…no, *angry*…that he wasn't given the chance to demonstrate his knowledge. *God this guy really knows how to piss off his defendants.*

Hackett looked toward Matthews, "If Counsel has no objections, I'll just read them off myself."

Matthews nodded, indicating his reluctant approval. With almost a month to prepare for this continued deposition, he still wasn't sure where Hackett's team was taking all of this. He did discover that the donor's girlfriend had been deposed by Hackett and revealed that her boyfriend had been in the county jail just two weeks prior to his death. He discussed this at length earlier with Ulek, who wasn't aware of the jailing, but also questioned the relevance. "Bill, recent incarceration is on the CDC list because jails and prisons are known to be havens for risky behavior, you know, like IV drug abuse and anal intercourse or rape. But the risks associated with those kinds of behaviors are mostly relevant to HIV infection. HIV is not an issue in this case."

Hackett pulled a document from his briefcase and recited the CDC guidelines for exclusion of high risk donor organs, slowly and deliberately for the sake of the stenographer:

"1. Men who have had sex with another man in the preceding five years.
2. Persons who report nonmedical intravenous, intramuscular, or subcutaneous injections of drugs in the preceding five years.
3. Persons with hemophilia or related clotting disorders who have received human derived clotting factor concentrates.
4. Men and women who have engaged in sex in exchange for money or drugs in the preceding five years.
5. Persons who have had sex in the preceding twelve months with any person described in the four previously stated criteria or with a person known or suspected to have HIV infection.
6. Persons who have been exposed in the preceding twelve months to known or suspected HIV-infected blood through percutaneous inoculation or through contact with an open wound, non-intact skin, or mucous membrane."

After a dramatic pause, he then added, "7. Recent inmates of correctional systems."

Hackett appeared to be pleased with his recitation and went on, "Now, Dr. Ulek, were you the physician who accepted the heart transplant for Mr. Fred Jackson on March 8, 2008?"

God, we've been through this before. "Yes, I accepted the organ after discussion with the surgeon who was on-call."

"Oh yes, and could you please tell us the name of that surgeon?"

Dan bit his lip, realizing that he had been trapped into

dragging another name into the case. He was looking to Bill Matthews for some helpful body language but received none.

"Sharon Costanzo," he responded curtly.

Hackett nodded to his partner, Jim Gannon, who was taking notes and took the nod to mean 'get that name down!'

Hackett asked further, "Were there any other doctors involved in accepting the organ other than you and Dr. Costanzo?"

Son of a bitch. Remember, "yes" or "no" whenever possible. "No," said Dan.

"And Dr. Ulek, would it have been you or Dr. Costanzo...sorry...is that C-o-s-t-a-n-z-o?"

"Yes."

"Was it you or Dr. Costanzo who reviewed the CDC high risk criteria with the Ohio Organ Bank before accepting the heart for Mr. Jackson?"

"Objection! Form of the question. You're really asking two questions," exclaimed Bill Matthews.

"OK. Dr. Ulek, did you review the CDC high risk criteria with the Ohio Organ Bank before accepting the heart?"

Dan responded, "I don't understand the relevance of the criteria to this case. The donor was not a hemophiliac, there was no history of IV drug abuse, there—"

Hackett interrupted. "Dr. Ulek, I did not ask your opinion about the relevance of the guidelines. Please answer the question. Did you review the CDC high risk criteria before accepting the heart for Mr. Jackson?"

Hackett had succeeded in infuriating Ulek. Not only did he question the relevance of the CDC criteria that were designed to identify behaviors posing a risk for HIV – irrelevant in this case – but Hackett was presenting the CDC criteria as though they were *absolute* standards for turning down a donor. In reality, these criteria represented only *relative* contraindications to accepting a donor. They were indications for turning down the donor *"UNLESS the risk to the recipient of NOT performing the transplant is deemed to be greater than the risk of HIV transmission."* Verbatim. Dan had memorized that line from the CDC website, hoping for a chance to bring it up as part of his deposition. Now he realized how crafty Hackett was at his profession. *The bastard is not going to give me a chance.*

"I'm sorry, could you repeat the question?"

"Did you review the CDC criteria, as they related to donor #OH7450, with the Ohio Organ Bank before accepting the heart for Mr. Jackson?"

"I did not formally review the criteria," said Dan.

"I'm sorry, does that imply that you reviewed them *informally*?"

"I don't remember how I reviewed them. We presume that the donor coordinators ask the appropriate questions. Then we are presented only with relevant information. There are checklists. In the middle of the night, I do not go through every item on the checklist." Dan realized that he was speaking loudly and decided to stop until another question was asked.

Hackett provided another dramatic pause, pretending to flip through old notes on his legal pad.

"Dr. Ulek, at the time you accepted the organ for Mr. Jackson, were you aware that the donor was released from a correctional institution, or more specifically from the Montgomery County Jail, ten days prior to his death?"

"At that time, no, I was not aware."

Bill Matthews suddenly understood his adversary's tactic. He had trapped Dan Ulek into incriminating the OOB and its donor coordinator for failing to notify the accepting physicians about the donor's recent incarceration. But he still did not understand the relevance of incarceration to this case. Mentally, he began preparing a defense based on the controversial nature of the CDC criteria (after all he could name a dozen recent celebrities, congressman, other politicians, and recent presidents who satisfied some of those criteria!) and based on their irrelevance to infection with LCMV.

Hackett went on, "Should you have been? – strike that..." He then rephrased his question? "Dr Ulek, *if* you had inquired about recent incarceration and knew that the donor was recently in the county jail, would you have accepted the heart transplant for Mr. Jackson?"

Bill Matthews interrupted, " Objection to form. I think you just asked two questions again."

"Sorry. Dr. Ulek, should the heart transplant have been accepted if the donor was recently incarcerated?"

Matthews considered objecting again. The foundation of the question was based on a theoretical construct. He decided to let Hackett proceed.

Dan was caught off guard and could not answer immediately, because he honestly couldn't answer "yes" or "no". A history of recent incarceration would have increased the possibility of HIV infection, even though the donor tested negative. All of that was based on the well-recognized window of time it takes after acquiring HIV infection before one's blood test turns positive. Mr. Jackson was fairly stable with the help of a left ventricular VAD, but it was unlikely that he would ever be offered a heart from a donor as young and healthy as the Wright State donor. *At this point in time, years later, we know that HIV was not the issue, but we didn't know that then. Hackett doesn't understand the role of clinical judgment in making these decisions! Right now, I'm not sure what I would have decided had I known the patient had been incarcerated. But I didn't know about the incarceration...Oh God, he wants me to say "no". He wants me to point the finger at the OOB!*

Dan finally attempted to answer, "That would have depended on..."

Hackett cut him off, "Please Dr. Ulek, just answer yes or no."

Before Dan could respond, Hackett suddenly announced, "Actually, I have no further questions."

Ulek and Matthews, both stunned by the abrupt end of the deposition, met afterwards to review Hackett's thought processes.

"I think he knows something about this incarceration that we don't know," said Bill. "If he's hiding evidence, I'll countersue the bastard for malpractice. The good news is that I think you'll be acquitted. They are going after the OOB. He didn't need you to answer his last question, because you already testified that you were not informed about the incarceration. They are going after the OOB. It's brilliant. Remember, he is prosecuting two, possibly three cases – not just one. If he is successful in incriminating the OOB in one case, he will win the other cases in a landslide – potentially three large awards, not just one. Brilliant. The man is brilliant. Obnoxious as hell, but brilliant."

We are talking about patients who have died or have been left in vegetative states. We are talking about families that are probably still grief-stricken over the outcomes of their loved ones. We are talking about professionals who are dealing with incredible anguish as they now second guess their decisions in this awful case. And here before me, my own attorney is talking about countersuits, large awards, and brilliant prosecutors. Dan liked Bill, but he could not eliminate the preeminent thought on his mind right now: *Fucking lawyers!*

Chapter Twenty

The Anderson Case
July 2009

Scott Anderson died eighty-nine days after his kidney transplant – at the age of nineteen. He was comatose for the final seventy-four days of his short life. About seven days after he was readmitted to the Ohio Medical Center with seizures, Mark Hubbard met with Ken and Sarah Anderson and told them the entire story about the LCMV infection. The angel dust probably had nothing to do with Scott's initial presentation – it was likely the viral infection all along. In retrospect, the cold symptoms that Scott noted before his fateful seizures probably represented a viral prodrome, ultimately complicated by infection of his central nervous system, exactly as investigators from the Centers for Disease Control had described. Six of the seven organ recipients had acquired the viral infection and there was no known specific treatment. The other kidney recipient at the OMC was dead and his initial "stroke" may not a have been a stroke at all, but another manifestation of the LCMV infection.

At that point in time, Scott's new kidney was working well, much to Hubbard's surprise. Sarah and Ken already knew about Warren Mitchell's death. In fact, at Sarah's insistence, they attended the funeral. With the bad news about the LCMV infection, their emotions ran the gamut from shock to depression. The fact that Scott's new kidney was working was no consolation now.

Sarah was the first to erupt with unanswerable questions. "What do you mean there is no treatment? How did this happen? Why didn't you know the donor had this infection? Is this how Mr. Mitchell died? Are the other patients going to die? Jesus Christ, is my only remaining son going to die?"

Mark was prepared for the onslaught of questions, but he was not prepared with acceptable answers. Still, he tried to respond. "Listen, this viral infection is extremely rare – honestly, I had never even heard of it before – and there is no way it can be tested for in the short period of time that we have to make decisions about accepting organs from deceased donors. I am told that normal people – I mean people who are not taking immunosuppressive drugs – rarely if ever succumb to this infection. If Scott doesn't wake up in the next day or two, I think we should begin weaning him off his immunosuppression. The hope is that his immune system would come back and control the viral infection. He might end up rejecting the kidney, but at this point I am more interested in saving his life than in saving the organ."

Ken Anderson was busy trying to control his tears and emotions. *I can't believe we are having this life-and-death discussion just a few weeks after what was supposed to be a life-saving transplant.* He let his wife do all of the talking. He was too angry to say what was on his mind.

"We don't want you to wait a day or two," Sarah said angrily. "Dr. Hubbard, this is our only son. He is our *only* son, and we have not spoken to him for a week. He is dying, just like Mr. Mitchell died. Maybe not in the same exact way, but from the same viral infection. If there is any chance of Scott surviving this illness, please stop his immunosuppressive drugs now."

During the next month, Scott remained comatose and respirator-dependent. Hubbard agreed to gradually wean him off immunosuppression. After four weeks in the OMC's surgical intensive care unit, a tracheostomy was performed so he could be attached to the respirator without the need for an endotracheal tube in his throat. Those kinds of tubes ultimately caused frictional ulcerations of the larynx. The tracheostomy tube allowed direct access to the lower respiratory tree with less chance of ulceration and easier access for suctioning of secretions. This was all standard management for ICU patients who were ventilator-dependent for long periods of time.

After six weeks in the OMC's ICU, Scott was transferred to a long-term acute care hospital or LTAC that specialized in the care of patients on respirators. There were no such facilities in Lima. Instead, the Anderson's settled for an LTAC northwest of Columbus, at least shortening their drives to and from home. Shortly after the transfer, Scott's urine output started to decrease and blood tests suggested acute kidney failure. A staff physician at the LTAC called Mark Hubbard for advice.

"Sorry to say it, but I've been expecting this call. Scott is probably rejecting his kidney. But at this point, there is nothing we can do. If we treat him for rejection with more immunosuppressive drug therapy, the virus will grow more rapidly. There is nothing we can do other than renew dialysis when his kidney fails," Mark said over the phone.

When a consulting nephrologist at the LTAC called the Andersons a week later to tell them that Scott was in imminent need of dialysis, Ken and Sarah were prepared with an answer.

Sarah answered the call and listened patiently to the doctor's summary of the clinical facts before responding.

"We honestly don't see any hope for recovery," she said. "My husband and I have decided that we do not wish to renew dialysis treatments for Scott. Yes, we understand that, without dialysis, he will likely die. No, we do not want you to initiate dialysis. Again, yes, we understand the consequences. Yes, we understand."

Scott died two weeks later. The doctors stopped drawing blood tests during his final days of life, but they speculated that the terminal cause of death may have been a cardiac arrhythmia related to a high potassium level or some other electrolyte imbalance related to kidney failure. Scott died peacefully. He never showed any signs of pain or discomfort.

For years before and after their sons became ill, Ken and

Sarah had many discussions about the political landscape in America, especially regarding issues that were now relevant to their life situation. For example, they both agreed that Americans were infatuated with suing one another. "Everyone wants to sue someone else for a quick financial fix," Ken would say. "A woman spills hot coffee on her private parts and sues McDonalds for six million dollars. A man finds a finger nail in his Taco Bell burrito and wins three million dollars. The US has gone crazy with law suits," he would say. It was all crazy.

But this is different.

This was our only living son. Somebody made a mistake. This is different.

The medical bills related to Scott's kidney transplant and his subsequent admission for fatal lymphocytic choriomeningitis had thus far totaled just under $670,000. More than one year after his death, the Andersons were still receiving new bills for some equipment or service provided during his prolonged hospitalizations at the OMC and the LTAC. Ken's health insurance covered between sixty to eighty percent of most bills, but the remaining portion that they owed was prodigious for their level of income. The Andersons quickly realized that they had accrued a life-long debt that they would have to pay off slowly but surely, perhaps spanning the remainder of their lives. Sarah went back to work part-time at the public library, but the extra income barely made a dent. They received constant calls and letters from collection agencies demanding immediate payment in full. Ken was seriously concerned about the cap on his health insurance policy. *If Sarah or I ever get seriously ill, we may not be able to afford our own medical care. Somebody made a mistake. We deserve to be compensated. This is different.*

Sarah resisted the idea of a lawsuit for months, but finally caved in to her husband's wishes. Despite Scott's horrible outcome, she had no malicious feelings toward the doctors or nurses who cared for Scott at the OMC. They were always kind and honest, and the circumstances of Scott's illness seemed beyond their control. She had no desire to hurt any of them. She *loved* Dr. Hubbard. However, Ken pointed out that the doctors and nurses all had hefty malpractice policies and that none of them would suffer any personal financial setback. "Besides, the big insurance money comes from the institution, the hospital. They stockpile money to cover cases like this."

Sarah could see that their financial woes were affecting her husband's mental and physical health. They were now a childless couple. Ken was constantly afraid to spend money, and their social life deteriorated. He stopped playing golf on weekends and never exercised. He was now smoking more than ever – more than a pack a day. In order to increase his own income, Ken started a personal tax consulting business that often required time away from home at night or on weekends. His diabetes was out of control, probably because he had gained twenty pounds since Scott's death – and now he required insulin shots in addition to the pills he had been taking for years. His personal medical bills were adding up. Ken figured they owed about $175,000 on Scott's medical bills. He convinced Sarah that he was only interested in suing to cover those medical costs that were not covered by insurance. She finally acquiesced. *If we can just eliminate our medical debt, maybe we can get back to some semblance of a normal life.*

Ken had already done his homework in finding Ohio law firms specializing in personal injury and medical malpractice. He had a series of phone calls with paralegals at Hackett, Hackett, and Lowenstein, discovering that it was a large firm based in Cincinnati with branch offices in Columbus and Cleveland. After two months of preliminary investigations by the firm, a paralegal called Ken to arrange a face-to-face meeting for further discussion.

"Alright, my wife and I would be happy to drive to Cincinnati to meet with your team," Ken said.

"Oh no, Mr. Anderson. Our senior partner is William Hackett and he personally wants to meet with you in our Columbus office. He will drive up to meet you in Columbus at your convenience."

He'll drive up at our convenience, huh? "Sarah, I believe this law firm thinks that we have a legitimate case," Ken remarked.

As branch offices go, the Hackett, Hackett and Lowenstein suite on the twentieth floor of the Continental Center in Columbus was pretty plush – plenty of mahogany and rich burgundy colors in the carpeting and draperies. A secretary escorted Ken and Sarah into William Hackett's spacious corner office with large windows facing to the north and to the west. As they walked in, Hackett was facing one of the windows and speaking into a handheld tape recorder, dictating a letter to one of his consultants. He swiveled around to meet the Andersons, cleverly concealing the recording device. Sarah's first impression of the man's physical features focused on his preeminent huge grin, literally baring his teeth. Like a grinning chimpanzee. *Shit-eatin' grin, my father would say.*

The meeting lasted less than twenty minutes. Yes, Hackett thought they had a case...a *big* case. He explained that his firm was already familiar with some of the details about the donor-transmitted disease that caused Scott's death because they were prosecuting the Cleveland Medical Center and some of their doctors in the case of another patient who received an organ from the same infected donor.

Although Hackett dominated the discussion, Sarah finally got a chance to comment. "Ken and I are only interested in recovering money to cover our medical costs – about $180,000," she said, expecting Hackett to be startled by the figure. His face was expressionless.

"And of course to cover any legal fees," she added.

"Of course," responded Hackett, again baring his teeth. "But Mr. and Mrs. Anderson, you have dealt not only with financial stresses that have resulted from a medical mistake, but also emotional stresses – tremendous emotional suffering resulting from your son's illness and death. And he was your only remaining son at that." He was looking at Ken who nodded in agreement, and went on, "You deserve to be compensated for your emotional stress. Mr. and Mrs. Anderson, juries understand this. It's the American way."

He paused before concluding, "If we go to a jury trial we may be able to seek not only a compensatory award but also an award for punitive damages. Your bills can be paid and you can be comfortable for life. Mr. and Mrs. Anderson, this case could be worth...millions!"

Hackett ended the meeting with a round of handshakes and another shit-eatin' grin.

Chapter Twenty-one

Liver Rounds
November 2009

Towards the end of each month, Andy Siegel and Mark Hubbard traditionally found a day when their transplant fellow and chief resident were off-call and invited them to a local drinking hole for a round or two of drinks – sometimes three. Together with any other available house staff or faculty from the transplant team, they were usually able to round up seven or eight people. Andy and Mark always picked up and split the tab, happily. They knew that this little tradition helped to boost morale on the transplant team. The get-togethers helped to relieve stress for the surgical attendings, and even more so for the trainees – giving them a rare chance to let their hair down among peers and mentors. This month's "liver rounds" were more relaxed than usual because it was the Friday after Thanksgiving – a quasi-holiday with a low hospital census, no elective surgery scheduled for the day, and the weekend looming. And with the spouses and families relaxing after yesterday's busy holiday, there were fewer guilt feelings about not rushing home after work. Siegel arranged for two tables at Lucky's Stout House – an Irish pub on High Street near the medical campus – and figured that he and his partner were going to be in for a generous tab this time around.

Being at Lucky's, draught Guinness stout dominated the drink orders – at least for the first round. This month's chief resident, Ivan Shannon, was a native of Dublin, and proudly entertained the group with his historical account of Arthur Guinness' St. James Gate Brewery, established in 1759, etc, etc. "The brew appears to be black or dark brown to the novice," said Ivan with his thick Irish brogue, while holding his glass of Guinness up against a ceiling light. "But it's officially a very dark shade of ruby," he went on, then savoring his first sip of the dark beer. During Shannon's month-long rotation on the Transplant Service, Siegel had spent a considerable amount of time teaching him about surgical techniques and about posttransplant immunosuppression. Until now, however, he hadn't even realized that Ivan was born and bred in Ireland – not to mention that he had a personality and a sense of humor. *Sometimes we behave like robots and forget that doctors are also human beings.*

Mark Hubbard wasn't in the mood for a Guinness and instead opted for a single malt scotch on the rocks. *Glenfiddich, thank you.* As the crowd began to thin out around 7:30 PM, Siegel shuffled his partner down to the end of Lucky's bar, out of earshot of the remaining residents and staff members.

"Buy you another?" Siegel offered.

"Sure. Why not. Mary Ellen knows I'm going to be late, and it'll be leftover turkey soup and sandwiches tonight anyhow."

"Something troubling you? You look bummed about something," Siegel noted perceptibly.

"Sorry if it shows. Yeah, I received some certified mail today – the Anderson lawsuit. Looks like they are going to pursue it seriously."

Siegel and Hubbard were equal in stature and in professorial rank in the Department of Surgery at the Ohio Medical Center – each being Associate Professors of Surgery and both answering to Henry Bolman who was a full Professor and the Director of the Transplant Center that included programs not just in kidney transplantation, but also pancreas, liver, lung and heart transplantation. Siegel and Hubbard focused on kidney transplantation but occasionally were asked to do pancreas and liver transplants during on-call weekends. Although equal in rank, Siegel was about five years older than Hubbard. He trained at the University of Minnesota before moving to Columbus and was widely considered to be the heir apparent to Bolman's position. Hubbard was a true Buckeye – born in a suburb of

Columbus, a graduate of Ohio State Medical School and fully trained at the OMC – internship, residency, chief residency, and transplant fellowship – before joining the full-time faculty. He was third on the academic totem pool in the Division of Transplantation, but at the age of forty-three, he was content with his station and happy with his job.

"That *is* a bummer," offered Siegel, hearing about the lawsuit for the first time.

Siegel himself had been named in two lawsuits in his career. One case involved a patient who complained of malpractice when her kidney transplant failed from severe rejection. From the beginning, Siegel knew that the allegation was frivolous. Episodes of rejection were not uncommon and occasionally caused failure of a transplanted kidney. It was an unfortunate but *expected* complication of the procedure. The plaintiff's attorneys could find no expert in the field willing to offer a different opinion and, after fourteen months, the case was dismissed without any settlement or court trial.

Siegel went on to tell his partner about his second lawsuit. "In the second case, I was named in a wrongful death lawsuit involving an 86-year-old man who had metastatic lung cancer. The family claimed that the patient died from an accidental overdose of morphine. I was one of sixteen doctors named in the original lawsuit. Sixteen! I had no recollection of the case when I received the summons because my involvement was so trivial. I was attending on the Surgical Consult Service, and we were merely asked to surgically place a central intravenous catheter for administration of fluids and medications. The procedure took less than an hour and went smoothly without complications. In fact, I just supervised a second-year resident who did the entire case. I never participated in the care of the patient before or after placement of that catheter. Yet I and almost every other doctor with a signature in the patient's chart were initially named in the lawsuit. I was ultimately dropped from the case and later learned that all of the other named physicians and surgeons were dropped as well. However, the hospital settled the case out of court because the medical records indicated a nursing transcription error that resulted in the patient receiving two extra doses of morphine that were technically not ordered by a doctor. It was a medical mistake. No matter that the patient had terminal, metastatic lung cancer – literally on death's doorstep. There was a medical mistake and someone had to pay. Someone deserved to be compensated. In cases like that, the hospital lawyers are not permitted to divulge the amount of the settlement to me or any of the other original defendants."

Siegel was, of course, totally innocent of any wrongdoing in each of these cases. But he still remembered the unabashed anger that he felt when he was confronted with those green-striped envelopes sent by special delivery. In each case, he cursorily read the front page, rapidly assimilated the reality of being sued, and then tossed the package into his inbox, initially refusing to read the details for fear of becoming overtly ill.

"So, did you read your lawsuit?" Siegel asked, already knowing the answer he would hear.

"No, I couldn't bear to read the details. I'll read it later," Hubbard responded. "Maybe Mary Ellen will enjoy some bedtime reading. I can't believe the sons-of-a-bitches had the balls to deliver the lawsuit on a Thanksgiving weekend. The whole thing pisses me off, Andy. I mean, I *did* get the one-hundred and eighty day letter from Hackett and Hackett this summer, but I didn't think my name would show up on the actual lawsuit. I know the whole LCMV story was a nightmare, but I personally didn't do anything wrong. I really have nothing to confess. And what *really* pisses me off is that, at every step of that boy's posttransplant course, I was as honest and as transparent as I could possibly be with his parents. I thought we had actually become friends."

"Welcome to America," said Siegel. "It's a society enamored

with lawsuits and free pots of gold. And God forbid that doctors ever become friendly with patients or their families. Is this the first time you've been named in a lawsuit?"

"Yeah."

"I know how you feel. Welcome to the club," Siegel responded.

As the two of them sipped their drinks, superficially taking in the action of the college basketball game being broadcast on the television screen hovering over the bar, Siegel suddenly realized that Hubbard may have been particularly angry that Siegel was not named in a lawsuit stemming from the Wright State donor case. When Hubbard told him in July that he received the one-hundred and eighty day letter, Siegel wondered whether he would get a similar letter regarding the Warren Mitchell case. After all, Mr. Mitchell had clear evidence of the LCMV infection at the time of his death, even if his presentation was different from those of the other transplant recipients getting organs from the Wright State donor. Moreover, it was Siegel, not Hubbard, who technically accepted the kidneys from the donor. *Maybe the lawyers haven't been smart enough to figure that out. Or maybe they will figure it out eventually and drag me into the Anderson case.* He was actually thinking of a way to bring up the subject delicately when Hubbard beat him to the punch, fortunately *not* focusing on the organ acceptance issue.

"So, there's been no legal action regarding that old man that you transplanted with the other kidney from the same donor?" Hubbard asked.

"No. But can I tell you something, Mark? Ever since July, I've been waiting for my own one-hundred and eighty day letter. I gotta tell you, waiting for that letter is almost as anxiety-provoking as waiting for an actual lawsuit," he lied. "No reason for you to be jealous. I worry every day that the letter is on the way."

"I doubt that you'll get a letter," Hubbard responded, trying not to show any signs of resentment. "I've been meeting pretty regularly with our lawyers since July. They think there will be *multiple* lawsuits in three different states emanating from this case. But your old man was one of the earliest deaths. If nothing has happened by now, they think it's unlikely the family will sue. That's okay. I'm not *jealous,* Andy. I'm happy if it doesn't happen to you. But I'm still pissed off about my situation and about the entire system."

"Mark, listen," Siegel implored. "There was, and there still *is* no way to detect this rare LCMV virus infection in a potential organ transplant donor before proceeding with the transplants. And even if there was, it was not your responsibility. I'm sure you will ultimately be acquitted."

"Easier said than done," Hubbard replied brusquely. "According to the lawyers, it all depends on whether the plaintiff attorneys can get at least one case into a court room. And then, as always, it depends on the mindset of the jurors. There are multiple active lawsuits involving this one donor and I've heard that there may be several more lawsuits on the way. The outcome of the first case that gets to court will have a huge influence on the subsequent cases, including the size of the awards. Right now, it looks the Scott Anderson case is being set up as the pivotal 'first' case, probably because of the Anderson boy's young age. He was only eighteen years old at the time of the transplant...nineteen when he died a few months later. Jurors will be really sympathetic about the death of a 19-year-old boy. So I think I'm going to be in the hot seat. In the mean time, I have a hard time sleeping at night and I'm taking Prilosec once a day for heartburn and dyspepsia – sometimes twice a day. And it could take months or even years to decide if the case goes forward. This part sucks. But if I have to go to court and *lose* the case, I'm not sure if I can continue to work. Could you?"

Siegel emptied the remaining beer in his glass before answering. Losing a malpractice case and being responsible for a large payout by the insurance company is something all physicians and surgeons feared. He recalled the famous case of a Chicago neurosurgeon who was caught red-handed "doctoring" medical records to hide a medical mistake that led to a patient's permanent paralysis and ultimate death. The court awarded the family ten million dollars, and the surgeon committed suicide four months later. His malpractice insurance covered only a fraction of the award and he killed himself rather than facing a huge life-long debt. Siegel also had a personal friend – a fellow trainee in transplantation surgery at the University of Minnesota – who lost a malpractice case involving a liver transplant recipient in Rochester, New York. It was a case of hepatic artery thrombosis that led to the development of a liver abscess in a patient with previous cirrhosis from hepatitis C. The patient did not die, but ended up needing a second liver transplant after multiple procedures that were required to drain the collection of pus in his liver. From Siegel's perspective it was a case of an *expected* complication. Every liver transplant surgeon in the field recognized hepatic artery thrombosis as an expected complication of the operation. Although the award was relatively small, his friend never recovered from the emotional damage. He quit doing transplants of any kind, and ultimately moved to a private practice in general surgery focusing on hernia repairs and resections or biopsies of lumps and bumps. *What a waste of talent.*

Siegel finally answered Hubbard's question after a long pause, "I'm not sure either, Mark...I'm really not sure." In reality, Siegel had thought about this scenario throughout most of his career. He grew up in Wisconsin outside of Milwaukee. His father worked in a container factory all of his life and Andy was able to work at his dad's factory during summers in late high school and throughout college. For a student, the pay was excellent, covering more than half of his college tuition. In five summers at the factory, he had various responsibilities but mostly worked in the Packing Department where an assembly line delivered freshly made cans that were then packaged into boxes. For some reason, only women were assigned the job of plucking the cans from the assembly line and snuggling them into their boxes. Male workers like Andy stood at the other end of the line and hoisted the boxes onto skids that were then delivered either directly to a shipping truck or, more often, to a vast storage space in the factory's warehouse. The pace was quick and there was no time for socializing with co-workers, save for the highly regulated break times. The work was tedious and boring. On the other hand, once he mastered the routine, Andy found something extremely pleasant about the monotony of factory work. It was the same routine day in and day out, but his responsibilities were limited and there were no decisions to make. When the work day ended, there were never any work issues to worry about at home or to discuss with family. There were no job concerns that would interfere with his sleep at night. So, if he ever lost all of his assets in a malpractice suit, Andy would consider giving up medicine and pursuing some brainless activity. *Factory work is probably not going to pay enough for me to get by...maybe truck driving!*

All of the other attendees had slowly drifted out of Lucky's, heading home for the remainder of the Thanksgiving weekend, or for some – a weekend of service on-call at the OMC. Siegel signaled the bartender for the check and grabbed his coat from the rack adjacent to the bar. He turned to Hubbard, gently slapping him on his back. "Let me pick up the tab this time around. Hey, I'm on-call this weekend. So go home, say hello to Mary Ellen for me and try to have a nice weekend off."

Mark Hubbard drove to his home in Worthington, on the banks of the Olentangy River – close to the home in which he grew up and where his mother still lived. He desperately wanted to talk to Mary Ellen. For months he had been a lousy husband and a lousy father to their two young boys, aged seven and nine. During that time, he found excuses to avoid going home. He lied to Mary Ellen about late-night emergency cases in the OR. He lied to her about needing time to write review articles and book chapters that were overdue. He was avoiding his wife and kids. And now he realized that it was all related to the emotional stress resulting from the threat of a lawsuit. Not a real lawsuit – just the threat. Now that lawsuit was here and very real. Hopefully, Mary Ellen would understand and forgive him for his inappropriate behavior during the past year. *Hopefully she will understand that if I'm sued and lose the case, we may lose everything – our house, all of our possessions, all of the material things that we have worked so hard for. I love you too, Mary Ellen, but yes it COULD happen.*

Being the day after Thanksgiving, Mark was hoping that Mary Ellen would be in a consoling mood.

She wasn't.

"Mark, I know you've had a lot of things going on at work and a lot on your mind for the past several months," Mary Ellen stated. "But I have my problems and needs too. You just haven't been here for me recently, Mark. You haven't been here for the boys. We really need to talk. We have some serious things to talk about."

Siegel drove to his home in Upper Arlington feeling a wealth of mixed emotions. First, relief that he had not been named in any lawsuit stemming from the Wright State donor…then guilt that maybe he *should* have been named. He felt sorry for the anxiety that his partner was experiencing. And then he felt anger…his one-hundred and eighty day letter could still arrive by certified mail at any time. He could be named in a lawsuit at any time. Maybe the Anderson case. Maybe the Mitchell case. Maybe some completely different case. It was a fact of life for any practicing doctor in America.

Chapter Twenty-two

Medical Grand Rounds, Cleveland Medical Center April 2010

As the Vice Chairman of the Department of Medicine at the Cleveland Medical Center, Dan Ulek was responsible for organizing and moderating Medical Grand Rounds, a weekly conference that was considered mandatory for all faculty and house staff in the department. The term "Grand Rounds" referred to traditional conferences developed in teaching hospitals in the early 1900s. At one time, the conferences were based on the live examination of a patient who presented with a classic disease or a diagnostic dilemma. A senior physician from the hospital would examine the patient and take a medical history on stage – typically in the center of an amphitheatre – sharing teaching points with the surrounding audience that consisted largely of other faculty, medical students, interns, and residents. Sometimes, audience members were allowed to ask additional questions or even to come to the stage to directly appreciate some finding on the physical examination. Live patient examinations were ultimately abandoned, in part because of patient privacy issues. Modern versions of "Grand Rounds" slowly evolved to consist of simple educational lectures given by expert physicians. At the CMC, about half of the Medical Grand Rounds lectures were delivered by visiting physicians who were invited from other academic medical centers.

This week's Grand Rounds speaker was Dr. Henry Bolman from the Ohio Medical Center in Columbus. He was invited to Cleveland and to the CMC as part of a two-day visiting professorship known as the "Jack Hurtuk Visiting Professorship," named after a cardiothoracic surgeon who served as Director of the Cardiothoracic Transplant program at CMC for several years before moving to Pittsburgh in 2006.

After encouraging the audience members to take their seats, Dan began his brief but laudatory introduction.

"It is a great pleasure for me to introduce my good friend, Dr. Henry Bolman, as this year's Jack Hurtuk Visiting Professor of Medicine. Dr. Bolman is a Distinguished Professor of Surgery at the Ohio Medical Center where he has spent most of his career and where he has served as the Director of Solid Organ Transplantation since 1996. He has published over two hundred manuscripts and dozens of books or book chapters, mostly dealing with surgical aspects of kidney and pancreas transplantation. He has served as President of the American Society of Kidney Transplantation and is the current editor of the Journal of Kidney Transplantation. The title of Dr. Bolmans's talk today is: Kidney Transplantation: Past, Present, and Future. Please welcome Dr. Henry Bolman."

Dan had known Bolman for years and respected him as an outstanding surgeon and educator. Earlier in his career, he supervised a productive research laboratory and published some landmark papers about a novel subset of white blood cells called natural killer cells, describing their role in the rejection of transplanted organs. Dan had the pleasure of attending several research presentations given by Bolman both regionally, nationally, and internationally. For today's address to a more general audience of doctors with little expertise in organ transplantation, he was expecting a mundane review of the field of kidney transplantation. He was wrong.

Bolman was an older man who appeared very business-like and sophisticated – the look of a seasoned Department Chair. He was dressed in a sharp pinstriped suit – a classic "professorial" look. He was tall and thin and had thick white hair and thick white eyebrows that contrasted with his black-rimmed spectacles. He began his lecture by showing a famous photograph of the identical twin brothers who served as the donor and recipient for the first successful kidney transplant performed in 1954 at the Peter Bent Brigham Hospital in Boston. In the photograph, the twins sat in front of the surgeons and physicians who cared for the donor and the recipient before and after the transplant. Bolman pointed out, mostly for the medical students and inexperienced trainees in the audience, that transplantation between identical twins could be performed without the need for anti-rejection drugs. The recipient's immune system was identical to that of the donor and would not recognize the brother's kidney as foreign tissue.

Bolman went on, describing the perplexing problem of acute rejection of organs transplanted between two human beings who were *not* identical twins. He described the role of immunosuppressive drugs in preventing the process of rejection and allowing transplanted organs to function for relatively long periods of time.

"This slide depicts the improvements in short-term outcomes that we have witnessed in the fifty plus years that have transpired since that first transplant at the Brigham," said Bolman, using his laser pointer to emphasize key points on the complicated graphic being displayed on the screen. "You can see that, with the development of newer and more potent immunosuppressive drugs, the incidence of acute rejection episodes experienced by kidney transplant recipients has gradually declined since those early years of transplantation. In the 1960s and 70s, only fifty percent of transplants performed with kidneys from deceased donors lasted more than one year. In the modern era, more than ninety-five percent of such kidneys function for more than a year and more than seventy percent function for more than five years. The good news in kidney transplantation is that short-term outcomes have improved dramatically in the past forty years. Transplanted kidneys are lasting longer. Recipients of kidney transplants are living longer."

Dan Ulek realized that this heretofore traditional review would take a provocative turn at about the fifteen-minute mark when Bolman clicked to his next slide, a title slide displaying a simple question:

HOW FAR CAN WE PUSH THE ENVELOPE?

The final thirty minutes of Bolman's presentation consisted, unexpectedly, of his sobering reflections and serious concerns about the future of the field of organ transplantation. He started by showing data indicating that the population of kidney transplant candidates was gradually getting older.

"In the early days of transplantation, patients over the age of fifty were excluded from transplantation, deemed to be too old to tolerate the rigors of transplant surgery and the requisite immunosuppressive drugs. Today, the upper age limit has been abandoned. Many centers, including my own, have successfully transplanted patients in their mid-seventies. In fact, these patients sometimes do surprisingly well. But old people die eventually and it seems likely that this trend for transplanting older recipients will ultimately be reflected in lower patient survival rates than we have experienced in the past two decades."

Bolman's next slide showed a graph depicting the explosive increase in the number of patients waiting for kidney transplants during the past twenty years, related in part to liberalizing the upper age limits for transplant candidates. "So here is the crux of the problem. We can develop even better and safer anti-rejection drugs, but they won't fix the fundamental crisis we face: a continued shortage of organs for the growing list of patients in need...a continued disparity between supply and demand that has resulted in huge waiting lists, long waiting times, and increasing mortality rates among patients who are waiting."

His finishing remarks were the most sobering of all.

"So, how have we reacted to the shortage of organs from deceased donors? We have pushed the envelope to include older donors...donors with medical problems such as hypertension, even diabetes...donors who yield kidneys that may already be scarred from the effects of aging and other medical problems. In our earnest efforts to provide kidneys for the ever increasing population of transplant candidates, we have sometimes used donors – unknowingly – who harbor malignancies or viral infections that can be transmitted to the recipient...sometimes with fatal consequences."

Ulek suddenly realized, unlike other oblivious members of the audience, that Bolman's entire perspective on kidney transplantation may have been altered by the tragic LCMV case that involved two patients at his own Ohio Medical Center in Columbus.

Bolman went on, "Ladies and gentlemen, I don't pretend to have the answers to the serious questions that I raise here regarding the future of organ transplantation. Xenotransplantation – that is, transplantation or organs from other animal species, sounds attractive but has not been perfected and carries its own baggage of ethical issues. Do we really want to breed pigs or monkeys in colonies to provide a pool for organ donation to humans? Sounds a little creepy to me! Will pigs, monkeys or other animals introduce previously unknown viral infections into the human population? New varieties of HIV-like viruses? No, I don't have the answers. I'll leave those answers to the next generation of transplant surgeons and physicians. But as I ponder my role as an aging transplant surgeon, increasingly I wake up each day and recall the principles of medical practice that many of you in this room agreed to, under oath, when you graduated from medical school."

He then went on to cite the Hippocratic Oath, quoting the original version that was translated to English. "I swear by

Apollo...that I will prescribe regimens for the good of my patients according to my ability and my judgment and *never do harm* to anyone."

"I urge my colleagues to pursue organ transplantation in the future with that important principle in mind: 'Do no harm'. Thank you for your kind attention, ladies and gentlemen."

There was a standing ovation.

Following the talk, Dan had lunch with Dr. Bolman in the faculty dining room.

"Henry, that was a pretty pessimistic view of the field. I am thinking that you have been influenced by the LCMV case from 2008?" Dan asked.

"Yes, and as you know, it's an *ongoing* ordeal. I know you guys are involved in one of the cases here in Cleveland, and I'm not sure how you're handling it. The effects on the Columbus transplantation community have been devastating. I'm sure the emotional stress was partially responsible for the marital difficulties of at least one of my colleagues. Morale at the OOB has been terrible for two years with no signs of recovery. The turnover in personnel has been disturbing. Bob Briggs has barely been able to maintain a full crew of donor coordinators. Ironically, the coordinator who has taken the biggest beating with all of these lawsuits is still working at the OOB, but his productivity has decreased because he spends more time in legal meetings than he does on the road evaluating potential donors. Organ donation rates have plummeted in the Columbus area and I am now supervising a team of frustrated surgeons and transplant coordinators who honestly don't have enough work to do."

"I guess I've been through this kind of thing before." Dan responded. "I'm not saying it doesn't affect me. But I'm older, hopefully wiser, and know that I personally did nothing wrong in the case here in Cleveland. I also know that we can still lose the case in court. Maybe *all* of the cases will be lost. But it won't be the end of the world, at least not for me. Life goes on."

"I envy your positive attitude, Dan. I am older than you – a *lot* older – but probably less wise. Happily, I plan to retire next year. I'm seventy-two and ready to call it quits. I will miss the surgery and some elements of patient care, but I won't miss the craziness of a system in which the threat of malpractice suits preoccupies the minds of our most talented young physicians and surgeons. I've been tracking the LCMV cases and have accumulated a rather large collection of notes about the outcomes of the patients and their caretakers. At some point I'd like to return to Cleveland and spend a few hours with you and the other members of your team who were involved in the Fred Jackson case. I plan to write a memoir eventually. But of course, I'm waiting for the outcome of the court cases – if they materialize – before I color the memoir with my editorial opinions about all the nonsense."

"It may come down to a single court case or at least an index case that will determine whether the other cases stand a fighting chance for the prosecuting lawyers," offered Dan. "I am told that the index case will likely be that of the teenage boy from your center. He received one of the two kidneys from the infected donor."

"Yes, the Anderson case. What an awful story. I'm sure that the prosecuting attorneys will whip the jurors into a frenzy over that one. It's all part of the craziness. And it's already been more than two years since the original transplant. It's almost impossible to remember clinical details from cases that long ago. They drag these things on for years, prolonging the stress and anxiety for the folks named in these lawsuits."

"I think the Anderson court case has been scheduled for later this year – maybe late November or early December," Dan replied.

"Well then, someone is going to have a very merry Christmas," said Bolman. "It's just not clear whether it will be the lawyers or the doctors."

Chapter Twenty-three

Caesar's Palace, Las Vegas
May 2010

Colleagues or patients would never guess that Dr. Dan Ulek was a Vegas kind of guy, let alone a gambling man. Truth was, Dan and his wife Kathy *loved* Las Vegas and made efforts to travel there from Cleveland at least once a year, sometimes twice. This latest trip coincided with their thirty-third wedding anniversary. On the flight from Cleveland, Dan and Kathy were recounting some of their most memorable family vacations, with the help of the photo albums that Dan kept on his traveling laptop. There was a separate folder entitled 'Vegas Vacations'. Kathy pointed to the screen and said, "There's the famous twenty-first birthday trip – I haven't seen those photos for a while."

When their two youngest twin children turned twenty-one, Dan paid for the entire family – including the twins' two older brothers – to a long weekend in Vegas – three nights and four days. He put the kids up at Bally's while he and Kathy stayed at the Flamingo – close by, but not too close. Dan viewed it as a rite of passage. The kids were finally all adults. *Welcome to our favorite adult playground.* Although he and Kathy got together with the four kids for most meals – and of course paid for them – he gave them plenty of time on their own and did not inquire of their whereabouts. *After all, what happens in Vegas...*

Dan was clicking through the slide shows, sharing each photo with his wife. Kathy asked him to pause periodically. "Stop there. That's a great shot of Brian and Lauren hoisting a couple of beers at Smith and Wollensky's – that was a great night."

"Yeah, I'm sure that was the first time they ever tasted beer," quipped Dan.

Dan and Kathy had been pretty liberal about teenage drinking as their kids were growing up, figuring that if they had been more restrictive, the children would be rebelliously abusive. It worked. By the time the kids turned twenty-one they each had plenty of experience with alcohol and rarely overdid it, even on this incredible lark in Las Vegas. Dan paid for everything except gambling money for the kids. They each had full- or part-time jobs and, when Dan announced plans for the trip eight months earlier, he told each of the kids that they would have to save their own gambling money. He was more than happy to provide some advice about gambling on a budget. The Ulek children thought it was a pretty good deal – what with the free airfare and hotel – and Dan and Kathy knew that they would be forced to gamble responsibly if they were using their hard-earned savings.

The last night of that infamous Ulek weekend in Vegas was a particular blast for the entire family as they gambled together at the Imperial Palace until three in the morning – mostly playing Black Jack – while the dealers, all young people wearing the costumes of various rock stars, took turns lip-synching classic rock-and-roll songs on a central stage. It was crazy, loud, young-people fun. Although neither of the twins had ever seriously played Black Jack before, they picked up the game quickly and one of them, Lauren, won over five hundred dollars on that last night alone. Going home with more money than you brought to Vegas was a rarity, so it was a nice ending to a weekend that the entire family would always remember. *Well they would remember some parts!*

In more recent years, Dan and Kathy moved from the Flamingo to the more posh and expensive Caesar's Palace across the street. There were certainly more expensive casino hotels on the strip – Bellagio, Wynn, and Mandalay Bay to name a few. When Dan suggested that they sample one of these newer places, Kathy balked. "I really like Caesar's central location on the strip, and it's luxurious enough for me. And there are enough good restaurants in Caesar's Palace alone to keep us eating for a week."

In recent years, Las Vegas had become a restaurant capital, rivaling New York, LA, and San Francisco for high-end restaurants, many of which were copied versions of storied restaurants from those more established cities. It seemed that the most famous chefs in America coveted a satellite restaurant or two on the strip in Vegas. These days, Dan and Kathy loved Vegas as much for the gourmet food as for the gambling.

But gamble they did. Never to the point of becoming an addiction, but still a little fix that they each needed every year or so. For a three-night stay (*that was about as much of Vegas as that they could take at a time*), they would typically bring a thousand dollars apiece for gambling money. Hardly high rollers by Vegas standards, but probably more money than the average American could afford to waste in three days, once a year. They rarely, if ever, took home more money than they brought, but on most trips they each ended up with some portion of their original thousand dollars. Dan used the leftover money to defray the costs of the airfare, hotel, and meals. He was never allowed to ask Kathy what she did with her "winnings" or leftovers. He figured that she was probably accumulating a stash of "Las Vegas cash" in one of the bed mattresses or cookie jars at home over the years.

At Caesar's they had a daily routine consisting of morning coffee and a croissant or Danish, grabbing early lounge chairs at Neptune's Pool for a swim in the morning sun, a late-morning Bloody Mary or Screwdriver, a light lunch, an afternoon of reading and/or sex (*what happens in Vegas…*), pre-dinner cocktails, dinner with a bottle of wine, and then gambling from around 8:00 pm till midnight…or later if they were both winning.

Kathy had pretty reliable luck at roulette tables and when she played together with Dan, they knew how to work a table so that one of them usually came away as a winner. It takes money to make money, so the key to roulette was placing a lot of chips on the board, spread out as much as possible on the grid of thirty-six numbers. Whenever they cozied up to a new roulette table, Dan and Kathy would typically each put down a hundred dollar bill to purchase a hundred one-dollar chips. If the table had a ten dollar minimum – that is at least ten dollars worth of chips for each spin of the roulette wheel – Dan and Kathy would double the minimum, putting down at least twenty chips apiece for one game. The key to winning was overlapping. With twenty chips, Dan would be sure to place ten chips on numbers different from those that Kathy played, while ten chips were placed on numbers common to hers. With this tactic, one of them was a winner about half the time, and perhaps twenty percent of the time they were both winners, having chips on a common number. Of course the more chips you played the higher the odds of winning something on any given spin. On a good night, the chips would pile up around either or both of them and the dealer would begin exchanging those one dollar chips for the more handsome green twenty-five dollar chips, or the even more handsome one hundred dollar chips – *black beauties*. At the end of the day, Dan and Kathy realized that it was all blind luck, but every now and then they would leave a table up a few thousand bucks – only to blow it later on another night, at another table, or maybe at another of Vegas' many casinos. The thrill of winning, even if short-lived, was what brought them back time and again. And it was truly *play* time – a time for each of them to forget the daily grind back home.

It was Saturday night, the last night of this latest trip to Vegas, and the couple's anniversary. Dan made reservations at Mesa Grill – one of several high-end (*i.e., expensive*) restaurants in Caesar's Palace. This was Bobby Flay's version of his restaurant of the same name in central Manhattan. Dan and Kathy had eaten at the New York venue a few years earlier and loved the unique southwestern cuisine. The menu appeared to be very similar (Dan loved the appetizer of barbecued duck served over a blueberry pancake), although the modern décor of Vegas version of Mesa Grill was very different than the two-storied, atrium-like restaurant in New York. The Vegas "branch" was actually located within the casino, which Dan found distracting, but surrounded by glass walls to make for a reasonably quiet atmosphere.

Over cocktails, Kathy made the first mention of a work-related issue since they arrived in Vegas.

"God, Dan, I always enjoy seeing you have fun and relaxing. You haven't mentioned the Jackson case for almost four days!" she said.

Dan didn't mind his wife's observation. This was their last night in Vegas and they were returning to the real world early the next morning. Besides, Dan had learned several years earlier to openly discuss his problems at work with Kathy. Early in his medical career, he rarely brought his work home. But his attitude changed in the 1990s, partly revolving around events affecting their son, Michael, who developed acute leukemia in 1994. Although Michael miraculously recovered, the ordeal was stressful for the entire Ulek family. Combined with a number of professional setbacks and a major malpractice lawsuit that he hid from Kathy for months, Dan almost went off the deep end. He almost quit medicine and gave some serious thought to pursuing a career as a novelist. It was the inspiration from his wife and his son that got him back on track. As part of the deal, he forever kept Kathy in the loop on how things were going at work – good or bad. The ordeal of the 90s also changed Dan's entire attitude about life and about dealing with stress. Although the Jackson case was distracting and time consuming, it was not like dealing with a family member's life-threatening illness. It was *not* the end of the world.

"Yeah, well the case is in a holding pattern of sorts. Bill Matthews tells me that judge is awaiting the outcome of another case in Columbus. Same donor, but the recipient was an 18-year-old kid who also died from the same viral infection. If the defense loses that case, it will set a precedent and open the door to dozens of jury trials," said Dan. "Including our case in Cleveland."

"Dozens of cases?" Kathy interjected. "I thought you said there were seven people who got organs from the donor?"

"Oh no, this entire thing has gotten crazy. First of all, except for one case – a second case from Columbus – in which no lawsuits have been filed to date, the other cases each have generated multiple lawsuits. Strangely enough, the worst situation revolves around a patient from Michigan who has never shown signs of the infection at all. The Infectious Disease guys believe she had some kind of natural immunity to the virus that was responsible for these infections. Anyhow, the patient apparently freaked out when her doctors told her about this LCMV infection and ended up suing the doctors and the hospital because she will forever be anxious about developing the infection. On top of that, the patient has no fewer than ten relatives who have submitted individual lawsuits, claiming that they visited the patient in the hospital or shortly after her discharge from the hospital, and now feel that they've been exposed to a rare viral infection. It's all BS because normal people almost always recover from the illness. Besides, it is highly unlikely that that the Michigan patient was capable of transmitting anything – she never had the disease!"

"It really *does* sound crazy," said Kathy. "I can't believe that there isn't some way of preventing some of the more frivolous cases from getting too far along before they are dismissed."

"Well a lot of those peripheral cases will prove to be truly frivolous and will never go to court – but the cost of all this must be staggering. I know for a fact that there are at least ten expert witnesses on each side of the Jackson case. These guys charge anywhere between three hundred and seven hundred and fifty dollars an hour for their services and some of them log over fifty hours of service time from reviewing records, meeting with attorneys, providing depositions, etcetera. If you do the math, the amount of money spent on expert witnesses alone is staggering, not to mention the fat attorney fees, court costs, etcetera – let alone if there are major awards in some of the cases. You know, for years now this whole case has been about a rare disease, a viral disease that tainted our honest efforts to do something good for patients. But now I see the real disease upon us – it's an *epidemic* of legal charges against health professionals in this and so many other cases. It's a disease alright – it's enough to make you sick."

"Amazing, and who pays for all of it?" Kathy asked

"Why do you think my department is always worried about bankruptcy? The malpractice premiums have gone through the roof, and it's all carved out of our clinical income. In fact, the CMC is now self-insured because none of the departments could afford the lofty premiums of the private malpractice insurance companies. Being self-insured is a big gamble. One huge award and the stash of reserved money could disappear instantly. I wouldn't want to be the hospital administrator in charge of playing those chips."

"So are you seriously worried about the Jackson case, Dan?"

"I stopped worrying about this kind of stuff years ago Kath. Life is too short. I am sure that I did nothing wrong in this case. I have nothing to confess. But I also know that a sympathetic jury can override innocence in these cases. If that happens, my life will go on. I still love my job. I still love my family, and I still love you. Speaking of which, I've been looking at the appetizer list. I love Bobby Flay's roasted tortillas, but I'm going with the half-dozen Blue Point oysters. I'm feeling a little frisky tonight," said Dan with a wink of one eye and raising his cocktail glass for a last-night-in-Vegas toast with his wife.

Kathy returned the wink. "OK, let's stop talking about doctors and lawyers...Happy Anniversary, sweetheart."

Chapter Twenty-four

Cora Mitchell's Decision
May 2010

Jim Gannon sat nervously at Cora Mitchell's kitchen table as she prepared some hot tea for each of them. Gannon disliked tea but decided to go with the flow. The Mitchells owned a well-kept, three-bedroom bungalow in the Driving Park neighborhood on the near east side of Columbus. Gannon had no concerns about driving into this mostly African America community. However, he was nervous because he was almost certain of the outcome of this meeting with Mrs. Mitchell. After she rebuffed phone calls from a number of paralegals at Hackett, Hackett and Lowenstein, William Hackett assigned Gannon to arrange this face-to-face meeting.

"Together with the other Columbus case and the case in Cleveland, we can be looking at multimillion dollar awards or settlements," Hackett told Gannon repeatedly. "A case like this will go a long way to bolster your resume and your chance for a partnership some day. Get out there and schmooze her. Turn on your Irish charm. Tell her you have lots of black friends. Appeal to her religious beliefs. Beg her. Whatever it takes, I want this case in our portfolio."

I could use something a little stronger than tea right now.

Following Hackett's advice, Gannon decided to open the discussion with something other than pursuit of a malpractice lawsuit.

"You have a lovely home. I presume your children are all grown and gone?" he asked.

"My children are all married and I have five grandchildren. My oldest son lives in Cleveland. My other son and daughter live here in the Columbus area – well out in the northern suburbs.

My daughter just had her second child – a beautiful grandson – about a month ago. Those kids and grandkids are the joy of my life."

"Good. And I hope they are healthy and doing well?" Gannon asked politely.

"Well the economy is so bad right now. My youngest son just lost his job. But he's college educated like my other two children, so I'm sure he'll find something soon. And everybody is in good health. My husband's family has a strong history of high blood pressure and he's passed it on to all three children but they each have it under control and get good doctoring."

Convenient segue!

"Oh yes, how long has it been since your husband passed?" Gannon asked.

"Almost a year and a half, but I suspect you knew that Mr. Gannon. I know why you are here so why don't we just get down to business?"

Gannon sipped his hot tea, cleared his throat, and spoke. "Mrs. Mitchell, you *do* realize that your husband – it's Warren, right? – died as a consequence of a medical mistake, don't you?"

"My husband died a happy man, Mr. Gannon. And if you're talking about that virus infection that everyone got so excited about, well you got to die from something. To me, a virus is like the sniffles or the flu – maybe even measles or chickenpox. There are viruses everywhere and we all come down with viruses from time to time. Ain't no doctor's fault if I catch a cold, so how can they be guilty of giving Warren a virus?"

"If they had properly detected the virus in Mr. Mitchell's donor, the organs would never have been transplanted and your husband might still be alive today," Gannon responded.

Cora took two long sips of her tea before renewing the conversation.

"So tell me Mr. Gannon, how is *your* family?"

"Oh, fine," he replied, not certain why Cora was asking this unexpected question.

"Do you have any family members on dialysis?" she asked.

In reality, until he became involved with these transplant cases, Gannon's knowledge about kidney failure, dialysis and kidney transplantation was miniscule.

"No, my family has managed to stay pretty healthy. No one is on dialysis that I know of."

"Well let me tell you that if Warren had not received that kidney transplant, there's a good chance he would have died soon on dialysis. It was keeping him alive but I knew he was slowly dying. So the way I figured, it was getting close to Warren's time anyhow. The kidney transplant gave him a few weeks of happiness and allowed him to die a happy man. If it was a virus that killed him after a transplant, well then it could have been a case of endocarditis if he'd stayed on dialysis – so whose fault would that be? People gotta die from something."

Gannon could tell that this line of reasoning was getting him nowhere. And he did not want to admit to Cora that he had no idea what the term *endocarditis* meant! He was impressed by her knowledge, by her intelligence, and by her ability to speak eloquently.

"Yes people gotta die from something, but if Warren's death was preventable then it was a medical mistake, and you and your family can be, no *should* be compensated. Cora, we could be talking about enough money to make you comfortable for life...make your children and grandchildren comfortable too. Thousands or even millions of dollars in compensation."

He was expecting a look of shock, amazement, joy or wonder but found no change in Cora's facial expression.

"And don't worry," he went on, trying to anticipate her thoughts. "That money doesn't come out of the doctors' pockets. It comes from big insurance companies. That's why the doctors have malpractice insurance – just for cases like this."

"Mr. Gannon, I am quite comfortable in my current state and

so are my children, with or without jobs. Warren and I raised our children right and they understand that money is not the source of all happiness or comfort. You seem like a nice young man – obviously well-educated – but I *do* think you have been misguided in getting into this awful business of suing hospitals and doctors. I got nothing against lawyers. *Should I tell him that some of my best friends are lawyers?* But you should really think about settling real estate disputes or divorces and wills – maybe even get into civil rights. Mr. Gannon, what you call a *medical mistake* I consider to be an act of God. It's been a year and a half since Warren passed. I miss him terribly but I am at peace. So are my children and my grandchildren. None of us have any intention of interrupting our peaceful lives by spending the next year in meetings with lawyers or going to court. You can save your million dollar awards and put the money to some better use…maybe feed the homeless, give scholarships to poor kids, support medical research to make organ transplants safer…so many better uses for money than *compensating* me or my children. There will be no lawsuits from the Mitchell family. We don't want or need money from some big insurance company."

Gannon had no idea how he would present all of this to Hackett and the other partners in the firm. He may have blown a golden opportunity to advance his career – to make a move towards being a partner. He tried his best to schmooze this potential client, but instead he felt like *he* was schmoozed by *her*. William Hackett was not going to be happy. The other partners in the firm were not going to be happy. But it was clear that this tea party with Cora Mitchell was over.

Chapter Twenty-five

The Virgin Islands
June 2010

Andy Siegel arranged the entire sailing trip. The four travelers would include himself, his 21-year-old son Jason, Mark Hubbard, and Mark's father Jack. It was a trip for *adult* men and Mark's sons were deemed too young to participate. The ten-day excursion included flights from Columbus to Miami, Miami to San Juan, and then a puddle jumper from San Juan to the small airfield on Beef Island, just east of Tortola in the British Virgin Islands. A driver met them at the airport and transported them to the sailing dock in Tortola where they met the captain who was assigned to their forty-four foot mono-hull sailing yacht, called "Annabelle". The captain, Henri, was a 30-year-old French Canadian with a short athletic frame and a thick mane of yellow hair...like a Beach Boy with a hint of a French accent. Henri escorted the group of men to the on-site supply store to stock up on water, food, booze and other essentials (like sun tan lotion, some CDs featuring Caribbean music, and big Cuban cigars). Andy and Henri spent most of the first evening plotting the course of the sailing excursion using Henri's extensive collection of maps. The others in the group feasted on martinis, beers and rib eye steaks prepared on the boat by Jack Hubbard, who was officially pronounced chief chef for the remainder of the trip.

Siegel had some sailing and yachting experience, including a one-week excursion around the Bahamas on a catamaran with his wife and two children when the kids were toddlers. He had always wanted to sail the Virgin Islands, known for their relatively calm intra-island waters, excellent snorkeling, and hundreds of venues for mooring the yacht, taking a dinghy to shore, and sampling island cuisine and revelry. It was early June, so the risk of hurricanes was low, although it was already hot and extremely humid.

Beyond a desire to add to his sailing expertise, Andy planned this trip hoping to provide some much needed male bonding. It would be like a camping trip on water – for guys only. For his son, who had just turned twenty-one three months earlier, it would be one of many ceremonial introductions to adult life. Jason graduated from Miami of Ohio just a month earlier and this sailing trip was a graduation gift. Andy had met Mark's dad, Jack Hubbard, on several occasions. He was a salty character who fancied himself a sailor, but who never sailed more than a thirty-foot sailboat in Lake Erie. Jack was now seventy-five years old and was suffering from metastatic prostate cancer. He also had a long history of congestive heart failure, reasonably controlled with medications. Mark Hubbard would be forever grateful to his partner for arranging this expedition – probably his father's last ever bonafide sailing trip.

And of course Andy hoped that this trip would allow his partner, Mark, to relax a bit. He had been under a great deal of stress related to the Anderson lawsuit. In the prior six months, he noticed that Mark would rarely leave the hospital before 7 PM, even when his OR schedule was light. Years earlier, Andy recognized that people who worked late hours unnecessarily were probably not workaholics. More often there was a reason to avoid going home. Andy knew that Mark and Mary Ellen were having some problems, but never discussed the details with his colleague. He was hoping that this ten-day "separation" would be therapeutic for his partner and friend. Maybe it would even lead to a reconciliation when they got back home.

After dinner, Andy and Henri excitedly announced the sailing itinerary for the next several days. Henri was very animated and discussed his plans for the excursion as though it was the first time he had ever captained a yacht in the Virgin Islands. In fact, he had been doing this for almost nine years.

Jack Hubbard liked Henri for his free-spiritedness. "Do you still live in Canada during the off-season?" Jack asked Henri.

"No, I own a small home on St. John's Island, but from November to July, I mostly live on boats, either as the sole captain for sailing yachts the size of the Annabelle or sometimes as a member of a larger crew on one of the bigger multi-family boats."

"Sounds like a nice life. Does the job pay well?" Jack asked somewhat nosily.

Henri just chuckled. "I get a flat stipend from the sailing company for each trip. But there are lots of perks – you know, mostly good weather and nice scenery."

Jack and the other travelers would learn that Henri's sailing company owned and managed the fleet of luxury yachts for high-end customers. Henri and other hired crew members received a number of perks aside from the nice scenery. It was customary for sailing groups to provide free food and beverages and, almost always, a handsome gratuity at the end of the sailing trip – often hundreds of dollars. For the next week, Andy, Mark, Jack, and even Jason would think often about Henri's life and fantasize about giving up their day jobs to live and work in the Virgin Islands.

The itinerary created by Henri was based, in part, on Andy's desire to see most of the major islands on both the British and US sides of the island chain, but mostly based on Henri's understanding of the expected weather conditions and prevailing winds for the next week. Henri reviewed the plans with the group. "Tomorrow morning we will sail first to Virgin Gorda – it has famous coastal rock formations and caves that are literally used as baths. You'll want to get off the yacht and spend some time there. Then we go back to Tortola for the second day. Next, weather permitting, will be Anegada, the only reef-based island in the Virgins.

Andy interrupted to explain this to Jason. "Reef-based islands like Anegada were built from eons of accumulating sea shells. All the other islands in the Virgin Island chain were volcanic in origin."

Jack Hubbard spoke up unexpectedly. "Well guys, it's a bit more complicated than that. The reef island that Mark is referring to is more often called an 'atoll', and atolls actually are shell-based islands built on top of an eroded or submerged volcanic island. Most atolls are ring-shaped with an interior lagoon, and that's the case with Anegada."

The other four men paused for almost thirty seconds, staring at old Jack Hubbard in disbelief. *And we thought he was just along for the ride!* Jason Siegel would have a new respect for his elders by the end of this trip

Henri finally broke the silence. "That's exactly right, Jack. Anyhow, the sail from Tortola to Anegada will be the only open-sea segment of the excursion, largely beyond any view of land. I have a supply of Dramamine just in case there are high waves for the segment. Otherwise, our sailing will be mostly through relatively calm waters between the easily visible volcanic islands. From Anegada, we'll head next to Jost Van Dyke for a stop at the immigration office because we'll be passing from the British to the US Virgin Islands. Each of us will have to go through passport control and customs – just like the routine in any foreign airport. Then we'll sail around the entire perimeter of St. John's Island. With stops for meals, that will take two days. Finally, we will head for St. Thomas Island and the final leg of the trip."

Henri made it perfectly clear that the itinerary would be reconsidered on a day-to-day basis depending on weather conditions. Andy was disappointed that the itinerary did not include a stop at St. Croix Island, the largest and most southern of the Virgins. But Henri insisted the St. Croix was too long of a sail (about thirty-five miles south of St. John's), and that sailing there would cost three to four days out of the ten-day trip – more than he thought it was worth. It became clear to Andy that Henri was in charge.

At the end of the first evening, Jack Hubbard pulled his son aside as they were both preparing to get some sleep on the boat.

"Mark, I must say...you look a little worried...or depressed...I can't put my finger on it. Is everything OK?" Jack asked his son.

"Oh sure, Dad, everything's fine. We've been busy as hell back in Columbus. So this is really a much-needed vacation," Mark responded.

"Busy is one thing. Worried or depressed...that's something else. So, you know I try not to pry, but is everything OK with you and Ellen?" asked Jack.

"Dad, everything is fine. Things have just been busy."

"OK, just asking."

After a long pause, Mark answered, "Alright, Dad, just so you know, I've been named in a rather big malpractice lawsuit. And you are very perceptive...it's been wearing on my nerves."

"You wanna share the details?" Jack asked.

"Not really. It's all silliness as far as I'm concerned and I don't want to bore you with the whole story."

"That's fine. Tell me though, has Andy also been named in this lawsuit?"

"No...he hasn't. Just me and some folks from the OPO. But Andy knows all about it."

"And you're sure everything's OK between you and Ellen?"

"Yes, Dad. We've had some spits and spats...like all married couples. But everything's fine now. Hey listen, Dad, let's get some rest. We need to get up early to start the sail. I really want you to have a good time on this trip."

"Let's *all* have a good time," Jack concluded, as he stripped down to his boxers preparing for bed. He remained worried about his son.

Each segment of the trip included time for swimming, snorkeling and of course, eating and drinking. Jack Hubbard mixed up a large batch of scrambled eggs each morning – served Hubbard style with plenty of Tabasco sauce. Lunch was less formal as each traveler grabbed some bread, cheese, or cold cuts that had been purchased in abundance at the Tortola supply store. All of the travelers were surprised to find themselves drinking beer by late morning and transitioning to cocktails at 5 PM. Rum and coke for Jason Siegel, gin martinis with lemon twists for Andy and Jack, and Johnnie Walker Black for Mark.

Jason quickly became the captain's first mate, and by day three of the trip, was adept at helping Henri moor the yacht in one of the hundreds of bays that surrounded the perimeter of each island. Jason had only a vague recollection of the family trip to the Bahamas years earlier, so learning the science and language of sailing was a new and exciting experience. He became facile with directional language – port versus starboard, forward versus aft – and proudly became familiar with the language of sailing lines (not ropes!). Within a week, he was skilled at creating square knots, sheet bends, bowlines, and clove hitches – and understood the utilities of each type of knot. Andy Siegel could see a serious sailor in the making. This was exactly what he wanted Jason to get out of this graduation gift.

Each night, the men would either cook their own food on the boat if they were harbored in a quiet unpopulated bay, or dinghy to shore to eat at a local restaurant in the more populated bays. Jack Hubbard had some difficulty managing the small hop onto and off of the dinghy and was happier staying on the boat for dinner. Sometimes during cocktail hours, Henri would mysteriously dive into the ocean with snorkeling gear and swim off for hours at a time. Jason was amazed at his swimming abilities.

"Considering that he smokes at least a pack of cigarettes a day, it's incredible how long he can stay under water without surfacing for air," Jason commented to the group one night.

"And I wonder where he goes for two, sometimes three hours at a time?" Jack Hubbard added.

"Well he's a single guy and my guess is that he's got a girlfriend in every port," offered Mark. Each of the men was thinking the same thing. *What a life!*

Henri would always return after dinner time as he was obliged contractually to sleep on the boat with his clients to assure their safety. Late at night, he would smoke cigars (gifts of his clients of course – another perk), listen to some reggae music, and point out constellations in the sky. During cloudless nights on the ocean, the stars and constellations were incredibly bright. It was the first time any of the travelers from Ohio had seen the Southern Cross. More than a little buzzed from an evening of scotch and wine, Mark Hubbard marveled at the famous constellation, recalling the Crosby, Stills and Nash song..."When you see the Southern Cross for the first time...you understand now why you came this way." He stared into the sky humming the song's refrain and wondering.

The yacht had sleeping quarters for four, although the captain's bunk was no bigger than an open casket. Jason slept on the couch in the living quarters of the central hull, and the other three men slept in the three additional bunks positioned at the front and back of the boat. The boat was not air conditioned and the nights were uncomfortably humid. Andy Siegel found himself getting up several times each night and jumping into the ocean, naked as a jay bird, in order to cool off for a few minutes. One night – actually more like 3 AM, he was startled to find Jason and Mark in the stern of the boat, chatting quietly and each sipping on Johnnie Walker Black and smoking big fat Cuban cigars. *Jason? Scotch? Cigars?* Andy was initially embarrassed to be found naked in front of his son and partner, but figured 'what the hell, we're all adult men'. When he jumped into the ocean, the other two put down their drinks and cigars and joined him for a twenty minute skinny dip. *Guys, it doesn't get any better than this.*

In some venues, they were plagued by flies. *Like camping on water.* One of the highlights of the trip came at Jost Van Dyke where hot showers were offered for two dollars a person in a facility adjacent to the immigration office. Talk about male bonding. Four naked men, twenty-one to seventy-five years of age, each savoring the luxury of soap and hot water in a communal shower, and literally groaning with delight.

On the second last day of the trip, as they were jumping onto their dinghy in Round Bay on St. John's Island, Jack Hubbard slipped and hit his head on the side of the yacht, creating a four-inch gash in his right forehead. Like most scalp wounds, it was a bloody mess. It didn't help that was taking aspirin and Plavix as blood thinners after having two coronary artery stents placed six months earlier. Both Andy and Mark knew that either of them could easily suture the wound closed in a few minutes, but their first-aid kit included only band-aids and two rolls of gauze. There was no suture set. Jack felt badly that his injury forced the group to change dinner plans for the night, as his son needed to apply heavy pressure to the wound for almost thirty minutes, after which he applied eight band-aids in an effort to close the wound, followed by construction of a gauze headband. It was getting too late to dinghy to shore and Mark was frankly worried about his father falling again.

"Don't worry, Dad," said Mark. "There are still plenty of steaks left in the cooler and tonight I'll play chef while you relax."

"Sorry about wrecking your dinner plans, guys. That's what you get for taking an old fart like me on a trip like this. You know, guys, I've spent the last week sweating my ass off in bed, swatting at man-eating flies, baking in salt water, pissing in the ocean, taking craps in the 'head' of a crowded boat – and wondering where the stuff went when I flushed. I've eaten more scrambled eggs than I've consumed in the previous ten years, and I've literally busted my head – wide open, spilling my blood all over the stern of this yacht. But in case I forget to mention it before we end this trip, let me just tell you guys – I've had the time of my life."

Andy Siegel felt at least partially fulfilled.

Jack went on, nodding to Andy and Mark, "And I don't know about you guys, but getting away from the wife for this little trip has actually been terrific. I mean, I miss Martha, but being out with just you guys has been a nice change of pace."

Mark responded, "Well it's not that often you can say to your wife, 'I'll be gone for ten days with no phone or e-mail access'. It *is* refreshing!"

"Holy cow, I almost forgot!" Andy chimed in. "I borrowed my neighbor's satellite phone for the trip, in case of some emergency. Do you guys want to call home to check in with Martha or Mary Ellen?"

"Maybe in the morning, before we fly back from St. Thomas," offered Mark.

"I'll pass," said Jack, smiling "After forty-eight years of marriage, Martha can wait another two days to hear from me again. If I know my wife at all, she's probably enjoying this as much as I am!"

The last leg of the sailing trip was an early-morning jaunt along the southeastern shore of St. Thomas Island. As the Annabelle approached St. Thomas Harbor and the town of Charlotte Amalie, Henri turned on the yacht's engine and instructed Jason to take down the mainsail. They would motor in the rest of the way – the sailing part of the trip was over. The magnificent Marriott Frenchman's Reef Resort sat high above them on a cliff overlooking the southeast corner of the harbor. Charlotte Amalie was the largest town that the yacht's passengers had seen since leaving San Juan ten days earlier. The trip was coming to an end. Almost time to return to civilization and real life.

Mark took up Andy's offer and used the satellite phone to call Mary Ellen. It was just past 8 AM back home, and he assumed that she would be up and preparing for her day. On the first dial, a strange male voice answered the phone and Mark quickly hung up, apologizing for dialing the wrong number. Focusing more carefully on the phone's key pad to dial the correct number, the same man answered.

"Who *is* this," asked Mark.

"Who is *this*?" the man asked, sounding as though he had just been wakened from his sleep.

Mark didn't answer. Instead he stared at the LCD display of the phone, displaying his home phone number, quite accurately.

Mary Ellen is sleeping with another man.

Chapter Twenty-six

Another Deposition – Part Two
March 2010

After almost forty minutes of introductory nonsense, William Hackett proceeded with the earnest portion of the Lance Turner deposition.

"So, Mr. Turner, could you please describe your role in the acquisition of organs from UNOS donor #OH7450 in May of 2008?" asked Mr. Hackett.

Lance answered as briefly and succinctly as possible, "I was the donor coordinator assigned by the Ohio Organ Bank to evaluate that donor."

"And can you tell us exactly what you mean by 'evaluating the donor'?"

"We are generally called to see patients who potentially meet the criteria for brain death or donation after cardiac death. In this case, the patient had a severe stroke. The ICU staff at Wright State called the OOB because it appeared that the patient was approaching a state of brain death. I was assigned to this case to begin the process of determining whether this unfortunate patient would qualify to be an organ donor if brain death was declared."

"I see. Very erudite...and Mr. Turner, did you decide that donor #OH7450 was acceptable as an organ donor?"

"Objection. Form", James Kennedy interrupted.

Hackett rephrased the question, "What did you determine as the result of your evaluation?"

"I determined that the donor was a potential candidate for organ transplantation," Lance answered.

"And can you tell us how you came to that conclusion?"

"We obtain information from the potential donor's family and friends about the patient's past medical history. Some elements of the past history could theoretically exclude donation. We also rely on a standard battery of laboratory tests to determine the overall health of the potential donor and to determine if there are any lab results that would preclude donation."

"And, Mr. Turner, did you find any lab results or items in the past medical history of donor #OH7540 that would *preclude* organ donation?"

"No."

Lance Turner and James Kennedy were prepared for the next line of questions. Through the network, Kennedy learned about the deposition of the donor's girlfriend, first entered as an exhibit in the Jackson case in Cleveland. If Hackett was going to bring up the donor's jail time, Lance was prepared to state that the girlfriend denied any recent incarceration.

"Mr. Turner, were you aware that UNOS donor #7450 was incarcerated just two weeks before his unfortunate death?"

Lance's eyes suddenly widened, "At the time, no! In fact..."

Hackett cut him off, "Was that a yes or no?"

"No."

"Mr. Turner, which family members did you obtain information from as part of your evaluation of donor #OH7450?"

"I talked several times to his mother by telephone...she was disabled – a dialysis patient with bilateral leg amputations – and was not able to get to the hospital. I also spent a great deal of time talking to Elroy's...umm, the donor's girlfriend."

"And that girlfriend's name is Tanya Stenfield?"

"Yes."

Hackett grabbed a folder from the pile of papers and documents lying on the desk in front of him. "We recently deposed Ms. Stenfield. She testified that her boyfriend was released from the county jail just ten days before his death after serving time for being an accomplice in an assault and battery case."

Lance looked over to Kennedy, expecting an objection. Instead, he offered Lance a quizzical rotary turn of an index finger that said, 'Let's see where he is going to take this.'

Hackett paused and looked up at Lance, expecting a response of some kind, but forgetting that he had not posed a question. Lance on the other hand, remembered Kennedy's repeated advice in the rehearsal meetings that he dubbed *Depositions 101*: "Never speak unless you are asked a question. When you are asked a question, think first, then answer the question as simply as possible. Do not wander away from the question asked. Do not give information that you are not asked for."

Hackett continued, "Mr. Turner, are you aware of the CDC's criteria for high risk behavior?"

"Yes, of course."

"And would you agree that recent incarceration is one of those criteria?"

"Yes, but..."

Hackett cut him off again, "So, Mr. Turner, do you think that transplant surgeons in Ohio, Michigan, and Pennsylvania would have accepted organs from donor #OH7450 had they known the donor met the CDC criteria for high risk behavior?"

"Objection. Object to foundation...you are asking a question based on a theoretical situation!" Kennedy barked.

Hackett smiled and made no initial response, recognizing that objections in depositions did nothing to remove the text from the printed record. Once this deposition circulated among other attorneys and expert witnesses, his point would be made.

Without acknowledging the objection, Hackett changed directions, "Mr. Turner, did you ask Ms. Stenfield whether her boyfriend had been incarcerated recently?"

"Absolutely. It's one of the questions that are part of a standard checklist that we go through when talking to donor families. I specifically asked Ms. Stenfield questions related to each of the CDC high risk criteria. I specifically asked her if

El...umm, the donor had recently been incarcerated, and she said that he was not."

It was becoming clear to Lance that if and when this case went to court, it was going to be his word against the word of Tanya Stenfield. He was now thankful that the OOB insisted upon both verbal and electronic verification of checklists. Plus he had the unique first-hand witness in the form of Frank Orlowski. The evidence would be clear that he asked all the right questions. Tanya Stenfield simply lied. Surely the jury would understand that. It would be his word against hers, but he had verbal and electronic evidence that he had asked all the appropriate questions.

Hackett continued, "And, Mr. Turner, I have just two more questions. Who had power of attorney to provide consent for donation in the case of donor #OH7450?"

Oh shit, is this how he plans to do me in? Lance paused before answering, "That would have been the donor's mother. Ms. Vivian Kirk provided the consent."

And then the final blow from Hackett, "And Mr. Turner did you ask the donor's mother, the relative with power of attorney, whether her son had recently been incarcerated?"

Lance knew that he could probably give an untruthful answer to this question. Vivian Kirk died of a heart attack in the spring of 2009, so she would not be able to testify in this case. But Lance was not a liar.

Staring downward, he answered, "No."

"I have no further questions," Hackett concluded

After the court reporter and plaintiff attorneys packed up their documents and left the conference room, James Kennedy stayed behind to talk to his client, who now appeared dejected.

Lance spoke first, "So they are going to go after me because I forgot to ask the mother about recent jail time?"

"Well, it's not going to help your case, but remember, the CDC criteria relate to behavior thought to pose a high risk for HIV infection. We know conclusively now that HIV was not a concern in this case, so that will be our counter to this whole line of attack from the Hackett camp."

"So you think I'll be in the clear?" asked Lance.

Kennedy paused and then opened his brief case, removing a piece of paper appearing to be the copy of a handwritten letter.

"Well this guy Hackett is very shrewd. There's a little piece of evidence here that I'm sure he knows about, but didn't bring up in today's deposition. He knew I would blow him out of the water if he tried to bring it up without due notice."

"What are you talking about?" Lance asked.

"Ms. Stenfield has been deposed by a number of attorneys involved in all the lawsuits that have been generated by this case. She offered this letter to an attorney in the Pittsburgh case. He sent me a copy. If I have a copy, I'm sure every lawyer involved in every case has it by now – including Hackett."

"What kind of letter?" asked Lance, who was getting increasingly anxious.

Kennedy handed the letter to Lance. "It's just one of several *love* letters that Elroy Kirk sent to his girlfriend while serving time in the Montgomery County Jail."

Lance took the letter from Kennedy and read it nervously, first noting the date scribbled at the top of the stationery: April 23, 2008

"My Dearest Missy T:

I can't wait to bust this joint. I can't wait to see you again and hold you in my arms. It won't be too long now and we will be together again. And I promise to go back to school so we can have a nice life.

I hate this place. It's dirty and it's infested. There are roaches everywhere. And at nights, there are mice crawling around everywhere. I woke up last night feeling a sudden pain in my ankle and I swear I got bit by a mouse..."

There was more to the letter, but Lance stopped as he had no need to read any further.

PART III

Chapter Twenty-seven

Lance Turner's Demise
November 2010

Debbie Turner stood at the graveside, pondering the events of the past several days and the startling letter she received one day earlier. There were lots of tears being shed around the casket. But Debbie could not cry. It was cold and a light freezing rain was falling – perfect weather for a funeral. Debbie's parents and Lance's mother stood on either side of her, holding umbrellas to protect themselves and their two granddaughters. Debbie's mother was holding Lucretia Turner, now six months old and heavily covered in blankets. Lance's mother held the hand of Symeca Turner, almost two years old and wearing a green raincoat and a matching hat. Debbie was happy that neither of her children was old enough to fully understand what was happening. *Thank God neither of them will remember this awful day. Or how their father died.* There were twenty-five or thirty other friends and relatives attending the graveside ceremony. Frank Orlowski was there, intermittently fighting tears. There were no camera men and no microphones. Frank was there as a friend, not a TV news man. Debbie also recognized Bob Briggs and several other younger men and women that she presumed to be Lance's colleagues at the Ohio Organ Bank.

Five days earlier she was startled from her sleep by an early-morning phone call. Lance was out of town on a thirty-six-hour shift and she was sleeping alone. She grasped for the alarm clock, confusing her ringing phone for the alarm. As she pried her eyes open, she realized her mistake. *Only 6:05, the alarm is set for 6:30.* She woke up and picked up the phone after six rings.

"Is this Mrs. Debbie Turner?" an unfamiliar male voice asked.

"Yes?" she responded, sensing some urgency in the man's

voice that had a distinctly Indian accent.

"I'm Dr. Anil Padiyar, calling form the Wright State County Hospital Emergency Room. I am calling about your husband, Lance Turner."

Debbie jumped up from her supine position and sat up on the side of the bed, now alarmed but confused. Lance spent a lot of time at Wright State and that was the site of his current assignment. But he should have been in the middle of his shift. She wasn't expecting him home until later that night. Lance would be spending time in the intensive care unit, or possibly would be on a break in his hotel room, but he shouldn't have been in the Emergency Room. "Is there something wrong? What's going on?" she inquired.

"Your husband was involved in a motor vehicle accident earlier this morning on Route 70. He has sustained a head injury. It's a serious injury, Mrs. Turner. I think you may want to get down here as soon as possible," said Dr. Padiyar in a very serious tone.

"Oh my God. Is Lance Okay? Can I speak to him?"

"Mrs. Turner. He has sustained a *serious* head injury and cannot speak. It would be good if you got down here right away."

Debbie's heart sank and she was about to ask, *"Is he dead?"* But she knew that Emergency Room physicians were taught not to alarm family members about serious injuries or illnesses over the phone for fear that they would become distraught, drive crazily, and cause accidents of their own. Even if Lance was dead on arrival, Dr. Padiyar would probably not tell her.

"I'll be there as soon as possible," said Debbie, hanging up the phone and asking for no further information. She quickly called her mother to help with the kids, threw on yesterday's clothes that were draped over the chair next to the bed, and headed west for Dayton in her Ford Escort. Waiting for the car's heater to warm up, she felt a cold shiver. It was more than her body's reaction to the chilly weather. She shivered again and had an overwhelming sense that her husband was no longer alive.

In fact, Lance's heart was still beating. But the left side of his head was crushed, his bloody brain oozing through cracks surrounding the bone fragments that once formed his skull. Massive head trauma. *If your brain is dead, you are officially dead.*

Bob Briggs was sipping his morning coffee and reviewing his schedule for the day when his office phone rang at 9:00 AM. It was Linda Mayes, now a seasoned OOB donor coordinator.

"Mr. Briggs, are you sitting down?" she asked.

"Yeah, what's up?"

"Lance Turner was injured in an MVA early this morning. He's in the ICU at Wright State."

"Jesus, is he okay?"

"Mr. Briggs, they think he is brain dead. Witnesses at the accident scene described a big gas tanker that crossed the median strip. It was icy. The driver may have fallen asleep, or maybe had a heart attack – we'll never know. It was a near head-on collision. The truck driver was killed instantly. The truck itself exploded – a massive fireball according to witnesses. Must have been a full tank. The front end of Lance's car was smashed like an accordion and Lance's head was injured badly."

Briggs was speechless. He and Lance had become colleagues and good friends. They had dealt with a great amount of stress revolving around the LCVM lawsuits and the upcoming Anderson trial. He realized that the stress had been wearing Lance down. He seemed very depressed recently, but he was a young man with a rosy future. This was not fair.

"You there, Mr. Briggs?" asked Linda.

"Yes, I'm here, sorry. Have they contacted his wife?"

"She is on her way. Mr. Briggs, did you hear what I said? They think that Lance is brain dead. They are calling us to evaluate Lance as a potential organ donor."

And to think this will all go down in the same ICU where Lance got involved with the LCMV donor. The ultimate irony.

Debbie sat in the ICU waiting room, grief stricken and in no mood to talk to anyone, let alone to a donor coordinator from the OOB. *I know all about organ donation! I know all about brain death! This is different. This is my husband! His heart is still beating. He can't be dead. Please save my husband!*

It had now been almost twenty-four hours since Debbie got that morning phone call from the Wright State Emergency Room. Lance was in the ICU, intubated and unresponsive. His head was heavily bandaged. His heart was beating but a consulting neurologist could find no signs of brain stem function. A neurosurgeon met with Debbie and told her that surgery was not an option – Lance was about to be declared brain dead and surgery would be of no benefit.

Debbie thought long and hard about her life, her loving relationship with her husband, her children, and her future. *Oh my God, what now?* She knew how passionate Lance had been about his work – at least at one time. She knew what Lance would want. When the ICU attending met with her to tell her that Lance was officially declared brain dead, she readily provided consent for organ donation. She kissed her husband goodbye, gathered the belongings that were pried out of the trunk of his damaged car, and headed home...to make funeral arrangements...and to ponder her future.

Lance's liver and right kidney were irreparably lacerated during the accident. His left lung was punctured and damaged inadvertently during placement of a subclavian vein intravenous catheter during his resuscitation in the ER. None of these organs were transplantable. However, the transplant surgery teams successfully procured the heart, the right lung, the left kidney, and the pancreas for transplantation. Four Gifts of Life.

At the funeral service, the minister depicted Lance as a modern hero. "Lance Turner was a loving father and husband.

He was passionate about his family and his work. He was a young man who provided the Gift of Life to four people suffering from end-stage organ disease. He was a real hero."

As she listened to the eulogy, Debbie decided that she would never reveal to anyone the secrets that she had discovered during the previous day. She had decided to unpack the small duffle bag found in the trunk of Lance's Honda, and was surprised to find an unopened bottle of Jack Daniels, an unlabeled clear plastic container containing about four ounces of a blue liquid that looked and smelled like windshield wiper fluid, and a bottle of pills labeled "Seconal 100 mg, Use as directed". She did not recognize the doctor's name on the bottle which contained thirty pills. None of this made sense until she got the morning mail containing a letter with a Dayton postmark and dated November 13, 2010 – same date as Lance's fatal motor vehicle accident. It was a handwritten suicide letter, written on stationary from the Xenia Fairfield Inn. The letter was somewhat cryptic and brief, and stunningly unemotional:

"Debbie:
Courage or cowardice? It doesn't make any difference any more. In this life you are damned if you do and damned if you don't.
I'm out.
Life insurance policy is in my desk drawer."

The letter was not signed. There was no expression of love, no mention of her or the children. No apologies. There was a second sheet of paper listing bank account numbers and passwords for online accounts.

My husband was killed in a fiery car crash on his way to a hotel room where he planned to commit suicide by overdosing on pills, alcohol and windshield washer fluid. A real hero.

Debbie would live the rest of her life keeping this secret. She looked around at her family members and friends standing in the misty rain. She stood at the graveside, unable to cry, realizing that the secret of Lance's intended suicide would haunt her forever.

Chapter Twenty-eight

The Anderson Trial
December 2010

Bob Briggs attended every day of the four-day Anderson trial at the US District Court in Columbus. The trial was delayed a full day because of an unexpectedly long jury selection process. The prosecutors eliminated several potential jurors who were either medical professionals, relatives of a medical professional, or anyone who demonstrated exuberant fondness for doctors. *No doctors or doctor lovers allowed in a medical malpractice case.* The team of defense attorneys eliminated anyone who had either received an organ transplant, needed one, or who knew someone who had a transplant of any kind. They also eliminated people who had been involved in a medical malpractice case or who knew a friend or family member who had been involved in a medical malpractice case. A total of fourteen prospective jurors were systematically eliminated. *Slim pickings.*

This was actually one of at least two planned "Anderson" trials. The District Court judge decided that it would be unfair to include the organ procurement organization and the hospital and its doctors in the same prosecution. The first trial would focus on the OOB and its personnel as the chief defendants. Although some of the OMC doctors and nurses were summoned to this first trial as witnesses, they were not true defendants. They would get their chance to defend themselves in a second trial. This arrangement was perfect for William Hackett. He believed that the first trial would be an easy victory – a "no-brainer" that would set up even larger awards once the doctors and hospitals were in court as real defendants. Victories in these initial trials could spawn an entire series of secondary lawsuits from other stakeholders who felt that they were harmed by or suffered mental anguish as a result of the mistaken acceptance of an infected donor.

Highest on this list of secondary stakeholders was Ms. Tanya Stenfield. *Ladies and gentlemen of the jury, this poor young woman with a bright future will live the rest of her days with the mental anguish of knowing that her decision – based on inadequate counseling – led to the death or permanent brain damage of six different individuals. Her life has been forever tainted by this medical mistake ladies and gentlemen!* Yes, Hackett was feeling pretty positive about how this would all play out. Plus, he was going up against James Kennedy, representing the OOB and its personnel. Kennedy was a young and promising litigator, but he was about forty years Hackett's junior, and Hackett was confident that he could dismantle his youthful foe readily.

Today was day three of the first Anderson trial, and it was Briggs' day in the witness stand. With Lance Turner's untimely death, Briggs would now be the point person to defend the OOB, to defend Lance Turner posthumously and, from his point of view, to defend all transplant professionals who could someday be charged with allegations similar to those invoked in the Anderson case. In the first days of the trial, the prosecution had summoned Sarah and Ken Anderson and a number of experts – mostly in the field of infectious diseases and virology. Genevieve Stager was summoned to discuss the microbiology and natural history of infections with LCMV, and to confirm that this was the infection that resulted in the death of Scott Anderson.

William Hackett did his best to depict the awful death of a young man who had just received a Gift of Life, only to be stricken down by a viral disease that he acquired through no fault of his own, no fault of his saddened friends and family members – only through the fault of transplant professionals who made a fatal medical mistake. Lance Turner's death forced Hackett's team to make some last-minute adjustments in strategy. They would have to rely on Turner's previous depositions and cross examine Briggs in Turner's absence. But after two days in the courtroom, Hackett sensed that the jury was sympathetic. In the next two days, he would go for the kill, conclusively demonstrating that the Ohio Organ Bank conspired with the Ohio Medical Center in mistakenly accepting a kidney from an infected donor. In the final two days of the trial, Hackett would question Mark Hubbard, Bob Briggs and other transplant professionals involved in the medical care Scott Anderson and his donor. Tanya Stenfield would, of course, be his star witness.

Mark Hubbard's testimony focused on the issues of organ procurement and acceptance. Sarah and Ken Anderson avoided eye contact with Hubbard who appeared to address many of his comments and answers directly to them.

"Isn't the transplant surgeon ultimately responsible for assuring that donated organs are free of disease and acceptable for transplantation?" Hackett asked Hubbard.

"In my opinion, no. The entire process is a team effort involving transplant surgeons, transplant physicians, nurse coordinators at the transplant center, and personnel from the OPO. We all rely on each other, and make every effort to obtain the best organs and safely transplant them," stated Hubbard, being careful not to point fingers.

At one point, Hubbard was asked to describe Scott Anderson's clinical course. It was a painful reconstruction of Scott's prolonged hospitalization: the transplant surgery, the arterial reconstruction, the delayed graft function, the initially mysterious seizures, the CDC investigation, and Scott's eventual death. During this part of the testimony, Hubbard found it difficult to look directly at the Anderson's but he could see Sarah sobbing out of the corner of his eye. By extracting details of the case, Hackett had succeeded in making his sympathetic jury sad and angry at the medical system.

Mark Hubbard left the witness stand with a bad feeling about the outcome of the trial. He was concerned about more than his own hide. The stress of this case had already led to significant anxiety and depression, and almost certainly contributed to the end of his marriage. *Maybe other divorces have been spawned at other institutions.* But now he was equally concerned that losing this case could negatively affect organ donation, not just in Columbus, but throughout the country. Surgeons would become gun shy about accepting anything other than the most pristine organs from the most pristine donors. *We'll be left with organs from old nuns and priests dying from strokes...well, nuns at least.* The number of patients receiving transplants would likely decrease, waiting lists would increase in size, and the death rates of patients waiting for organ transplants would increase. And of course, job security for transplant surgeons would be jeopardized by the reduced number of cases.

Hubbard knew that he had nothing to confess, but he had a bad feeling that this case was a lost cause. And the biggest kicker: he wasn't even a defendant in this trial. He would have to go through it all at least one more time in his own jury trial. The same painful depictions of Scott Anderson's illness and death, the same awkward interactions with Sarah and Ken Anderson, the same sense of fear and loathing that he felt as he was examined and cross-examined by lawyers – as though he was a common criminal.

Bob Briggs' testimony was unexpectedly short and benign. Hackett realized that cross-examining Briggs was going to be much less effective than having Lance Turner in the stand. He would just use Briggs to set the stage for Tanya Stenfield's testimony.

Hackett read Tanya's "love letter" from Elroy Kirk, focusing on the mouse bite that was obviously the source of the LCMV infection that killed Scott Anderson. He also emphasized the portion of the letter that promised a better life for his long-time lover and companion. *Ladies and gentleman of the jury, this young couple had a troubled background but clearly had plans for a better future!*

He leaned on the wood railing adjacent to the witness stand and, peering at Briggs, asked, "Shouldn't a competent donor coordinator be expected to elicit a history of recent incarceration in an infested jail cell? A cell infested with roaches and mice and other creatures capable of transmitting diseases to the prisoners?"

Briggs requested a glass of water to clear his throat and then responded. "Mr. Turner's depositions as well as our recorded checklists indicate that the family denied any recent incarceration."

"Which family member are you referring to, Mr. Briggs?" Hackett retorted briskly.

"Sorry, I was referring to the donor's girlfriend, Ms. Stenfield."

"Oh and was Ms. Stenfield the closest kin with power of attorney?" Hackett asked

"No, but..."

Hackett did not allow Briggs to complete his comment. "No further questions, Your Honor."

Briggs was stupefied.

His testimony was over.

Tanya Stenfield was dressed in a sharp gray plaid women's business suit. *Undoubtedly the first time she's ever worn clothing of this sort.* She appeared uncomfortable and nervous. Hackett needed no written notes. He had memorized his line of questions, all designed to convince the jury that the OOB and OMC wrongfully accepted organs from an infected donor. *Driven by greed and the need to maintain high transplant volumes, these professionals made a critical medical mistake that led to the tragic death of young Scott Anderson – a young man whose entire promising life was ahead of him.*

"Now ,Ms. Stenfield, did Mr. Turner from the Ohio Organ

Bank talk to you about the CDC's high risk criteria?" Hackett asked.

"Far's I know, he aksed me questions about whether Elroy had AIDS," she responded.

"Oh then it sounds like Mr. Turner was being very thorough?"

"He was a nice man and he aksed me a lot of questions," Tanya offered.

"Now Ms. Stenfield, did Mr. Lance Turner ever ask you whether Mr. Kirk had been incarcerated prior to his untimely death?" Hackett asked with a gleam in his eye. Of course, he knew the answer was "no". He had rehearsed this with his star witness dozens of time before the trial. He would then go on, dramatically characterizing the severity of this mistake while walking past the jury box. *Should have been an actor. This case could have won me an Oscar.*

"Yes he did," Tanya said without any hint of insight.

Hackett clenched his eyes and his fists for two seconds, then peered at his witness with a look that said, *"You moron, you meant 'no' not 'yes'!"*

"I'm sorry, would you like a glass of water?" Hackett asked, caught completely off guard.

"No sir, I'm fine. I don't need no water."

"Okay, I may have misunderstood your answer. Did Mr. Turner ask you whether Mr. Kirk had been incarcerated prior to his death?"

"Yes he did. And I told him, 'no'," Tanya replied, appearing quite satisfied.

Hackett was completely flustered but tried not to display his frustration in the middle of the courtroom. He returned to his table and fumbled through some notes on yellow legal pads, hoping to convince the jury that Tanya's answer was no surprise and that he now had a new line of questions. But he didn't have a new line of questions. He wanted to strangle Tanya Stenfield. He wanted to strangle his staff for not rehearsing her answers more carefully. *I'll lose the case because of this moronic witness and my moronic staff!*

Hackett approached the bench and requested a fifteen minute recess. During the break, he met with his witness.

"Now, Tanya...Ms. Stenfield, I know you are probably nervous being in a real courtroom and all, but, Ms. Stenfield, you *do* recall saying during your deposition that Mr. Turner did not ask you about your friend's recent incarceration, didn't you?"

"That's not exactly what I said. I forgot what I said. I forgot what you aksed. You twist questions and trick people into saying things that they don't want to say. Mr. Turner aksed me if Elroy had been in prison and I told him, 'no'. Elroy was never in no prison. He was in a county jail serving short time as an accomplice. He wasn't in no prison."

Hackett entertained thoughts of invoking perjury and of pulling Stenfield's deposition to read it to her word-for-word, but he knew those strategies would be useless. She apparently lied during the deposition, or was confused by the questions – but trying to figure out why she was confused would not help his cause now. Her testimony changed everything. *I could have won the case if I hadn't put this moron on the stand!* He would go back into the courtroom, hope that the cross-examination of Ms. Stenfield was not too damaging, then go on to a summary statement that would focus on evil doctors, hospitals and organ procurement agencies.

It was now James Kennedy's chance to shine. He had no idea what went on during the recess, but when Hackett announced to the judge that he had no further questions for Tanya Stenfield, he realized that the plaintiff's star witness now had become his own ally.

After some friendly introductory questions, Kennedy got to the heart of the matter.

"Ms. Stenfield, can you please tell us *exactly* what Mr. Turner asked you about Mr. Kirk's behavior and his risk for having

AIDS?"

"I can't remember all the details. A lot of silly questions about havin' sex with men or prostitutes, bein' queer, and shootin' drugs mostly," she responded.

"And regarding any recent incarceration, what *exactly* did Mr. Turner ask you?"

"As I told Mr. Hackett, Mr. Turner aksed me if Elroy had recently been in prison, and I said 'no' because he wasn't in no prison, he was serving three weeks of time in the county jail. Accomplice in a robbery. So I never lied about nothin'," she responded, glaring in the direction of Hackett.

Hackett put his hands up over his cheeks, hoping that members of the jury would not notice his flushed look of exasperation.

Tanya went on, now shifting her position in the witness chair to address members of the jury. "Listen, I knew Elroy was gonna die the minute I seen him fall to the floor havin' a fit. Far's I know, Elroy didn't die of no virus. He died because he was in trouble and swallowed a bag of dope. It was nobody's fault 'cept his. When they told me his brain was dead and that he could donate organs, I figured it was like Elroy's salvation…and mine too. Somethin' good comin' out of his bad life. No way was I gonna interfere with that. Even if I had known back then about that famous mouse bite, I wouldn't have told Mr. Turner. I wanted somethin' good to come of Elroy's life… and mine too. I'm sorry about all the people dyin' from the virus infection, but it ain't my fault and it sure wasn't Mr. Turner's fault."

Kennedy was stunned. He couldn't have elicited a more perfect response if he asked the other dozen questions that he originally planned. Out of the corner of his eye, he saw Hackett slumping in his chair.

Kennedy happily announced, "Your Honor, I have no further questions."

Bob Briggs called Debbie Turner the day after the trial to tell her the outcome. He had not spoken to her since the day of Lance's funeral.

"I thought you would like to know that the OOB was acquitted. All named parties were acquitted. Had Lance been alive, he would have been acquitted without prejudice, meaning that he would not be tried in other trials related to this donor. Debbie, Lance was a good man. He was a real hero. I hope the acquittal provides you some solace."

No solace. No consolation. The damage had already been done years before the trial. My husband sunk from a life of vigor and enthusiasm for the future to one of depression, bitterness, and hopelessness. And he was innocent all along! The dramatic motor vehicle accident was an act of God. A Godly cover-up. Long before the car crash, Lance was already a dying man.

Chapter Twenty-nine

Henry Bolman's Book
2012

Almost two years after her husband's death, Debbie Turner read a story about Dr. Henry Bolman's new book in the Arts and Culture section of the Columbus Dispatch. She never met Dr. Bolman but remembered Lance speaking fondly about him as the "godfather" of organ transplantation at the Ohio Medical Center and a prominent national leader in the field. It was not Henry Bolman's name, but the title of his book, "Running the List", and the topic – the 2008 LCMV transplant cases – that caught her attention. As a single working mother raising two small children, Debbie's pleasure reading was limited mostly to action novels, romantic fictions, and even some science fiction – books that provided a little escape from reality. She wasn't as fond of documentaries or non-fictions, but she couldn't resist buying this book – it was too close to her heart.

The reviewer from the Dispatch was very positive about the Bolwell's book, describing it as an account "of historical interest to the state of Ohio, the city of Columbus, and its medical community." He failed to mention the book's dedication, which Debbie spotted on page three as she flipped through the front matter:

"To Lance Turner, a dedicated organ donor coordinator, a loyal family man, and a heroic organ donor."

Debbie's eyes welled with tears. These were possibly the first tears she had shed over Lance since receiving the call about his car accident back in November of 2010. *Maybe he was a hero after all.*

Bolman's book began with seven lengthy chapters describing the medical details of each of the organ transplant recipients that were infected with LCMV in Ohio, Michigan, and Pennsylvania. Pretty dry stuff for the non-medical reader – lots of medical terminology that Debbie did not fully comprehend, even with her background as a dialysis technician. The more interesting second half of the book discussed the lawsuits emanating from the LCMV transplants on a case-by-case basis. There were twenty-seven lawsuits in all, at least at the time that Bolman's book was published.

Bolman made an effort to estimate the costs incurred by the LCMV lawsuits, focusing first only on the costs of expert witnesses in each case. For example, the family of Henry George filed three lawsuits against the OOB, Cincinnati General Hospital and Dr. Kevin Fung. For each lawsuit, there were teams of three or four attorneys assigned to each side of the case. On the prosecution side, twelve expert witnesses were hired for the opinions pertaining to the three lawsuits, while the defendant teams hired fifteen expert witnesses. The expert witnesses were predominantly transplant surgeons or physicians weighing in with their opinions about wrongdoings – or lack of them – in the case of Henry George. There were also some administrators from outside organ procurement organizations, infectious disease experts, and transplant coordinators. Each of them rendered expert opinions in their own realms of expertise. On average, these experts charged $450 per hour for their review of records and preparation of reports. The average number of hours spent on these tasks, per witness, was fifteen. Thus, not including additional fees for depositions, the cost for the opinions of expert witnesses for the Henry George case alone was almost $116,000. After the decision in the Anderson trial of 2010, the three suits were dropped without settlements or jury trials.

The Scott Anderson case was one of the most costly of the LCMV lawsuits because it actually progressed to a jury trial. For testimonies at jury trials, many expert witnesses increased their fees to as much as $1000 per hour, not including travel expenses that were reimbursed separately. Some witnesses demanded first class airfare and four-star hotel accommodations when traveling to jury trials. Bolman estimated the costs of expert witnesses in the Anderson lawsuit to be $210,000. As Debbie already knew before reading the book, the defendants in the first Anderson trial were acquitted. Based on the outcome of the first Anderson trial, Hackett, Hackett and Lowenstein decided not to proceed with the second trial that would have targeted the Ohio Medical Center and its doctors. But they already had paid their expert witnesses for the second case – another $105,000.

Of all the LCMV cases, the most expensive was the case of Anna Korhonen. Her case generated eleven separate lawsuits, many from angry and anxious family members who had little to do with the case, other than knowing Anna and feeling threatened by their exposure to her rare viral infection. The expert witness fees paid for these lawsuits exceeded $300,000. Ironically, the patient continued to do well and never showed any signs or symptoms of LCMV infection, even four years after her pancreas transplant. All cases related to Ms. Korhonen were dropped without settlements or trials.

There were no costs associated with the Warren Mitchell case. The family refused to file suit against any entity. But then there were Pittsburgh lawsuits and additional lawsuits emanating from the death of the lung transplant recipient in Cincinnati. The Pittsburgh and Cincinnati cases were all dropped without settlements or trials. Bolman estimated the total costs of expert witnesses for all twenty-seven lawsuits to be approximately $998,000.

In each of the last book chapters, Bolman went on to estimate legal fees for the twenty-four lawsuits generated from this donor-transmitted infection. Here, his estimates were based on typical attorney fees and on the likely number of hours spent on each case. In general, the legal fees were almost three times more than the dollars spent on expert witnesses. To date, all cases had been dropped. Only a single case went to trial and there had been no settlements. After including court costs for the Anderson trial, Bolman figured that the total costs related to this donor-derived infection to be somewhere between five and seven million dollars.

There were four deaths resulting from transmission of LCMV and, because of the statute of limitations in Ohio where each of the deaths occurred, more lawsuits could emerge for another two decades. Bolman felt that more suits were unlikely, considering the outcome of the index Anderson trial. Surprisingly, his book ended abruptly, with no summary, no opinions, and no substantive conclusions. He did not even include his previously rendered concerns about "pushing the envelope" too far in organ transplantation. It was as though he was challenging readers to make conclusions of their own. As Debbie finished the final chapter of Bolman's book, she thought, *Four people dead, two permanently disabled. So much money, time, energy, stress and anxiety spent to find out that no one was guilty.*

She flipped back to the book's dedication page, thinking of her husband. Lance Turner was not a hero. He was a victim.

All for naught.

Epilogue

The Prologue of this book referred to a 1999 report from the Institute of Medicine. In the very same year, eBay aborted an auction for a human kidney after the bidding peaked at 5.7 million dollars.

Despite organized efforts to expand the pool of organ donors, the demand for organs continues to significantly surpass the number of available donors. In 1989, there were 17,917 people waiting for life-saving organ transplants. By 2009, that number had increased to 105,567. During the same time period, the number of organ donors increased only from 5,927 to 14,630 – a supply that has not kept pace with the increase in demand. As a consequence of these disparities, people are waiting longer and longer for organ transplants. Each day, seventy-five people die while on waiting lists for organ transplants.

In this environment, transplant programs have been under increasing pressure to accept organs from donors that would have been considered unacceptable in an earlier era. As the general population ages, there has been a trend toward accepting organs from older donors. In the modern era, donors with medical problems such as hypertension and diabetes are sometimes accepted when they would have been turned down in previous years.

The story presented in this book is fictitious. Surely, transmission of a fatal viral infection from an organ donor to multiple organ recipients is an egregious error that no transplant center would allow knowingly. But lesser errors, often errors in judgment about the medical health of a donor or the quality of a donor's organs, occur quite commonly and sometimes result in suboptimal outcomes – either organs that never work or that function poorly. These are concerns that enter the minds of transplant surgeons and physicians whenever they accept an organ for transplantation.

There is little doubt that transplant doctors are interested in developing high quality programs and in enhancing their own careers by accumulating successful track records with excellent patient outcomes. However, their main motivation has been, and always should be, a desire to prolong the lives of patients with end-stage organ disease. While pursuing these selfish and unselfish goals in the modern era, every transplant professional faces a number of questions on a regular basis: How far we can we push the envelope? Will marginal donors yield inferior outcomes in organ transplant recipients? And finally, when do those inferior outcomes become interpreted as mistakes that mandate legal scrutiny?

Glossary of Medical Terms
and Abbreviations

Terms

Ampicillin. An antibiotic

Allograft. A tissue or organ transplanted from one non-identical member of a species to another

Aphasia. Inability to speak

Apnea. Cessation of breathing

Anastamosis. A connection between two tube-like structures, either natural or surgically created

Anticonvulsant. A medication used to treat or prevent seizures

Cannabinoids. The active chemicals derived from marijuana plants (Cannabis sativa)

Creatinine. An end-product of muscle metabolism, blood levels of which are used to measure one's level of kidney function

Crossmatch. A test performed between a potential kidney transplant recipient and donor to assure that the recipient does not have antibodies against the donor's cells; when the crossmatch is negative, there are no detected antibodies

Cryptococcus. A fungus

Dehiscence. Disruption or breakdown of a surgical wound

Delirium tremens. The most severe form of the alcohol withdrawal syndrome characterized by hallucinations

Dialysis. A treatment for replacing the function of diseased kidneys

Dilantin. Brand name for phenytoin

Dramamine. Brand name for dimenhydrinate, a drug used to treat vertigo or sea sickness

Encephalitis. Infection of the brain

Encephalopathy. A state of confusion

Endocarditis. Infection of a valve in the heart

Epidemiology. The study of health events in a defined

population of subjects

Fistula. A connection between an artery and vein, either natural or surgically created

Gram stain. A laboratory test in which body fluids are stained to detect the presence of bacteria

Granulocyte. A type of white blood cell

Hemiplegia. Weakness or paralysis of one side of the body

Hemodialysis. Dialysis performed by circulating a patient's blood through an artificial kidney machine

Hepatology. Medical subspecialty of internal medicine focusing on diseases of the liver

Hypertension. High blood pressure

Hypotension. Low blood pressure

Immunosuppression. Inhibition of the immune system, usually induced by drugs

Infarction. Death of a tissue or organ

Intubation. Placement of a tube into the trachea of a patient; the tube is often connected to a respirator to provide artificial ventilation

Ischemia. Altered condition of a tissue or organ resulting from low blood flow or reduced delivery of oxygen

Jejunum. The longest portion of the small intestine, positioned between the duodenum and the ileum

Labetolol. A medicine used to lower blood pressure

Leukopenia. Low white blood cell count in the blood

Listeria. A bacteria

Lumbar puncture. A procedure for withdrawing spinal fluid for analysis, often called a spinal tap

Lymphocyte. A type of white blood cell

Malignant hypertension. A severe form of hypertension characterized by extremely elevated blood pressure, confusion or other neurological symptoms, and sometimes kidney failure

Meningitis. Infection of the membrane that lines the surface of the brain and spinal cord

Myocardial infarction. Heart attack

Nephrology. Medical subspecialty of internal medicine focusing on diseases of the kidney

Nitroprusside. An intravenous medicine used to lower blood pressure

Normal saline. A commonly used intravenous solution containing sodium, chloride, and water in proportions that mimic the concentrations in human blood

Octeotride. A medication used to reduce pancreatic secretions after pancreas transplantation

Ophthalmoscope. A device used to view the structures of the eye.

Papilledema. Swelling of the optic nerves, usually reflecting swelling of the brain

Peritoneal dialysis. An alternative form of dialysis performed by exchange of fluids drained into a patient's peritoneal cavity

Phencylcidine. An illegal drug with sedative and hallucinatory properties

Phenytoin. A drug used to prevent or treat seizures or epilepsy

Piperacillin. An antibiotic

Polymerase chain reaction. A laboratory technique used to detect small amounts of DNA or RNA

Potassium. A serum electrolyte, important in controlling the electrical conduction of nerves, muscle, and the heart

Status epilepticus. Continuous seizures

Tachycardia. Rapid heart rate, more than 100 beats per minute.

Tacrolimus. An immunosuppressant or anti-rejection drug commonly administered to organ transplant recipients

Valium. Brand name for diazepam, a drug used to treat anxiety but sometimes used intravenously to control seizures

Vancomycin. An antibiotic

Ventricular fibrillation. An often fatal cardiac arrhythmia characterized by a confluence of abnormal heartbeats emanating from one of the heart's ventricles

Ventricular tachycardia. A sometimes fatal cardiac arrhythmia characterized by rapid and abnormal beats of the heart generated from an abnormal focus of one of the heart's ventricles

Abbreviations

AIDS. Acquired immunodeficiency syndrome

ARDS. Adult respiratory distress syndrome

BP. Blood pressure

CDC. Centers for Disease Control

CMV. Cytomegalovirus

CPR. Cardiopulmonary resuscitation

CT. Computerized tomography

CVP. Central venous pressure

DCD. Donor after cardiac death

DNR. Do not resuscitate

EEG. Electroencephalogram

EMS. Emergency Medical Service

ER. Emergency room

HIV. Human immunodeficiency virus

HLA. Human leukocyte antigen

ICU. Intensive care unit

ID. Infectious disease

KUB. "Kidneys, ureters, bladder": an old designation for a plain x-ray film of the abdomen

LCMV. Lymphocytic choriomeningitis virus

LP. Lumbar puncture

LTAC. Long-term acute care

MICU. Medical intensive care unit

MRI. Magnetic resonance imaging

OPO. Organ procurement organization

OR. Operating room

PCP. Phencyclidine

PCR. Polymerase chain reaction

PVC. Premature ventricular contraction
UNOS. United Network for Organ Sharing
VAD. Ventricular assist device
WBC. White blood cell count

Also by Donald Hricik

"Racing to Pittsburgh" Strategic/Eloquent Books 2010. Available on the Amazon and Barnes and Noble websites.

"We may deny it but we all chase that American Dream and we "run" off after so many of its facets that we fail to really wake-up. We end up like Alice in wonderland running twice as hard just to stay in the same place. Well, Dan Ulek (read, "you and I") virtually ran himself to death before he realized what it was to have a real life. No, there's no revelation here that we haven't heard but the poignancy of the story is like Ulek, we, too haven't learned. In "Racing to Pittsburgh" Dr. Hricik has written a masterful reminder of the meaningful joy that life can hold if we, too, hold life to be meaningful.
Al Bartucci, High School English Teacher, Euclid, Ohio

www.donaldhricik.com
www.facebook.com/donald.hricik

Roundfire Books put simply, publish great stories. Whether it's literary or popular, a gentle tale or a pulsating thriller, the connecting theme in all Roundfire fiction titles is that once you pick them up you won't want to put them down.